NO INTERMISSION

Mary Spilsbury Ross

PINA PUBLISHING ☯ SEATTLE

For information about special discounts for bulk purchases contact:
sales@pinapublishing.com

Manufactured in the United States of America
Library of Congress Cataloging-in-Publication Data Splisbury Ross, Mary

Summary:
A passionate story of ambition versus the universal desire to be loved—a young aspiring ballerina from a sleepy town in the Pacific Northwest and an elegant dance master with a secret past, come together in post WWII Europe. This well-researched historical fiction takes the reader backstage, hanging out with the Rolling Stones, and other celebrities of the 60's and to Cairo sitting next to the King of Jordan, the President of Egypt, and Heads of State from the Arab world to Palm Beach Casino, Cannes on the French Rivera. Smuggling of Nazi-looted art masterpieces by Degas, Picasso, Pissarro, Van Gogh, seem to follow the multi-racial dance troupe everywhere they perform. Margaret Alice Dinsdale from North Oyster on Vancouver Island learns the truth of wartime devastation in Europe, anti-Semitism, unimaginable poverty, smuggling, and the not-so-glamourous life of a professional dancer. Funny, articulate, and partly based on a true story.

ISBN: 978-1-943493-54-8 (hardcover)
       978-1-943493-41-8 (softcover)
       978-1-943493-57-9 (ebook)

[1. Historical - Fiction. 2. Romance - Fiction. 3. 1960's Europe - Fiction. 4. Ballet. 5. Dance. 6. Theatre. 7. Mystery. 8. Murder.]

DEDICATION

For my late husband
Dr. Michael Andrew Ross
(1935-2020)

His confidence in me was my inspiration.

ACKNOWLEDGEMENTS

While some characters who appear in this novel are based on actual figures and most towns and venues existed in 1964 as described, it is important to stress that all characters in the ballet including the ballet master are fictional. The one exception is the late Rudolfo Canessius Soemolang, (Rudi) a brilliant Indonesian dancer, teacher, entertainer, who gave me verbal permission to use his name before he passed.

Without dozens of sites on the internet my research into historical events and smuggling of artworks (1939-1961) would have taken years- Wikipedia.org, WW2today.com, wwwbritannica.com, and www.national archives.gov.uk to name a few.

Many books were important to my research. I have quoted directly from Irvine Stone 'The Agony and the Ecstasy' and the poetry of Rudyard Kipling, and 'Leotard' a memoir I co-authored with Sally Faverot de Kerbrech in 2014. The Alexandrian Quartet by Lawrence Durrell (1957-1960) refreshed my memories of Egypt in the 1960's. Lyrics to songs, titles, musical shows, composers, and choreographers are listed in the Appendix.

I am forever grateful for the sleuthing by my husband and his immense vocabulary in writing the appendix, proof-reading, and sage advice. Special thanks must go to Susan Harring who designed the dramatic cover and was sensitive and caring while I dithered over ideas. My publisher Jeanne Bender-Zehrer of Pina Publishing has been so very kind and patient while I rewrote the last chapters. Thank you Jeanne, for all your help. Without my young and enthusiastic, bilingual, editor, Valerie Irvine-Karinen, I would never have completed my first novel, *No Intermission*. She has been dedicated from the start and encouraged me when I felt defeated and elated when I finished.

Thank you, *'merci, mille grazie, danke shön, dank je, shukraan'*.

That night beneath the stars, you broke

the walls

I'd build around my heart.

There against my plan, your heated kiss

began to take command.

It happened then, it happened there,

on that first night,

I fell in love with you.

—Napoleon, The Musical
By Timothy Williams and Andrew Sabiston

MSR

Table of Contents

CHAPTER I

Getting There is Half the Fun

Between 1939 and 1946, three Cunard steamships, the RMS Queen Mary, RMS Queen Elizabeth, and SS Aquitania, nicknamed the 'Winston Specials,' transported over a million young soldiers across the North Atlantic to the battlefields of Europe. For thousands and thousands, it was a one-way crossing.

Aboard the Cunard Royal Mail Ship, '*Ivernia*,' 1963:

On the foredeck, curled up on a canvas chair under a thick blanket, is nineteen-year-old Margaret Alice Dinsdale. Back home in North Oyster, British Columbia, she's known as simply 'Maggie.' Although not curvaceous and blonde like many of the models in magazines, she is her own kind of striking. With flaming red hair, a tall, angular body, and long, shapely legs, her eyes twinkle. She has a shy smile, yet, one that spells trouble and mystery.

"You'll be a late bloomer dear," her mother had assured her. "You'll grow into yourself." *Whatever that means?*

Maggie has spent most of her life dancing and yearning to become a professional ballerina. Her biggest dream is to perform with the famous Royal Ballet in London, England. It all began at the age of five, when her grandmother took her with her two sisters to see a Christmas pantomime called 'Babes in the Woods.'

There, in the spotlight, two sweet, little children danced barefoot in a beam of light, while wolves howled and wind tore at their nightdresses. Terrified, they danced to exhaustion, and wrapped in each other's arms, froze to death. The pantomime was magical. Maggie clapped and clapped and tried to climb over the brass balcony rail onto the stage before the heavy, red velvet curtain lowered to the floor and the scene disappeared. That was the moment Maggie decided she had to be on the stage, not stuck in a seat with the audience.

She whines and cajoles enough that her father finally relents and agrees to dance lessons, despite Maggie's sisters, Geraldine and Allister, thinking she is a spoiled brat for getting them. The classes are with Miss Thelma Wynne in Ladysmith*, the nearest town to 'Longlands,' their family farm in North Oyster Cove. Miss Wynne is well-known for her discipline and her no-nonsense approach to dance. For the following twelve years, Maggie works hard, taking all of the British Academy ballet exams, competing in festivals and performing in recitals, but this is the moment she has been waiting for. She is going to an audition in London for the Royal Ballet School, which is why she is one of the nine hundred and twenty passengers aboard the RMS *Ivernia*; the smallest ship in the Cunard fleet.

As the ship rolls gently side to side, pitching and purring in a lullaby, Maggie is engrossed in *Atlas Shrugged* by Ayn Rand. It is a giant of a book, over a thousand pages, which she figures should keep her busy for the entire trip. *There is no point,* she decides, *to make friends with people she will never see again.* Maggie does not feel strong and independent, like the heroine in her novel. There is so much at stake, but she is anticipating a new and thrilling life once she arrives in London. Only her grandmother encouraged her to 'fly the coop,' toss her stuff in a suitcase, run away, and see the world. Onboard, Maggie feels conspicuously single. Couples and families appear to be having a ball; laughing, singing, playing quoits, shuffleboard, and checkers on the Promenade deck. She lights a Rothmans King Size cigarette, hoping it might make her look sophisticated. But, glancing around for an ashtray and finding none, she absent-mindedly slips the smoldering match into her shoe and buries her head into the words of Ms. Rand.

Part of the job of the Cunard staff is to keep all passengers happy, whether they're in first-class or steerage. Everyone is included in the shipboard activities, ranging from playing canasta or poker to musical performances and dance nights in the lounge. Even on their smallest ships, the passenger's enjoyment comes first.

While Maggie is reading, a Cunard employee saunters by, seizing the opportunity to attract the girl's attention. He has been admiring her for the entire journey: the girl with the sensational red hair—but never catches her without her nose in a book. Picking up a large, metal ashtray with a weighted stand, he hurries over and places it beside her.

"This might be better than your shoe," he jokes, smiling.

Maggie blushes with embarrassment, flicks an ash into the offered receptacle, and whispers, "Thank you."

Only then does she look up and into the intense blue eyes of the young man, and notices a metal name tag pinned on his jacket: Cunard Lines Assistant Medical Officer: Phillip M. Holmes. *Oh, crap,* she thinks, *he probably doesn't approve of smoking.* He smiles and introduces himself.

"My friends call me Pip, and I'm not a doctor, just a medical student. What is your name?" Maggie pushes her hair out of her eyes and gazes at him.

"My family calls me Margaret, but I prefer Maggie." There is an awkward silence as Maggie stares at him, noting that his silver-grey hair is speckled with a streak of black. It is unusual to see on someone so young. *Wow. He should be a movie star.*

Finally, the AMO with the unlikely name of Pip says, "See you tonight in the lounge on the Promenade Deck. It's the last night." He turns abruptly, and walks away.

In her tiny stateroom on the lower deck, Maggie is standing in her cotton underpants, trying on various combinations of blouses, skirts, dresses, and belts. She hadn't really packed for parties, instead focusing on her dance career. Her suitcase is stuffed with *pointe* shoes, tights, leggings, leotards, warm sweaters, and a special, crisp, white tunic for her audition at the Royal Ballet School. Exasperated, she finally chooses an emerald green cotton dress with a full skirt, puts on a dash of lipstick, brushes her hair to get rid of the tangles, and looking at her travel clock with only minutes to go, races out of the stateroom door. Two seconds later, the same door opens. Maggie, in her excitement, has forgotten her shoes.

The wind has picked up from the northwest, causing the SS *Ivernia* to jerk and pitch about like an angry mutt scratching for fleas. Double doors to the lounge are propped open, revealing couples sliding to the port side, then like a teeter-totter, careening to the starboard, with the occasional suspicious thud and thump from below deck. Many are staggering to keep their balance, squealing with delight or terror depending upon how many rum and cokes they've consumed.

"It's that damn gale out of Davis Strait," grumbles an old, formally dressed gentleman as he takes two refills from a passing tray. His companion is a blue-haired matron dressed in an unfortunate, puce satin gown with matching satin pumps. Suddenly, the *Ivernia* corkscrews, sending chairs, tables, and people slithering across the waxed dance floor, and the blue-haired woman straight out the door with her hands clapped over her mouth. She almost collides with Maggie, who is making her entrance in a prim, Johnathan Logan dress.* The six-piece band, ignoring the rollercoaster ride, is pulling out all the stoppers, with a Louis Armstrong's version of "When the Saints Come Marching In." Maggie gazes around, fearing that she is making a fool of herself to expect him to meet her.

As if on cue, the turbulence subsides, the band begins to play a slow dance, and Maggie sees the Assistant Medical Officer heading her way. Her heart beats rapidly and she feels her face flush. In a low and sultry voice, the pianist sings, "The Nearness of You."*

"It's not the pale moon that excites me, that thrills and delights me, oh no, it's just the nearness of you." Pip takes Maggie in his arms and without a word, they sway to the music, listening to the enchanting lyrics and each wondering if they will ever meet again.

London, England, 1963:

Bang on time, the ship's train shudders to a stop at Waterloo Station in London. Oblivious to the torrential downpour, Maggie steps onto the platform, carrying her square, brown ballet box, a large handbag, and her suitcase—with a new Cunard label stuck in one corner. It boasts their logo: 'Getting There is Half the Fun.' Remembering the last dance onboard, she grins happily as she splashes through murky puddles to the taxi stand, known locally as 'The Loo.' An overhead clock shows fifteen past three. She changes her watch to English time and flags a famous, black Austin FX4 taxicab. It screeches to a halt inches from her toes, welcoming her to London in the most London way possible. The cabbie, with a distinctive Cockney accent, asks "Where to, luv?" as she piles in with all of her belongings.

"I'm not sure," she mutters, searching through her cluttered handbag for a small address book. "Somewhere near Hyde Park, I think."

The rain continues to pour down, instantly flooding the streets and making the sidewalks look like a moving train of umbrellas and Wellington boots. The taxicab takes off, ducking and diving down side streets and slamming on brakes to avoid near collisions at crossroads.

"Shoulder of Mutton Alley, Cock Lane, The Hanging Sword, Mudchute Street? There are twenty thousand miles of roads within a six-mile radius of Charing Cross," he grins in the rearview mirror. "I know them all from our Queen's Buck House to Titley Close." Suddenly, Maggie remembers.

"Queen's, that's it!" she calls out. "The address is Queen's Gate Gardens!"

Could it possibly rain any harder? Maggie wonders as the windows fog up and nothing can be seen. She is having a few doubts about her arrival. "What shall I do if no one is home and I am left standing in this deluge?" The driver shrugs his shoulders.

A few minutes later, the taxi pulls to the curb, and the driver says, "Fifty-three, G. Queen's Gate Gardens." Maggie wipes the window with her coat sleeve and peers out.

"Wow, this is very elegant," she remarks.

"They're called Regency townhouses, named after that obese nincompoop King George IV when he was Prince Regent. Spent his life drinkin', whorin', and swillin' tincture of opium. And what's the nutter remembered for? Posh townhouses, Greek columns, fancy balconies, and rose gardens? Now, luv, you owe me four shillings, and then I'll get home to the misses for tea." Just before he drives away, he calls out: "Fifty-three G means garden flat, down in the cellar with the rats and creeping damp! Ta-ta!"

The garden flat looks deserted. There is not even a crack of light under the door. Maggie stands on the pavement, getting soaked through to her knickers, and finally descends the steps to the lower level. She walks past a row of garbage bins and knocks timidly on the door. *Silence!* Then, she knocks again, noticing that she can hear someone inside singing. A large, furry rat with beady little eyes and a long tail scampers over her shoe and hides behind a discarded bundle of newspapers.

She yelps, pounding on the door with her fist, "Hello, hello, I'm Allister's sister, let me in, damn it!"

London in 1963 is like no other city: a twenty-four-hour madhouse. Maggie wastes no time moving into the only available space at Fifty-three G, an ancient, cement wine cellar with a metal door and three penny-sized holes for ventilation. To cheer it up, she paints it purple and sleeps on one of the hard, concrete shelves. The other shelf serves as both a desk and dressing table, with an Underwood portable typewriter, light coming from a single overhead socket, a small mirror, and a biscuit tin filled with make-up. Next to the Underwood is a leather framed photo of her heroine, Moira Shearer, in her costume from The Red Shoes. Hidden behind the photo in the silk taffeta lining is her stash of cash, the money she received from Granny.

Within a week she has a part-time job at the neighbourhood coin-operated laundromat on Brompton Road, hanging up dresses and suits that stink of chemicals and old sweat. She splits her time by taking ballet lessons from Madame Audrey de Voss, in Notting Hill Gate, in preparation for her long-awaited audition. She realizes one day, *Life doesn't get better than this.* At night, she and her roommates; two girls from Vancouver, and whoever else is hanging about, play bridge beside the gas fire in the sitting room and drink cheap vodka and orange juice. Other nights they pool their money and go to pubs with eccentric names like Dirty Dicks, The Pig and Whistle, and The Lamb and Flag. Some pubs have pianos, and inevitably, Maggie's roommate Sandra would play and have the whole room singing lustily.

By the end of the first week, Maggie decides to hack twelve inches from the bottom of her skirts and hem them in pretty little stitches that would make her Home Economics teacher, Miss

Pendray, proud, and her mother have a heart attack. Mini-skirts are in, and tweed A-lines are out. After buying a pair of boots so tight that she needs a zipper to get into them, there is barely enough money for rent. So, it'll be Wall's pork sausages and a bag of green stuff called 'spring' greens, despite being in September, to keep her going. *Lordy, lordy, what a crazy country.*

Park Lane is one of the most posh addresses in London, and the equivalent of Fifth Avenue in New York, Hollywood Boulevard in Los Angeles, and Jingle Pot Road in Ladysmith. On November 22nd, Maggie is invited to her roommate Sandra's twenty-first birthday on the top floor of the brand new Park Lane Hilton Hotel at number twenty-two. It has only been open since April.

Of course, it is raining as the three scramble up the stairs of Fifty-three G in search of a taxi. Queen's Gate Gardens is deserted and the trio rush up to High Street, where there are always black Fairlanes cruising for a fare. But High Street is empty, not a car, not a person in sight.

"What's happening? Where is everybody? It's like the plague has descended upon London town." After more than fifteen minutes, a lone cabbie pulls into view.

The trio bundle in and the birthday girl Sandra announces, "Twenty-two Park Lane, please." The driver just sits, staring in the rearview mirror. Seconds pass.

"Don't you know, luvs?" he sighs. "The President of the United States has been assassinated. He is dead. Dead as a mackerel."

Maggie's audition for the Royal Ballet School does not go as planned. She is alone in a small, dark studio, with no piano, dressed in her white tunic and clean, flesh-coloured ballet slippers. Her unruly hair is pulled so tightly that her *chignon* feels like a barnacle on the back of her head. The door opens. A no-nonsense middle-aged woman bustles in and does not introduce herself.

"Miss Dinsdale, you will do a few plies?" Without warning, the woman proceeds to push and prod her like a flank steak, mutters about alignment, and twists Maggie's ankles like a corkscrew. Finally, standing face to face, she pronounces, "You are too tall."

"Too tall for what?" Maggie snaps, and the woman retires without another word.

Twelve long years of hope, of dreaming, of never-ending classes, exhaustion, ingrown toenails and blisters are destroyed with just four fatal words: "You are too tall." Maggie arrives home to the garden flat in Queen's Gate to a letter from her father, saying "Get a job or come home."

In desperation, Maggie answers every advertisement in The Stage. Ads for singers with some dance training, a pantomime opening in Liverpool requiring dancers proficient in toe tap, modern dancers for a West End show who must be size six, presumably to fit the ready-made costumes, male dancers needed for Christmas Elves at Harrods Department store. Maggie has never taken tap dancing in her life, let alone put the metal bits on the top of her pointe shoes, nor has she the faintest idea where Liverpool might be, nor Harrods for that matter. Last week she went to an audition and found about fifty girls applying for one position.

Perched on a stool in her purple cupboard, Maggie is typing furiously on the Underwood portable. It is freezing cold and she has all of her clothes on, as well as a hat designed by her mother. The space is littered with books and the latest copies of 'The Stage,' which comes out every Friday. An ashtray fills with butts as she smokes furiously, filling the cupboard with the stench of nicotine and making her eyes water.

Fifty-three G, Queen's Gate Gardens, London, England:
Dear Pops:
Of course, I am trying to get a job. I am studying all of the

books you sent but I don't want to become an old maid school teacher. I just got here, and I'm not coming home. I will not...

Maggie re-reads the letter, tears it out of the machine, and tosses it onto the floor with the rest of the rejects and newspapers. Her attention is caught by an advertisement on the first page of The Stage. It reads: "Female dancers with classical and modern training wanted immediately in Switzerland. Les Ballets Jazz Europa." *Switzerland at Christmas*, she fantasizes: fresh, clean snow, perhaps a modern version of The Nutcracker Suite and the Sugar Plum Fairy. She will dance like she has never danced before, and she is going to get this job. The following day, Big Ben chimes four o'clock and Maggie dashes across Trafalgar Square, turns down a side street, and stops in front of a soot-blackened brick building: a survivor of the bombing during WWII. A metal sign indicates Shaftesbury Studios. She pounds up the stairs, well-worn from thousands of dancing feet. At the top landing, a crusty, old man slouches behind his desk like a centurion guarding the gates to Rome. He peers over his glasses and growls, "Yer late," then disappears behind the Daily Express.

Without knocking, Maggie pushes open the opaque glass door, tosses her coat and purse in a corner of the room, slips into ballet shoes, and stands in line with five other girls. They are all facing a large mirror that stretches from one side of the room to the other. Instantly, her reflection shows she is the outsider; wearing a classic black leotard and tights, with her hair pulled tightly into a ponytail. The other five look like seasoned professionals in bright, casual tee shirts, skin-tight jazz pants and sneakers or high heels. Standing in front of them with her back to the mirror, a young girl introduces herself as Anna Bell, a dancer with Les Ballets Jazz Europa.

"I'd like to see you improvise and show me what you can do. Please include some *pirouettes*, some elevation, flexibility and some floor work." *Holy smokes,* thinks Maggie. *What the hell is floor work?*

Ladysmith, Vancouver Island, 1950:

Memories of her first classes with Miss Thelma Wynne come flooding back. She is transported, finding herself holding tightly to a long ballet barre that runs the length of a sunlit room. The studio is on the top floor of the old Traveller's Hotel, with a large window that overlooks the railway tracks. She, and a dozen other six-year-old girls are lined up according to size, from the shortest to the tallest. This order doesn't last long, as the moment any mistake is made, the offender is sent to the back of the room, often in tears. Miss Wynne carries a pointer made of wood and uses it to prod the girls' backs and *tap, tap, tap* out the rhythm.

Her motto: "If my girls can survive me and still want a career in dance, they will survive anything. Ballet is not for sissies."

London, 1963:

In the rehearsal room at the Shaftesbury Studios, a large lady is sitting on a stool in front of an upright piano. She plays a few bars from Gershwin's "Rhapsody in Blue" and Anna points to the girl at the end of the line. The girl steps forward, runs about and takes a few leaps, and then rolls on the floor, spread-eagle like a puppy with an itch. The other four girls have very strong *pirouettes*, and are extraordinarily flexible in their floor work, doing the splits and backbends like circus acrobats. Then, it is Maggie's turn, and she gives it her all. *I'm no sissy and I'll be damned if I'll go to the back of the room. It's now or never.* The pianist speeds up poor Gershwin's Rhapsody to a tempo that would give the composer a nervous collapse. Maggie flies through the air and pretends she is back home at Longlands, wild and free, whirling and twirling down the steep meadow of poppies and cornflowers and rolling over the wild mint and sage. The ribbon holding her ponytail loosens and she finishes, breathless, damp with sweat and full of joy.

"I got the job!" Maggie is ecstatic, and tells the old curmudgeon on the landing. He stares at her, unimpressed, but her enthusiasm is unshakable. "I did it, eh?! I am off to Paris with Anna to meet the company, and then we're on our way!"

Underground, the Piccadilly Line tube rattles to a stop, the door snaps open, and Maggie throws herself into the crowded car. She squeezes into a worn, leather bench in the non-smoking car and lights a cigarette. They are cheap Woodbines, but in an expensive gold Benson and Hedges box. The only problem is the smell. They stink like Woodbines. Impatiently, she watches the stations zip by: Piccadilly Circus, Green Park, Hyde Park, Knightsbridge, and finally, South Kensington. After a few weeks of riding the underground trains, Maggie feels a bit like a Londoner. She often catches herself singing "I get a funny feeling inside of me, just walking up and down. Guess it's because I'm a Londoner, that I love London town."

That night, with the fog closing in and the temperature dropping, Maggie and her roommates drink a toast to each other.

"Cheers to all our dreams of success, adventure, and the grand life." It seems so long ago that Maggie had pounded on the door to be let in, looking like a drowned cat, yet, it was only months ago. She clears out the cupboard, packs as many of her belongings as she can fit into her suitcase, and presses a new luggage sticker in the opposite corner of the Cunard logo. It is a red, white, and blue Union Jack with Big Ben on the left-hand side. Maggie is ready to see the world, or at the very least, Switzerland.

Chapter II

Not All That it Seems

*Between 1933 and 1945, hundreds of millions of dollars in
paintings by the Great Masters and countless others were swindled
by Nazi Germany and their neutral neighbour, Switzerland. To
this day, thousands of paintings that were stolen during WWII
and hidden or resold have never been found. These include the
works of Picasso, Van Gogh, Klimt, Raphael, Matisse, Degas,
and Toulouse-Lautrec. After drugs and guns, art theft is third in
liquidity for cross-border smuggling operations. Worldwide efforts
to find and return stolen art for a "just and fair" remuneration
have failed. Switzerland has been the most reluctant to open their
archives, bank vaults, and dormant accounts of holocaust victims.
This would force them to admit to money laundering for the Nazi
regime and to paying 'fluchgut,' or flight money, a pittance paid for
paintings so that refugees, mostly Jewish, could escape German
occupied countries. 'Fluchgut' was the equivalent of a highway
man with a pistol aimed at an innocent heart, threatening "Your
money or your life." In this case, Switzerland took their money,
even their gold fillings—which they smelted into bars, and refused
asylum to anyone with a J on their passport. That was the sinister
side of neutrality.*

The English Channel crossing this Christmas season is memorable for its ferocity. The moment the ferry leaves the protection of the coast and sails into the open channel, the wind howls and icy sleet rains down on the decks. The ferry begins to pitch forward and backward, bow to stern, and then port to starboard.

"I hate this sort of thing," moans Anna, who is clutching a chair as though it is a life raft. Maggie finds it thrilling. She loves the ocean and spent her childhood playing in it. As a kid, she could be found clinging to a driftwood pontoon in the worst possible weather, or running along rolling log booms that were being towed in front of their farm at North Oyster Cove.

The bow smacks the icy water with a huge *whoomp* and then bucks like a wild horse. Waves break over the deck rails as crew members frantically tie the doors shut with thick hemp, so that queasy passengers can't stagger on deck for a breath of air and get thrown overboard. Children start screaming as bottles and glasses slide down the polished metal bar, looking as though they're moving in slow motion until suddenly smashing onto the deck. Nearing Calais, Maggie is the only one left standing, the other passengers appearing visibly ill. With her legs braced for balance, she is drinking a shot glass of neat, Mount Gay rum from Barbados and laughing uproariously like a mad pirate.

"Mount Gay is owned by some relative of mine," she tells the bartender, slurring her words ever so slightly. "His name was Aubrey Fripps-Ward and he had one hundred children."

"Great way to build up a clientele for rum," he laughs.

Paris, France, 1963:

There are seven train stations in Paris: Saint-Lazare, de l'Est, de Lyon, Austerlitz, de Bercy, Montparnasse, and the Gare du Nord. It might have caused less frustration for Anna, Maggie, and the confused taxi driver had they realized that the boat train and the eastbound train to Switzerland left from the same station of the Gare du Nord. Essentially, they didn't have to go anywhere. The taxi driver throws his hands in the air, muttering obscenities about them wasting his precious time. The Gare du Nord is a bewildering and complicated series of platforms, rails, signs, ticket booths, and newsstands simply jammed with arrivals. The passer-bys are carrying a variety of clumsy bags, ranging from skis and ski poles, to piles of luggage and wrapped Christmas presents. Everyone is pushing and tripping over each other, calling out *"au revoir"* or *"Joyeux Noël."*

"Follow me," calls Anna, as she strides along the platform in very high heeled boots, and huge, dark sunglasses, head thrown back like a Hollywood star. People turn and stare at her wondering where they might have seen her before.

Whistles blow and a loudspeaker calls out platform numbers that cannot be understood.

"Here we are," Anna points down a platform. The space is overflowing with porters, carrying mountains of luggage, and a jumble of people of all nationalities and colours. She disappears into a muddle of young people midway down a long line, standing in front of dark green carriages. Bold, gold letters boast the name *'Compagnie Internationale des Wagon-Lits.'* Maggie is left standing alone, smelling French perfume mixed with wet wool, leather, and sweat. Suddenly, the warning whistle blows, the carriage windows are slammed open, and suitcases fly from hand to hand through the window like an assembly line.

An older, rather handsome man with some authority rushes by barking orders, handing out tickets, and speaking in English, French, Dutch, Italian, and German.

Sighing, he asks, "Where is Anna? Is she late again?" to no one in particular. Maggie wonders if he is Nikolaus Pávlos, the choreographer and ballet master for the group, but before she can say a word he hurries off. He heads toward the freight cars with an ever so slight limp, muttering about the skips, or *panniers*; the costume trunks. A very cute guy with sexy black eyes snatches Maggie's suitcase and heaves it through the window.

"*Merda!*" he snaps "What you have inside? *Elefante*? Too heavy, *troppo pesante!*" Then, he peers at her, just a little perplexed. "Who are you?" he asks, before turning on the charm and introducing himself. "I am Romeo."

Maggie picks up the rest of her belongings and giggles, "Of course you are, and I am Juliette."

The final whistle blows and a smartly dressed porter in a dark suit and cap calls "*d'abord*" in a monotonous voice. The eastbound train lurches forward through a cloud of steam, and Maggie is off to Bern, Switzerland and a new life as a professional dancer with Les Ballets Jazz Europa. Standing in the wood-paneled corridor, wondering what to do next, Maggie finally meets the Maestro.

With a jolt and a screeching of metal on metal, Maggie and a distinguished looking man are almost thrown into a pile of luggage littering the narrow passageway. Regaining his balance, he grabs both her hands in a firm grasp, and in a low, silky, voice with a slight foreign accent introduces himself. "Nikolaus Pávlos, Maestro of Les Ballets Jazz Europa. There is a pause, "Nikko, I am called that, too," and he kisses her cheeks, first left then right. "Welcome *la Canadienne!*"

Sliding open a carriage door, Maggie sits next to a Nordic blond beauty who smiles at her. "My English is not very fine," she apologizes. "I am Aneke, from Holland." She wastes no time in telling Maggie that she is engaged to Rudi, the leading man. Rudi is Indonesian, a charmer, a flirt, and a brilliant dancer. A lovely, auburn-haired girl sitting across the aisle shyly introduces herself as Sophia.

"I am from Munich, Germany, and most of us in the ballet speak some English or French. From Canada, you speak both, no?" Maggie is ashamed to admit that her French is limited.

"But I am going to learn very quickly."

As the train picks up speed, everyone settles down like roosting chickens, either playing cards, sleeping, or staring out the window as eastern France flashes by. Maggie pulls a large map of Europe from her bag and inks in her journey so far with a black marking pen: Southampton, London, Dover, Calais, Paris, and now, she searches for Bern; the capital city of Switzerland. The motion of the train on the tracks and the repetitive *clickity clack* is hypnotic, and soon her eyes close and she drifts off, thousands of miles away to Christmastime at Longlands, in North Oyster Cove.

North Oyster, Vancouver Island, 1950's:

Fog horns hoot across the water, echoing against the land. Visibility only stretches a few miles, and even the outline of Decourcy Island is lost in a white mist. There is always plenty of snow for sliding down the hill, even if it turns to slush when it reaches the beach. Maggie and her sisters are sent trudging through the snow to St. Phillip's Church in Cedar, singing "Canada's Huron Christmas Carol" written in 1642. *"Twas in the moon of winter-time when all the birds had fled, that mighty Gitchi Manitou sent angel choirs instead. Before their light the stars grew dim, and wandering hunters heard the hymn: Jesus your King is born, Jesus is born, in excelsis Gloria."*

After the service, the three have aggressive snowball fights until one of them gets a nosebleed. Home again, to knitted, wool socks filled with gifts. Every year their presents are the same, but the squeals of joy remain genuine. Stuffed down into the sock is a new toothbrush, a face cloth, a tangerine, some nuts: almonds, walnuts, and Brazil nuts in their shells, and a package of five fruit lifesavers. Most important of all, a book from their grandmother. Not any old book, either, not second hand, not from a rummage sale, but a *brand-new* book. Every year, she quotes the same thing:

"Literature, music, dance, and art are the most important possessions in life."

While the goose roasts in the oven, Maggie's mother, dressed in a floor-length black, velvet gown, plays her favourite Brahms and Vivaldi concertos on her grand piano. She is looking far off into space as if she were in a concert hall in one of the capitals of Europe. She could have been a concert pianist if she had not, much to her distress, had three babies, one after another. She had been devastated. Her husband, a not very successful writer, artist, and lecturer, had tried to console her by turning the living room into a music hall. The three little girls knew the music of Mozart better than they knew "The Three Blind Mice." Maggie's father had always made his presents by hand, which meant they were often a little eccentric. One year it was a bat roost, "to keep the mosquitos, flies, and moths away," he had argued. Then, there was a mud scraper and boot remover, a home-made ironing board that fell out of a cupboard without warning, and an automatic chicken coop door made from a washing machine engine, that was supposed to lock the hens in at night and free them at dawn. Maggie's favourite was a trapeze that hung from the barn rafters so she could join a circus, if ballet didn't work out.

Switzerland, 1963:

Jolted awake by Anna Bell, Maggie gets up and follows her into the corridor.

"You have to be onstage for all the ballets or we don't get paid. So, let's get started with the first ballet, called 'Jazz Blues.' Most of the music is by Yusef Lateef," she says with authority. "If you don't know his music, you will love it," she adds. And so, in a cramped corridor of a Wagon-Lit speeding toward the French Alps, Maggie learns the complicated choreography of Nikolaus Pávlos, while Anna hums off-key. Suddenly, the compartment door across from theirs opens, and a rather determined girl comes in. She steps toward Maggie, armed with a tape measure, a box of pins, and a scowl on her face. Without saying a word she takes measurements, occasionally sucking air between her teeth with displeasure. Maggie is confused and doesn't understand if the fuss is because she is too tall or too skinny. The girl returns to her compartment and just as the door snaps shut, she swears "*Sale Anglaise.*"

"That means you are a filthy English," translates a voice from behind. "Hello, I am Prudence Rosebourgh, but everybody here calls me Rosie." She continues, "Don't worry about Simone. Her bark is worse than her bite. She is wildly jealous that someone might take her responsibilities."

"What are they?" Maggie asks.

"Costume repairs and keeping the boss happy," Rosie replies, winking wickedly.

Without thinking, Maggie bursts out, "Oh, surely not, he is so old! He looks the same age as my father." Deadly silence ensues. Both Anna and Rosie look embarrassed.

"Do you want to be my roommate in Bern?" Rosie continues, as though nothing has been said.

"Yes," Maggie nods. The train picks up speed as Les Ballets tear across eastern France toward the Alps. Anna teaches her a small part of the second ballet which is called 'The Leather Boys.'*

"It's a bit like rival gangs, the mods and the rockers in London," she explains, "and most of the music is from Leonard Bernstein." Maggie is thoroughly confused.

Accommodation is paid for by the ballet and almost everyone has a roommate. At the Hotel Wildenmann in Bern, Rosie and Maggie are sharing a small, cramped room on the top floor with two twin beds and gorgeous, puffy duvets—a first for Maggie. Rosie is a lively companion and full of gossip. She points out Liliane, who has been in the company the longest.

"She is a true Parisian, and her mother…" she says snobbishly, "is an usherette at a cinema on the *Champs Élysées*."

The following day, Rosie proudly announces, "My mother makes toothbrushes in a factory in Hertford just outside London." After the first night, it is obvious that Rosie is sleeping elsewhere.

The theatre is within walking distance of the Hotel Wildenmann, which is a blessing, as it is snowing. As Rosie and Maggie enter the stage door, stomping the ice from their boots, Maggie sees a sign: 'Mocambo Cabaret,' and her jaw drops. It never occurred to her that they'd be dancing in a nightclub and not a theatre. The Club Mocambo is decorated with Mexican hats and gaudy streamers, and stinks of old cigars. But, it is the most popular club in Bern.

"We've sold out from now to New Year's Eve," announces the Maestro proudly. "A newspaper reported that we are dancing *West Side Story*, and we do use some of Bernstein's music….so…now, *daahlinks*, we get to work. We have one day to fit Maggie into all the ballets." He lights a cigarette and signals to the Belgian boy, Xavier, to start the reel-to-reel music recorder. The music of Yusef Lateef explodes from the speakers that are mounted beside the Mexican hats, which start to shake accumulated dust onto the floor below. Maggie has never worked so hard in her life. Luckily, she is a fast learner, but a dozen dancers on a small, round stage leaves no room for the tiniest of errors. Sweat flies, feet burn, and legs ache with fatigue—but no one stops dancing.

"What happens if someone gets sick?" she asks Rosie.

"You don't get sick. You keep on dancing till you drop."

Opening night is terrifying. Maggie's heart is thumping and she feels faint. *What if I forget the steps? What if I fall off the stage and land into someone's lap in the audience? Or worse still, what if someone recognizes me and tells my mother I am dancing in a nightclub?* There is a sudden hush of the audience as the lights dim, someone coughs, programmes are rattled and folded, and Maggie feels all her anxiety lift. From the moment she hears the first beats of the drums, she feels in another world. From stage left, she appears, her long legs in black tights, red hair pulled into a ponytail, wearing a snow-white turtleneck sweater and sneakers. Like a lioness stalking prey, she moves in slow motion, snapping her fingers to the drum beat, confident and at one with the moment. Every dancer is alert, each body moves to the rhythm; the cadence of the sound. They are on another planet, and it doesn't matter if they are dancing in a cabaret or in Carnegie Hall. All private grievances are forgotten as they perform the genius of Nikolaus Pávlos' vision.

An explosion of applause brings everyone back to earth. Sweat is running down all of their faces and soaking into their turtleneck sweaters. They bow and dash off to change, as Rudi, the solo drummer, coyly says, "Aw, shucks," and bows as the curtain closes. When everyone is changed into their costumes for 'The Leather Boys' all thoughts of who is in the audience become unimportant. Maggie is dancing her heart out to the unbelievably modern choreography and she is proud to be part of it all. 'Jazz Mood' and 'The Leather Boys' go without mishap, and Maggie wishes she could say the same for the Finale. When she first hears Stan Kenton's music 'Artistry in Rhythm' she thinks, *Slow down buster, no one can dance that fast in three-inch high heels.* The real problem is that Maggie hates her costume. It's a sloppy, old, yellow satin bathing suit about ten sizes too big for her. Simone sewed rubber falsies into the bodice to give her some cleavage, but she still feels ridiculous. To add to the embarrassment, The Mocambo orchestra plays Stan Kenton's music even faster than the taped version, and Maggie can't keep up. Her arms are up when they are supposed to be down. She looks left when she should be looking right, and the whole dance is a disaster. The audience doesn't seem to notice, and are wildly enthusiastic, but Maggie feels humiliated. Only Rudi finds it hilarious.

"You are a very, very funny lady," he says, as he walks to the boys' dressing room, chuckling to himself. Out of the corner of her eye, she catches sight of Aneke, his fiancé, watching her intently.

Maggie is alone, sitting on her single bed in the Hotel Wildenmann, painting her toenails and attempting to read Sir Winston Churchill's "Their Finest Hour." Her reading choices are deliberately scholarly as she tries to self-educate herself. Most people, including Maggie's father, think dancers are a bit thick because they've spent their whole lives using their bodies and not their brains. Maggie is determined to prove them all wrong. She curls up in the feather duvet, exhausted, waiting to fall asleep, and wonders whose bed Rosie is sleeping in.

Very close to the Wildenmann Hotel is an old restaurant called 'Ratskeller.' It is after midnight when Les Ballets arrive, starving. Almost as if the restaurant had been waiting, a long table is set by an open fire. Romeo pulls out a chair for Maggie and she sits quickly. She reaches into her wallet and peeks at the few Swiss Francs left. The menu is written in German, Italian, and French. Running her finger down the list of prices, the cheapest dish is Italian *'cervelli,** or in German, *'gehirne.'*

"Beautiful, veal," Maggie translates, and promptly orders it. Romeo gives her a quizzical look.

"You know this, *cervelli*?"

She smiles faintly. "Maybe?"

He pours her a large glass of red wine and pointing to it, asks "How you say...paid for already?"

"On the house," translates Maggie. He fills the glass to the brim and sends the bottle down the table. Maggie looks around, smiling happily.

From the kitchen, hot platters arrive carrying *'schnitzel mit spaëtzle,'* which looks like steak and noodles, chops with sauce béarnaise, french fries, an enormous bowl of onion soup topped with cheese a large blood sausage that produces a lot of jokes, hot potato salad, and still nothing for Maggie. Everyone digs in and Maggie's wine glass is topped up, yet again. Finally, the '*maître d*' places a large dish in front of her. Right in the middle of the plate is a deep-fried blob that looks like a half tennis ball covered in crumbs. She looks around and realizes that everyone has stopped to wait expectantly for her to start. With her knife, she timidly taps the ball lightly—it's spongy. She finally pokes one side with her fork and then stabs it with her knife.

"Yuck," she squeals, "it's milky slime, not even cooked." Revolted, she asks, "Is it brains?" She shudders and puts her fork and knife down slowly and carefully before hiding her face in a napkin. Romeo laughs and laughs, in fact, he laughs so hard that he falls right off his chair while wheezing.

"Beautiful veal, ha, ha, ha!" The whole room erupts as though it is the funniest thing in the world. Maggie thinks this is the perfect moment to try out her Italian swear words and says "*Stronzino*," little asshole.

"Why didn't you tell me '*cervelli*' means brains?" Evidently, being a little asshole is much worse than being a big one, but it only makes Romeo laugh even harder.

At class the next morning Maggie sits in a corner, stretching and idly watching the rehearsal. Rudi and Anna are practicing the '*pas de deux*' from 'Raubkunst,' a ballet which translates from German as "stolen or looted artworks." It is a subtle, yet perplexing ballet about stealing paintings from private collections in Nazi occupied countries. The scenery consists of piles of empty picture frames and the dancers climb in and out in a sequence of intricate patterns. The music is haunting, and the choreography: spectacular. Even Maggie's little part is a joy to dance, although no one understands the political implications. All she does understand is that she wants Anna's role for herself. Maggie wants to dance the '*pas de deux*' with Rudi.

On her one day off, Maggie wanders around the art gallery in Bern called the Kunstmuseum. She looks for the works of her favourite painters: the ballet dancers of Edgar Degas, Picasso's clowns, and the explosive 'Can-Can' dancers at the Moulin Rouge nightclub painted by Henri de Toulouse-Lautrec. So absorbed in the display, she accidentally bumps into a fellow art lover, and is embarrassed to discover it is the Maestro. He is very upset, almost angry to see her there, and Maggie has no idea why.

"I didn't know you were interested in art," he says to her, in an accusatory voice. For a moment, Maggie is tongue-tied.

"My father is an artist, and gives lectures on art history." The Maestro glances at his watch and hurriedly makes his exit, explaining that he has an appointment. Maggie is left wondering, *What was that all about?*

In the middle of the night, a few days before the ballet is to leave Bern, there is a robbery. In a small, backstreet art gallery not far from the Mocambo, a painting disappears, a watercolour by Edgar Degas called 'Mlle Gabrielle Diot 1890.'* It is not reported to the Swiss police because it is a '*raubkunst*;' a stolen painting, and does not belong to the gallery of Gunter Simes and Sons of Bern, Switzerland.

Dear Mom, Pop, and Granny:
I am dancing like never before. The choreography is wild and wonderful and I am having the time of my life. I have torn up my five-week contract and am going with Les Ballets Jazz to Germany, to the Black Forest, I think. I will write when I get to wherever I am going. Don't worry about me. We stick together like a family. Love, Mags, xox

CHAPTER III

A Rolling Stone Gathers No Moss

Longlands, North Oyster Cove, 1945-1950:

Maggie's mother is teutophobic, like her neighbours, and blames the Germans for all the ills of the world. Her own great-grandfather had been a German immigrant to Canada, a fact that she likes to ignore. It never occurs to her that the music she adores and plays on her battered, grand piano consists mainly of German composers— the three B's: Beethoven, Brahms, and Bach. When Maggie's mother is sad and alone, waiting for Maggie's father to come home from his long lecture tours, she plays Strauss waltzes and the three sisters dance around the music room making up lyrics to suit themselves. The very word waltz comes from '*walzen*,' a teutonic word meaning to glide in three-quarter time with the accent on the first beat.

Germany, 1964:

Maggie is curious to see for herself this country that her mother thinks is so evil, and meet as many German people as she can along the way. Unfortunately, her language skills are non-existent, other than 'please,' 'thank you,' and '*Ich habe einen Bleistift*;' I have a pencil. It is going to be a very long journey for Les Ballets Jazz Europa from Bern, in Switzerland, to Bremen, in the north of Germany. Everyone is paying a little extra to be in the first-class car because the seats turn into beds at night. It's called the '*Schlafwagen*.' Without any breakdowns, the entire trip should take about twenty-four hours. Although Maggie still feels like an outsider, she is asked to play cards. Now, this could be the beginning of friendships for her, but Maggie decides to sit by herself at a table in the next compartment. She unfolds her map to ink in the route: Basel, Freiburg, Offenburg, Strasbourg, Karlsruhe, Mannheim, Frankfurt, Kassel, Hanover, and finally Bremen. She can't find the Black Forest anywhere. *Perhaps the Black Forest is not real,* she thinks, *just the setting for the Grimm's brothers' fairy tales and the place where Hansel and Gretel get lost.* How she loved that story, especially how the wicked witch gets roasted alive.

Maggie falls asleep and slumps over her map, waking just as the train slows down at a border crossing. She staggers, half asleep, to the door of the compartment, just as the Maestro pushes past and darts into the smelly '*toiletten*' sliding the door shut with a click. Frank, whose Algerian name is Fahad, is standing outside like a guard. He casually lights a hand-rolled cigarette and picks bits of tobacco from his teeth. The train is not moving. Two inspectors climb aboard and start checking passports. When they are close to the W.C., big Frank blocks their way, wheezing and coughing phlegm. Disgusted, the inspectors hurry past all the luggage to continue down the corridor. As soon as they disappear, Frank knocks twice on the door—a signal. *Tap, tap.*

Maggie disappears into her compartment but can hear Nikko say, "Go and check number four." Maggie knows that he means the rattan costume trunk, which is sort of a private joke because it is filled with smelly shoes and everyone always holds their noses at the mention of it.

"Make sure it is not taken off until Frankfurt." *Why take the shoes off in Frankfurt when we are going farther north to Bremen?* Maggie wonders. *I guess we are going to dance barefoot. How thrilling. I tell you, crossing borders can shatter one's nerves.* The train starts up again, rattling and joggling along, making good time as it presses farther and farther northeast. Each village seems to get poorer and dirtier, with increasing amounts of graffiti, garbage and grey clothes hanging haphazardly on lines. *And, the piles of rubble,* she thinks. *Surely they aren't leftover debris from the Allied bombing?*

Another stop at another nameless station, and Herr Porter rumbles in a monotonous voice *"Acht minute."* The dancers have eight minutes to stretch their legs. Most normal folks would take a brisk walk up and down the platform, but not Les Ballets. They shoot off the train in a *grand jeté,* yelping and leaping about like gazelles. Even the Maestro, Nikko, starts tap-dancing on the benches and everyone cavorts around like children let out for morning recess. Eight minutes later, when the porter calls out *"Alle einsteiger,"* they march back onto the train like they're soldiers. Other passengers have already boarded and have taken their seats.

"Das ist mein platz, my place, get out of here you blubber butt!" There is a lot of multilingual bickering, but finally, everyone settles down until the next stop. Everyone, that is, except Rudi, who complains that he has been kept awake all night by three drunken '*schmugelglumpfs*,' and has a swollen eye to prove it.

Frankfurt, 1964:

The rattan costume basket 'number four' of Les Ballets Jazz Europa lies open on top of a luggage cart, with the lid thrown back. In the dim light of a railroad lantern, the contents are exposed. Neatly sorted shoes, silver heels, long leather black boots, white leather boots, white umbrellas, hats, and dismantled props lie in careful rows. Two elderly men are tossing the contents onto a table. One belches rudely and the other blows a '*furzte*' and laughs loudly. At the bottom of the '*pannier*,' dirty fingers feel for the latch, click, it opens and the false bottom is removed showing six or seven inches of extra space, a whole bottom layer. The two carefully lift out a large flat package from the bottom of the trunk. The cover is locked back in place and the shoes, boots and umbrellas tossed on top. From the platform outside, the porter calls "*alle einsteiger*," all aboard, once more. The lid is closed on number four, as it is rolled onto the platform to the open door of the freight car, is pushed in with a label marked 'Bremen' over the one that was 'Frankfurt.' The whole operation takes exactly four minutes. The likeness of Mademoiselle Gabrielle 'Diot' has moved from Switzerland to her new home in Germany.

Bremen, Germany, 1964:

The theatre *Astoria*, in Bremen, is absolutely fabulous. Maggie will not have to deceive anyone in her letters home. It is like a theatre in Victorian London, but brand-spanking new. Well, everything in Bremen is brand new, because the British air force flattened nearly the entire city in WWII.* Fortunately, the ancient town hall, the *Rathaus*, and the statue in the middle of the *Marktplatz* were not destroyed. The new *Astoria* even has showers with hot water. The stage is gigantic and equipped with the latest theatrical lighting system. Les Ballets Jazz Europa has two performances a night for two weeks. Maggie is still paid the equivalent in marks of ten dollars a day, which equates to two dollars and fifty cents per hour when she is actually on the stage. No one else complains or even mentions money at all, and she has her suspicions that some are paid more. *Thank heavens Granny sends money,* she thinks.

Les Ballets Jazz Europa is featured in all of the German newspapers and one magazine. There is actually a photo of Maggie dancing on the roof, overlooking the city. Everywhere they go there are journalists and fans waiting for autographs. It is all quite exciting but beginning to feel intrusive. Maggie is reading the latest

Dance magazine in her hotel room, when she notices a large photo of the 'Maestro Nikolaos Pávlos; the Father of Modern Dance in Europe.' She continues to read: "He highlights new roles for men in ballet—bringing out male virtuosity, strength and stamina instead of the passive role of lifting partner. His choreography is endlessly inventive, capturing the mood of the modern generation." *Wow, that's more than impressive.* She puts down the magazine and smiles to herself, lights a cigarette, and continues with the English translation of *The Train* by Rose Valland. The book is about stealing paintings and sculptures from wealthy Jewish families during the war. It's a real fingernail-biter.

Maggie can smell them before actually seeing the sausage carts in the market square. The intoxicating aroma of pork fat, sizzling veal, and allspice makes her faint with hunger as she crosses the square on the way to the *Astoria* each morning. Finally, she has found something she can afford. She swoons over German *wurst*, Swedish *potatiskorv*, and an Austrian sausage called *Frankfurter Würstl*, which is very perplexing, because Frankfurt is in Germany not Austria. After sampling every type of sausage on the cart, the Swedish Korv with sweet pickle relish is the clear winner. On this particular day she buys two Korvs in two little buns called *korvbröts*, eats one, and carries the other to the theatre to eat later.

The door to the dressing room is slightly ajar and she opens it with the tip of her boot. The room is not empty. In the corner, sewing a torn costume, is Simone. There are tears running down her cheeks and onto the fabric in her lap. Impulsively, Maggie places the sausage next to her.

"I brought this for you, *pour toi*." This makes Simone cry all the harder. Between sobs, broken English and slang French, it all comes pouring out. She feels too old at thirty to master the new choreography and thinks Nikko is about to send her away. The *sales Anglais*; filthy English, bombed her home in Strasbourg, killing her entire family, and now she is alone in the world. Without Nikko and the ballet, she has nothing, '*rien de rien*' to live for. Maggie is aghast.

She stammers lamely, "What would we do without our costume mistress?"

Fortunately, right at that moment, a group of dancers burst through the door, laughing and chatting. Simone quickly wipes her tears and throws the repaired costume at one of them.

She snaps, "*Salope salissante*, hang it up yourself, messy bitch," and bites savagely into the Swedish korv, chewing it like a stray dog.

Nikko is hunched over the telephone conspiratorially, his hand cupped over the mouthpiece. He is speaking in Italian.

"*Si, si, Luciano, ho capito*," he says in a hushed voice. Anna is coming down the corridor with a coffee in her hand.

He switches to English and straightens up, explaining, "I will do anything to keep my ballet going. Anything at all. You understand. *Si*, it was raining in Frankfurt. Got that, Frankfurt. No, no, not Dusseldorf," he sighs, rolling his eyes at Anna as if to say, 'what an idiot this guy is, he needs to look at a map.' "*Si, si*, we will be in Hamburg for one day only doing a television special. Gotta go, here comes my coffee," and he hangs up.

"Anna, Anna, my *daahlink*! What would I do without you?" He gulps the coffee and places the cup down on top of the phone cupboard.

"Are we really being televised in Hamburg?" she asks, hopeful.

"Yes, my sweet Anna, and we are getting costumes for the two new ballets: La Résistance and Raubkunst." She looks at him, skeptical.

"Did you win the Irish sweepstakes?"* He laughs and pulls her into his arms, kissing her firmly.

Hamburg, 1964:

On a large estate in the Wandsbeck area of Hamburg is one

of the most modern film studios in Europe. The ballet arrives, exhausted after packing all the skips, scenery, and personal luggage the night before and at five in the morning. A filming of 'The Leather Boys' has to be done in one day only, as Les Ballets are opening in Travemünde on the sea in forty-eight hours. Everyone is very grumpy except the Maestro. He seems to thrive on very little sleep and has his most creative ideas when everyone else is ready to pass out. 'The Leather Boys' is one of the most popular ballets to date and really has no storyline except there are two rival gangs, The Mods, and the Rockers and it ends in a glorious fight on stage. The costumes for the Rockers are all leather; jackets, trousers, and tall boots. The rival mod guys wear turtleneck sweaters and pressed trousers, and the girls sport Mary Quant mini-dresses.*

Maggie is a Rocker in black, thigh-high boots and mesh tights. She gently strokes the soft leather shirt tied in a knot at her waist as she peers in the mirror. Her huge, false eyelashes make it hard to see anything but as Rudi walks by he whistles softly, so she knows she looks half decent. The dancers file into the large, windowless room where the filming will take place. It stinks of dirty ashtrays, rat droppings, and burning electrical cables. While the Maestro flaps around with the camera men, the director, the music arranger, and the set director, the many minions wearing ear protectors rush like ants in every direction. The dancers gather in a far corner to warm up. Maggie stretches, tries a few pirouettés, and then a series of jumps, warming and softening the joints and muscles. The sounds of *West Side Story* and Gershwin fade in and out, and honking of cars and the roar of a motor bike are deafening. The doors close sealing them into the cement bunker.

"Places!" the Maestro warns, then the director calls for silence: *"STILLE! Sei ruhig!"* You could hear a pin drop.

None of the dancers are sure that they like working on film

because there is no audience, so the thrill of performing is not the same. Most of them like dancing for people, not the blank glass eye of a camera. It's all a bit of a letdown. Maggie has performed an excruciating back bend leap so many times that she feels as though her spine will never straighten again. She thinks, *If I live to be a ripe old age, I will be creeping along like a pill bug just because of this one lousy second on a television screen that few people are going to see.* After hours and hours, the dancers are let out of the complex and inhale the fresh, cold air. The Maestro stays behind to pack the '*panniers*' and send them to the train. Then, Maggie sees it, just beside the path, hidden in some fallen leaves. Like a giant lizard, she scoops it up and pops it into her handbag, feeling like a thief. The dancers haven't had anything to eat since they arrived at 8a.m. and are now heading to the train station. *How is it possible that no one thought to provide any food at all, not even a tiny plate of sandwiches, only endless cups of coffee?* But now, Maggie has one fallen apple to eat on the train.

As soon as all the dancers have left the television studios and most of the staff are gone, Nikko pulls a letter from his pocket, rereads it, and walks slowly down a long corridor. A door is ajar at the end. He knocks with two taps.

"*Eingeben*, enter," says a voice. The maestro hands the letter to a very tall white-haired gentleman in a formal suit, who is standing by a warm fireplace ablaze with dry wood. Nikko shakes his head.

"The gallery will never go for a deal like this. Never. The Italian people want that particular painting by van Huysum back with an apology from your government."* He smiles ruefully, "There can be no money involved. I won't have anything to do with this." The letter is tossed into the fire and burns to ashes. "My compliments to this fine facility." He bows slightly, "*Auf Wiedersehen*."

Travemünde, Germany, June, 1964:

Amazing what a few hours' nap and a bit of fuel will do to rejuvenate those half-dead from exhaustion. Les Ballets arrive at midnight to the northern, seaside casino town of Travemünde, and are met like superstars. They are ushered into a dining room at the staff quarters, where they are staying, and treated to a feast; a table of food, more than Maggie has seen in weeks. There is every conceivable kind of fish, from pickled herring to baby shrimp called *krabben*, as well as sprats, sausages, and a pyramid of fruit with dozens of apples. Four very young waiters are in uniform, and even the manager of the casino is there to greet them. Everyone speaks English, Italian, Greek, French, Danish, and Dutch, and Maggie thinks they are charming. It is truly a United Nations of civility. Later, the dancers collapse on clouds of feathers.

La Résistance begins on an empty stage with seven dancers only half visible, their arms edged in a cool light. High above, a searchlight flickers through a barred, jail-like window. It is a cold light that brings the feeling of dread. The music of a waltz is in a minor key making it sound haunted and forbidding. It begins softly and the noise of the city streets fade. A young, French girl is being held back by hands as she pulls and strives to leave and join a young soldier on the other side of the dark stage. His jacket is off, but the insignia of a German officer is visible. She pulls free and runs to him. The story of the ballet is a wartime Romeo and Juliet. It is modern, poignant, soul-stirring, and tragic. The choreography is brilliant and the Maestro has played with the lighting, making rockets flash, a moon beam, shattered glass sparkling, and a searchlight. At the end, of course, the French girl lies dead and the soldier runs off. A swastika shines in a small, barred window upon a fragile, lifeless body.

Backstage, the dancers wait, breathing hard, with sweat running down their chests. They are counting the seconds, "One, two, three, four, five…" and silence.

"*Merde*, they hate it."

Someone in the audience starts to clap and yells, "Bravo," and then, like an exploding bomb, everyone is on their feet clapping and whistling. The entire ballet rushes onstage and bows, the applause ear-splitting. The Maestro stands backstage, hands around the huge, hemp rope holding up the velvet curtain. He is grinning foolishly, unable to stop the tears from welling up in the corners of his eyes. *La Résistance* is a resounding success. At the moment when the applause reaches its peak, he lowers the heavy curtain to the stage, letting the dust fly like little sea birds before settling again into the dirty, velvet folds.

Longlands, North Oyster Cove, June 6, 1944:

It is all over by late afternoon. Maggie's mother is sitting up in her bed at Longlands, eating freshly picked strawberries and cream from Betsy the cow, quite ravenous after the ordeal of giving birth to her third daughter, Margaret Alice Dinsdale. Meanwhile, almost five thousand miles away, on a small stretch of sand in Normandy between Courseulles and Saint-Aubin sur Mer over ten thousand soldiers, a thousand of whom were Canadians, died. An equal number of German soldiers perished and civilian deaths numbered fifteen thousand in the fog of battle. June 6th, a day of joy for some and a day to mourn for many others.

Aarhus, Denmark, 1964:

June 6th, 1944 is D-Day, as well as Maggie's birthday. *I must be the only twenty-year-old virgin in the entire world,* she thinks, depressed. She feels like Alice in Wonderland, without a rabbit hole to fall down. *At this rate, I am going to end up a sour, old spinster looking after my parents until death from boredom,* she writes in her diary. One of the

Dutch girls, Talitha, asks if Maggie is a lesbian or something, to which Anna replies sarcastically, "Oh no, she's a Canadian." As it turns out, Maggie's birthday is a success of sorts. She doesn't get laid, but the entire ballet and a boisterous group of students from the University of Aarhus have an all-night bash. In the middle of the celebration, two guys, brothers Peter and Jens, who call themselves "gnags," *whatever that means*, crash the party and sing and play the guitar. Everybody dances until dawn. Maggie learns how to gulp schnapps in one swallow. And then, of course, they all have Danish beer. *Oh boy, what a night!* Dear, sweet Ronáld gives Maggie her very own semi-automatic switchblade knife with a staghorn handle. It snaps open to eleven inches and is to keep her safe, or at the very least, to peel apples. *He might be gay, but he sure knows how to look after a girl*, she is forced to admit.

Dear Mom and Pop:
Please excuse the messy handwriting. I am on yet another jiggling train heading south, destination: Montreux, Switzerland. Les Ballets have a two-week contract and are filming a ballet for Eurovision. It is a festival, but for television shows called the Golden Rose or Rose d'Or de Montreux. This is a really big deal. I know you don't have a television set but there are some famous stars meeting in Montreux. From Africa; Les Surfs, from England; Petula Clarke, from France; Sacha Distel and some group of guys called the Rolling Stones. I've never heard of any of them. Anyway, I must tell you about my date with a German dentist in Travemünde. I had a raging toothache and went to the village dentist who spoke only a few words of English but clearly said 'root canal' and I almost fainted. Looking around, the office was like a Victorian torture chamber. The drill was actually operated by a treadle, somewhat like a sewing machine with the feet. Well, to make a long story

short, he was as gentle as a lamb and even made me laugh. As he approached my mouth with the archaic drill, pumping with his feet, he leered "I am a wicked old Nazi, ja" and he threw back his head and cackled. I had to return for a second appointment to finish and he didn't charge me 'ein pfennig.' He had seen our ballet 'La Résistence,' and said it was beautiful, that it was his story, too. He had a tear in his eye and blew his nose into his handkerchief. Then, he hugged me so hard that he almost popped my filling out. Mom, you may want to rethink your ideas about Germans. I miss you all. Love, Mags

All night and all the next day, the train rocks and rolls southward, a rhythm of wheels on rails. As it twists through mountain passes, the mournful whistle echoes back and forth. A comforting smell of old leather and brass polish emanates, and when the carriage doors slide open, the unmistakable stench of urine prickles their noses. At most stops of more than four minutes, the windows are pushed open and hot coffee passes through. On and on, the engines haul drowsy passengers to their destinations. Every so often someone pulls out their switchblade and slices apples, passes them around, and then falls back to sleep or puts their noses into a book. In one of the compartments, an endless game of 'hearts' drones on. In another compartment, a heap of dancers sleep in a pile like a litter of exhausted kittens curled together, with feet on laps, heads on shoulders, some snoring softly and others gazing out into the night, seeing nothing. The corridor is filled with luggage, boxes, and parcels. On Maggie's suitcase, luggage stickers are slapped over top of each other. Cunard Lines, London, Bern, Bremen, Aarhus, Hamburg, Copenhagen, Malmo, and in the middle: 'Les Ballets Jazz Europa.'

Montreux, Switzerland, 1964:

Maggie is shocked. *Holy cow, the Maestro must have robbed*

a bank. The dancers are living in the most expensive, magnificent hotel in all Montreux, maybe in all Switzerland. The Grand Hotel Suisse is like a castle, right on Lake Geneva, with balconies that open onto a flower-filled garden beside a path. The location is right next door to the Casino, where the filming is to take place. The Casino, formerly the *'Kursaal,'* a watering hole for the rich and famous that looks over the placid water to the startling snow-capped mountains of the Alps. Usually, Montreux is sedate and regal, but this week it is jam-packed with television people from around the world. Maggie has been rehearsing non-stop since their arrival, tripping over television cables, having ears blasted off with sound equipment, and practicing on the opaque, glass stage with lights coming from below. The opening ballet is *'Mambo Diablo,'* the Afro-Cuban dance in blacklight that makes teeth, white fringe costumes, and umbrellas appear to be dancing on human bodies like magic. The ballet ends in a terrific jungle storm with the screams of wild animals, thunder, and lightning.

The master of ceremonies for the Eurovision show is a guy called Sacha Distel, who is a good-looking, actor, singer and jazz musician. He is staring in fascination at Anna. Maggie is not interested, but what does burn her up is that she is not chosen to present one of the damn gold roses to the winners. Sacha, the film star, and Nikko choose Simone, who is preening around in a dress that looks like it has a dead cat sewn around the hem. Anna looks staggeringly beautiful in a simple black dress. Rosie borrows a pink lace sheath, and Shirel is poured into a tube of navy blue satin. Maggie feels she is a far better dancer than any of them, but is overlooked. *Maybe I am not chosen because I look like an American,* she wonders.

While the winners are being announced in the grand ballroom, Maggie is sitting in the 'Ye Ye Club,' named after the Beatles song, *"She loves me ye, ye, ye,"* getting hammered and watching her first striptease. She is at a table with an English singer named Petula

Clark who is in town to sing her single chart topping "Downtown" for the T.V. special. "Ready, Steady, Go." The lights dim in the mahogany wood-paneled room and all is silent except for the odd cough and striking of matches. A rather plain girl of about twenty stomps on stage carrying a knitted holdall. She is stark naked—not a stitch on. The music, if you can call it that, begins with a jolt, a mad clown-like *"Oom pah pah"* and she rummages in her sack and pulls out a pair of knickers. She tries to put them on, getting all tangled up and putting two legs in the same hole, then sideways with a leg through the waist and the other in the wrong hole. Her face is deadpan. Maggie and Petula are laughing so hard that they're finding it difficult to breathe. Then, the girl bends over and attempts, in vain, to fasten the hooks and eyes on a black lace garter belt. Her silk stockings rip and her left foot goes right through the bottom. The audience is howling and weeping with laughter. The orchestra plays a cacophony of rhythm of bumps and grinds. The pink cotton brassiere gets tied in a knot and a baggy wool sweater is put on backwards. By this time, Maggie is in hysterics. The stripper ends her act as she began; completely without expression, but fully clothed—a brilliant comedienne. Maggie and Petula, whose real name is Sally, clap and clap until their hands ache. All thoughts of the stupid Golden Rose have disappeared, and the famous words, *"Laugh and the world laughs with you, cry and you cry alone,"* ricochets around in Maggie's tipsy head.

The next morning Talitha shakes Maggie awake and hands her a coffee. Bright sun pours in the window of the fancy Grande Suisse hotel room giving her a blinding headache.

"Where did you get to last night? We looked all over for you."

"I was in the bar," she mumbles, and rolls over to go back to sleep.

"Whoa," cries Talitha. "Starting in twenty minutes, get up. Rudi is taking class this morning." Maggie is suddenly awake.

Montreux, Switzerland, April 20th, 1964:

"READY, STEADY, GO!" A voice booms. "From the world-famous Casino of Montreux, Switzerland, The Rolling Stones, from England. Please give a warm reception on their first performance in Europe." The huge speakers are deafening and some of the dancers plug their ears.

"*Trop fort! de quoi parle-t-il*? What's he talking about?" The cameras are pointing toward two large, ornate doors that lead to the veranda that encircles the lake. The director is frantically pointing to the ballet dancers standing there to make some noise, so they clap politely. The doors open for the grand entrance and five skinny boys hesitate and then creep onto the set. The dancers are taken aback at the long, greasy hair, rumpled clothes, and sharp-pointed, winklepicker boots*. The five boys glance around uncomfortably, wondering what to do next.

The director is encouraging Les Ballets Jazz to look animated, so they all clap harder and shout, "Yey, yey!" The music starts at top volume, with a song called 'Mona,' and the outer doors are flung open. A screaming mob of scruffy teenagers burst in, all laughing drunkenly, yelling and howling like animals and mugging the cameras. It is impossible to hear 'Mona' or anything else.

"What is this ready, steady go, all about?" Talitha asks, bewildered. "Look at their dirty fingernails!" Maggie and the others escape to their dressing rooms below.

Later, they hear that the English mob turn from raucous to a full-blown riot after the taping. The fans move outside, where they argue, punch each other, urinate on the English hollyhocks and tulips, break antique furniture, and vomit into the potted palm trees. The police arrive too late to save the gardens and the pimply-faced fans are sent off in the paddy wagon to the edge of town and told to go and never come back. *While Les Ballets Jazz is heading to Italy, the Stones are heading to super stardom.*

At precisely 4:02 in the afternoon, the southbound train pulls into the Montreux station. The station master, in an immaculate uniform, steps daintily onto the platform.

He blows his whistle and calls out, "*Sei minuti, sechs minuten,* six minutes." Like a well-rehearsed performance, the BJE shoot into action. A chain gang moves more than eighty-four pieces of luggage, record players, radios, boxes, bags, and a cat cage from the platform into the carriage. The freight doors slide open and the costume trunks are hauled inside and stacked. The Maestro charges up and down the aisle counting trunks, paying porters and handlers, and giving out tickets while barking instructions in four different languages. He is like an orchestra leader conducting Tchaikovsky's 1812 Overture. Everyone works in unison. Anna, late as usual, teeters into view, wearing back-strap high heels and clutching two dozen hothouse roses.

"*Putin,*" hisses Simone, seeing the lavish flowers, "*salope,*" she adds. The Maestro glances from the flowers to Anna with a quizzical expression. Then he shrugs his shoulders as if to imply that he couldn't give a damn, turns and steps onto the train.

"*D'abord,*" calls the station master, as Anna's bulging bags are flung unceremoniously through the window. Six minutes later, in a puff of steam, the station is empty and the citizens of Montreux close their sleepy shutters for more siesta time.

CHAPTER IV

Pasta, Paintings, and Pirouettes

Milan was finally brought to its knees on the night of August 13, 1944 by the British Royal Air Force, who dropped almost thirteen thousand tons of explosives and incendiary bombs in one raid. The bombing started raging fires that eventually left a half million Italian civilians rattled and homeless. The focus of the raid was on the ancient historical sites: the magnificent Duomo di Milano (1386), Santa Maria delle Grazie(1466), the Sforza Castle(1499), the Royal Palace(1717) and the theatres; La Scala(1778), Teatro Lirico(1779) and Teatro Dal Verme(1872). The final insult was that the American Air Force renewed the bombing in October 1944, dropping one thousand tons of explosives, after the Italian Fascist Regime had already declared defeat in September 1943—The Armistice of Cassible. **

All her life, Maggie has imagined Italy to be the envy of all other countries. It is a land blessed with endless sunshine, joyous people, lush vineyards of purple fruit, hand-hewn stone castles perched on hilltops, and gilded cathedrals filled with precious paintings by the finest artists in the world. All Italian men look like Gods and stroll about drinking wine and singing like Dean Martin, while Italian women make pasta and babies and spend an inordinate amount of time popping into church to pray and prattle.

Maggie's fantasy is shattered as the train pulls into the main station, the '*stazione centrale de Milano*' in the summer of 1964. The rain is bucketing down and the windows of the train are opaque, as though covered in thick, pea soup. The carriage door opens and Maggie jumps down, landing in a large puddle.

"My boots, my new Bally boots!" She yelps as everyone splashes about, searching for their possessions and rushing toward a sign that reads 'USCITA.' She looks around, distracted by the filthy, soot-covered walls, leaking roof, and the utter befuddlement and confusion. Ronáld, who has befriended her, appears, fedora pulled low, and takes her gently but firmly by the arm. He guides her to the exit like a lost child in a tempest.

Rosie and Maggie are standing on the stage of an enormous theatre, the '*Smeraldo*,' built in 1942, that seats close to a thousand people. They are staring through the overhead into the 'fly gallery.'

"Is this really a movie theatre?" asks Maggie, craning her neck to peek between the massive ropes that hold up a jungle of equipment and a full movie screen.

"We are performing *avanti spettacolo*. That means we dance before a feature film, usually a cowboy movie with Italian subtitles," Rosie informs her in a know-it-all tone.

Maggie chortles, "Oh, it is like two for the price of one. One ticket for a spaghetti Western*, plus a ballet thrown in. That's quite a bargain!" As it turns out, Les Ballets Jazz performs not one, but two shows per night, interspersed with Clint Eastwood firing his pistols at phoney Mexican bandits and '*rojos*' while galloping over the hills of Tuscany. The feature film tonight is called, "A Fistful of Dollars." The contract at the *Teatro Smeraldo* is for two weeks, and every day and night, freezing rain and sleet cascade down, drenching everyone's hair and clothes that never seem to dry. Everybody gets sick. Not enough sleep, not enough food, and living in close quarters spells disaster. The pay is six thousand lira, which sounds like a lot, but amounts to ten dollars a day.

Dear Mom and Pop:

Thank you for the money order waiting at the American Express office. I am quite desperate, as I can't seem to live on what I make. Miss Thelma Wynne is right, "Ballet is not for sugar plum fairies." I am dog tired, run down, have a terrible cold and need to buy cough syrup, vitamin pills, and underpants. The Italian and French girls love suppositories. They don't take medicine the normal way by mouth, but push waxy torpedoes up their bottoms. Very kooky, eh? Lots of love, Mags. xxx

What Maggie fails to mention is that her cough medicine is 'Stock 84,' a cheap brandy that renders one speechless and sets the throat on fire. Similarly, she doesn't elaborate on her need for new knickers. She will never forget nor forgive the humiliation of the very first rehearsal in Bern, Switzerland, at the Mocambo Cabaret. As she stepped out of her street clothes to change into dance gear for the first time, the girls began to stare and titter at her underwear.

Then, two of them, Mimi and Shirel, started to hoot with laughter, pointing and asking, "*Mais, qu'est-ce que tu porte*? What are you wearing?" They pull and snap at her panty girdle that reaches mid-thigh, attached to garter snaps.

"It's a Playtex long-line panty." There is so much laughter and joking that the boys in the dressing room next door come in, without knocking, and join in the hilarity.

Now, Maggie can take a joke, but standing there semi-naked with a bunch of idiots snickering at her is not her idea of amusement. She has been waiting to go shopping for the most adorable bikini panties ever made, no matter what they cost. Underwear is important.

Maggie is discovering that there is a lot more to being a ballerina than the actual title. The final indignity comes with the music; a bare whisper of a drum brush, and her cue to enter. She flies across the stage like a bird in an almighty, flying great split.

Some wanker shouts "*Troppo magra*," making his buddies cackle like a gobble of turkeys.

Rosie is happy to translate; "That means you are too skinny, dearie," in the bitchiest tone of voice. It is the way she says it, mocking and spiteful, that is so cruel. By the time the ballet is over and they all hurry back to the dressing room to change costumes, Maggie has decided she despises Rosie. The BJE has a second show to do and it will be hours before she can disappear to her hotel and cry. Maggie decides: *I will never share a room with that bitch Rosie again, not ever!* By the end of the second show of the night, the Maestro hands the entertainment over to Clint Eastwood, in a ten-gallon hat, shooting everyone in sight. The dancers are starving—almost fainting for food.

On this night, Anna takes Maggie under her wing and says, "Hurry up, come with me. Nikko has found a brilliant little place, 'Trattoria Nonna Maria,' very close by, with the best old-fashioned Milanese cooking, and cheap as chips." Make-up is removed at lightning speed with cold cream, false eyelashes are ripped off haphazardly, and everyone takes a turn splashing water about in the antiquated corner sink. Above the faucet are signatures of Billie Holiday, Duke Ellington, and Thelonious Monk, humbly beside other graffiti of hearts and lipstick kisses, scratched into the plaster wall. Maggie carefully avoids Rosie. Arm in arm, Anna and Maggie splash across the street and then slip single-file between two very old, grey, stone apartment buildings into a narrow and dimly-lit alley. The muffled sound of the city gives way to uneasy silence. The *passaggio* reeks of mould and misery.

Creeping along past-tightly closed doors, Anna murmurs, "I

hope this is it." They stop and listen for some sign of life. Maggie runs her hand over the thousands of little holes in the walls. "This looks like a machine gun has sprayed the walls. Look, nothing has been patched or repaired in all these years since the war." She looks up at a faded, stenciled silhouette of a man, painted by a door, and peers closely. "Is that supposed to be Benito Mussolini? Is this graffiti?" Her questions go unanswered and Anna has gone ahead. Anna finally calls, "I've found it. Come on. I'm famished." The sound of laughter erupts as the door to the trattoria opens and a shaft of light reveals an alcove in the blackened wall. The two disappear and the heavy door snaps shut. The plaster walls, painted marigold yellow are covered in family photos, autographed portraits of celebrities and opera singers, and local bands. From metal hooks, garlic braids and aging salamis hang in abundance. Shelves hold various knick-knacks, bottles of dusty vintage wine, a clock, liquors, miscellaneous pottery jugs and a garish, ceramic replica of Sant'Ambrogio, the patron saint of Milan.

On one side of the room narrow tables are crammed with semi-inebriated men who have finished eating, but are drinking coffee and 'Frenet Branca,' a bitter liquor made of herbs. They are pounding their fists on the table and arguing politics in the ancient dialect of the Milanese.

The room falls silent as Anna in her best Italian calls out, "Can you serve sixteen starving dancers, *ballerini affamati?*"

"*Va bene*, of course," booms a deep, baritone voice from the kitchen. The smell wafting through the room is enough to make them both faint.

Maggie inhales deeply, "Garlic frying in butter," she sighs. Once more, the door bursts open, letting in a blast of cold air as the others arrive, greeting the chef who has come out bearing an armload of glasses and a couple of bottles tucked under his arm. He is a large, round man with a mustache and sparkling eyes. His starched apron is clean besides a few blobs of fresh tomato sauce. Immediately, the locals abandon their *frenet branca*, and start rearranging the small tables into rows and scraping wooden chairs across the tile floor. Mamma snatches soiled tablecloths and replaces them with fresh ironed ones, all the while clucking like a mother hen.

Romeo sneaks up behind Maggie and tickles her ear. "Are you going to order *cervelli* tonight?"

Maggie rolls her eyes. "Brains? No, I want something more fattening."

"Oh, leave her alone, Romeo," says Anna, giving him a 'hands-off' look, while she and Maggie sit together beside Ronáld. The Maestro is nowhere to be seen.

Without ordering anything, platters of local cheeses arrive; gorgonzola, both *cremificato* and *piccante*, mounds of soft *stracchino* and thin slices of *Grano Padano*. Other dishes of tomatoes, olives, and salami from Lombardy are rushed from the kitchen. Then, with a flourish, Mamma brings in a steaming tray of hot buns shaped like roses, bursting open in the summer sun.

"*Rosetta*," she cries, "straight from the oven." They all cheer, scream and dive in like savages, pouring wine into glasses and drinking to their health.

Anna pauses, "Where is Nikko?"

Just as the main course, the '*Secondo*' is being served, the heavy, wooden door opens and the Maestro enters, followed by a group of local folk singers from a nightclub in town. They all are hugging and kissing the chef and Nonna Maria as though they are family. Somehow, everyone squeezes in and finds a knife and fork. From a monumental pan, braised veal, osso buca and the famous *risotto alla milanese* are ladled onto plates. A hand passes Maggie a bowl of parsley and lemon sauce.

"Put that on top, it's called *gremolata*." In all her life, she has never tasted anything as rich and complex.

"Incredible," she says, as a hand pours more wine into her glass. As the last drops of veal sauce and *gremolata* is wiped up with the bread and the plates cleared, the chef returns carrying a guitar. The night is just beginning. Ronáld stands up, cigarette in hand and in perfect pitch, sings a folk song in the local dialect of the Milanese. Nonna is so overwhelmed, she throws her apron over her head and bursts into tears.

Early next morning, the green stage door of the Teatro Smeraldo opens, and chattering echo down the corridor toward the dressing rooms. Simone is already there, with her needle and thread, stitching rips and patching holes in costumes. The rancid smell of yesterday's sweat combined with butt-filled ashtrays and backstage grease competes with freshly made coffee carried in by a dozen or so giggling, hungover dancers. From the stage above comes the sound of Mendelssohn's piano *'Allegretto'* or 'Spring Song' on the tape recorder and the voice of Aneka.

"We're starting, hurry up, *dépêchez-vous!*" On stage, a make-shift barre runs along the back wall. The dusty house curtains and backdrop are high up in the 'fly gallery' and the darkened auditorium that seats a thousand, is now as silent as a tomb. In periodic waves, the ballet members enter, gulp coffee, and take their places. Class begins with the inevitable *pliés*; knee bends to warm the muscles and joints.

"*Grande pliés*, to the count of six," Aneka, not noted for her sense of the ridiculous, begins without a hint of a smile. There are yawns, stretches, and smart remarks bantering about.

"*Un, deux, trois, quatre, cinq, six*, slowly, *'port de bras'* with soft, *zachte armen en handen.*"

They tighten their abdomens, keeping their arms and hands as soft as thistledown. Aneka hops from one language to another without realizing it. Maggie drifts along with the music, her body automatically bending and stretching, but inwardly she is pondering the alarming conversation with Ronáld in the trattoria the night before.

"I still don't understand why there are silhouettes of Mussolini painted on the walls outside. It's creepy." He had looked at her sadly, for a long time before answering.

"You really don't know what went on in Europe, do you?" He gave a great sigh. *"In 1944 with the fascists still in power, every Italian citizen had to swear allegiance to Benito Mussolini and to the fascist regime."* Maggie listened to every word. *"Anyone who did not pledge allegiance, starved, was not given food rations or else, was sent to prison and tortured. Italian Jews were not given an option, but sent to concentration camps or left to starve in hiding. A likeness of Il Duce was painted beside the doors of those who swore allegiance. No stencil—no food! It was as simple as that! Any neighbours who tried to feed them were shot."*

Shocked, Maggie asks, "But, Ronáld, you are Jewish, how can you come here to Nonna Maria's knowing that they supported Mussolini?" He inhales deeply and from a million miles away, reflects "Ah yes! You see, in order to survive, you must forgive, but, you never forget."

Maggie is half asleep when her door opens softly and Rosie tiptoes in. With only the moonlight to guide her, she slips into her pyjamas and climbs into the other single bed. In a barely audible mumble she breathes, "I'm sorry Mags, I didn't mean…."

At first light, Maggie bolts upright. The rain has finally stopped and the morning sun pours through the shutters. The other bed is rumpled but the room is empty. Maggie picks up her latest book, "The Tropic of Cancer," by Henry Miller and reads about pornographic sex. She figures it is time she wakes up to reality. By the end of the week, Les Ballets Jazz Europa moves to the center of Milan to the historic opera house, *Teatro Lirico* and are booked into the *Pensione Rastrelli*, on the same street. They are living close to the Piazza Duomo, Italy's largest glass-covered shopping market, and oldest department store '*La Rinascente*.'

Number 42 via Rastrelli is a private *'pensione'* or lodging, squeezed like a pimple between two travertine townhouses and owned by a friend of the Maestro. It is conveniently located one minute away from the stage door of the *Lirico*. All along the street, large posters advertise the "World-Famous Les Ballets Jazz Europa" with a glossy black and white photo of the dancers clad in all-white costumes of fringe, some carrying fringe umbrellas and others wearing tall, pointed, white dunce hats on their heads like African garden gnomes. The lighting of the photograph cleverly accentuates the white on black drama and lots of naked legs.

Maggie, Talitha, and Liliane stop outside number forty-two and Anna boldly knocks and opens the door. The girls step inside. A small, squirrel of a man is perched like a bank teller on a stool, reading *'Corriere della Sera:'* the anti-communist news of Milan. He leaps to his toes, exclaiming, *'Ballerini!'* and scrambles about, handing out keys, snatching passports and making everyone sign an official register, all the while chattering incomprehensibly. Then, he darts behind a curtain and begins typing furiously, as names, numbers, and nationalities are registered with the local police.

Maggie groans, "Well this certainly ain't the Palace Hotel," as she heads for the spiral staircase to the third floor dragging her suitcase. She finally has a room to herself.

Anna calls up the stairwell from below, *"Rinascente* is two minutes away, I'm going shopping."

In the centre of the Piazza del Duomo, Maggie stops and gapes at the famous *'Duomo di Milano, Santa Maria Nascente,'* the second largest church in Europe. For once she is speechless. It is the most magnificent building she has ever seen. Like an enormous pale, pink, marble wedding cake, it is decorated with one hundred thirty-five, long, fragile, spires, two thousand two hundred forty-five statues and ninety-six, evil, little, pointy-eared buggers called "gargoyles" according to her guide book. At the far end of the piazza is an archway and the entrance to the super famous, knicker store that has been rebuilt after being hit below the belt by the Allied bombers. The four dancers, two British, one French and one Canadian, dive into the piles of lacy panties in every colour, size and shape. Bikinis come with matching underwire push-up bras that give the smallest breasts some cleavage and some even have embarrassingly tiny garter-belts to complete the ensemble. Like kids in a candy shop, they rummage around, holding up flimsy fabric, laughing together like sisters. Underpants come in black lace, sheer white with tiny, embroidered flowers in pastel colours, pink peek-a-boos, cotton eyelets with baby ruffles and satin woven with bows. A short time later, Maggie strolls back across the square toward the pensione, armed with a bag full of knickers and a huge smile. She doesn't even glance at the *Duomo* that is glittering like a jeweled crown in the late afternoon sunlight.

Pensione Rastrelli, 42 via Rastrelli, Milano, Italia:

Dear Mom and Pop,

I have my own private room on the top floor, within spittin' distance of the world-famous Church of Saint Mary of the Nativity so you can just imagine the view across the rooftops. We will be here a week, dancing at the 'Teatro Lirico' which is very old and full of history. The most famous opera singers and ballerinas have performed here, even Benito Mussolini gave a solo oration, but I don't suppose that was very uplifting. Anyway, he is just a ghost from the past.

Near the end of the war, the people of Milano hung him upside down from a meat hook near the church where Leonardo da Vinci's inspiring Last Supper survives. His mistress, Clara Petacci was shot too and then hung beside him like an ageing salami with her skirts modestly tied around her knees. No one could ridicule HER bloomers. I have to go and check it out, the painting, I mean. Life is full of surprises. Love to you. Mags xxxxx

Room number 304 in the *Pensione Rastrelli* is most definitely not a room with a view that anyone would want to write home about. It is barely big enough for a single bed, one chair, and an ancient, corner sink with cold water only. The walls and the slanted ceiling are painted the colour of a sow's belly, with streaks of wallpaper showing through. The main feature is a tiny, shuttered window that looks into an air shaft, a courtyard of metal garbage bins and a discarded, blue bicycle four flights below. A lattice of laden clotheslines criss-cross at every floor, home to hundreds of cooing pigeons as well as wet bedding. The air, perfumed with rotting fruit and mould stings the inside of the nostrils, but, for the next week, it is home.

"Yuck, *walgelijk*, disgusting," gasps Talitha, gagging. It's a one-holer, and she runs back down a narrow flight of stone stairs to stage level. Backstage at the famous *Teatro Lirico*, there is one toilet only, for stagehands, singers, dancers, orchestra and anyone loitering beyond the proscenium arch who needs to relieve themselves.

"*Déguelasse*," sniffs Simone, "*merde*." Inside the offending crapper is a smelly, old hole in the middle of a once white-tiled floor, now stained with rust. Straddling the exit pipe are two enamel footprints, raised about three inches above. Facing the door on the left, is a small iron tap to be used in lieu of toilet paper.

"Brilliant! It's straight out of the pages of history. I love it. There is even a trap door in the middle of the stage and dozens of private dressing rooms and a dungeon under the stage filled with antique props!" But no one is listening to Maggie's enthusiasm.

On opening night, the faded plush velvet seats are full to capacity, even the four tiers of chipped, gilded boxes, and the unstable gallery are sold out. Les Ballets Jazz Europa is really the only show in town as most families do not own television sets of their own. The few screens blaring out in bars and billiard rooms are channeled to political postulating or news broadcasts. There is a hush as the house lights dim, and the double-thick, fire-resistant, heavy curtain is hauled to the wings by a sweating stagehand, with a stub of a cigarette stuck between a rotting gap in his two most prominent teeth. Behind the fire barrier, soft grey silky curtains almost float to the wings as the ballet begins. The haunting waltz in a minor key of '*La Résistance*' fills the enormous theatre, and within minutes, the audience is falling under the spell of the love story; an emotional masterpiece of choreography. Maggie is dancing with all the depth of feeling she possesses, knowing that Nikko is watching every movement. He never misses a thing and she is desperately wanting a solo part, even a really small solo, to be truly fulfilled. She glances into the wings where he usually stands, but no one is there.

Just inside the heavy, metal stage door, a telephone is fastened to a plaster wall covered in graffiti, phone numbers, and names.

Nikko shouts into the mouthpiece, "Max, we open at the Verdi in Florence, for Christ's sake. How can I do this?" He glances up, listening as the music stops, a pistol shot cracks, and then the thunderous applause explodes like a bomb, echoing down the corridor. The suspicion of a satisfied smile crosses his face—the ballet is a hit. That is all he has ever wanted. He takes out a cigarette from his shirt pocket and taps it absentmindedly on the wall.

"Okay, calm down, Max," he sighs. "Where is the pick-up? And, to the usual place?" The phone goes dead. He hangs the receiver up and puts the cigarette to his lips, searching for a match. Big Frank appears with a lighter, "Sunday, '*il-Had*'," he says in the Algerian dialect, "Fahad, we have a job to do!"

It is pandemonium, as usual, on platform four at the train station. Les Ballets Jazz is moving south to the city of Florence, the birthplace of the Renaissance. Suitcases; seven enormous *panniers* and miscellaneous parcels are piled haphazardly on the platform waiting for the train to arrive, but not everyone is accounted for. Two platforms away, another figure stands quietly beside a waiting train. The porter blows a whistle and a black, nondescript suitcase is placed beside the open door to the carriage. Immediately, the figure picks it up, hops aboard and disappears inside. The train ricochets backwards and forwards for a second as another whistle warns of departure. *"Tutti a bordo,"* the station master warns everyone to board, and the 1:43 from platform number six departs on time, heading northeast, for the border to Switzerland, and on to Luxembourg.

Minutes later, when the southbound train pulls out of Milano, Maggie settles in a corner and opens her new book. Having finished "The Tropic of Cancer," she opens Irving Stone's life of Michaelangelo, "The Agony and the Ecstasy." With a crash, the door to the compartment opens, and Frank flings himself onto the opposite bench, breathing hard with perspiration running down the side of his face.

Maggie looks up and winks, "Sleep in, did you?"

CHAPTER V

The Agony and the Ecstasy

In 1348, a pandemic called The Black Plague spread throughout Europe, killing twenty-five million people. Seventy percent of the population in the thriving city of Florence died, including all of the inmates and gaolers of the immense and horrifying 'Stinche' private prison.* Five-hundred years later, in approximately 1850, this ancient dungeon of death was reborn as the Teatro Verdi, the largest and most opulent opera house in Tuscany. Although it was originally called 'Ye Olde Stinche Prison Theatre,' it was thoughtfully renamed in honour of Giuseppe Fortunino Francesco Verdi, one of the greatest composers in the history of opera.

At number five via *Porta Rossa*, in the heart of Firenze, a discreet brass plaque identifies '*Pensione Tenti,*' home to Les Ballets for the next week or so. Several dancers are standing with their possessions outside of the closed door. Almost directly across the street is a small trattoria, '*La Bussola,*' specializing in pizza and calzone, according to the sign in the window. A finger presses the buzzer of number five and the door clicks open. Rosie, Anna, Simone, Talitha, Maggie, Liliane, and all their paraphernalia disappear inside. An ancient elevator cage rumbles down from above and bumps to a stop. It is the size of a telephone booth.

"Just put the bags inside and we can walk," is the suggestion.

"*Putin*," sighs Simone, "I'm not climbing any stairs, *pas moi*." She sits down on her overstuffed *valise* and waits defiantly for the return of the lift from the upper levels.

Maggie unlocks the door to a room on the top floor of the *pensione*. She groans out loud. The bedroom is a dormitory with five iron beds lined up in a row like a boarding school for wayward children, not for the ballerinas of one of the leading dance companies of Europe. The only consolation is that there is a bathroom with a tub, not a communal washroom down the hall.

"*Impossible,*" Liliane is outraged. "Where is Nikko?"

Rosie replies cattily, "He's probably in a whorehouse in Palermo," as she claims the bed closest to the only window. Maggie dumps her suitcase on the bed at the opposite end of the room by the open door. Noisily, Simone rattles a key in the lock of the room next door.

"That old cow, *vieille vache*," sniffs Liliane in disgust. "How did she manage a private room?"

Everyone settles in, refreshes their makeup, and hands their passports to Signora Maria Tenti, an attractive middle-aged woman at the front desk. Then, they set off down a narrow street. The five look like exotic birds, wearing provocative pencil skirts, bright blouses, and high heels.

"Where is the *Teatro Verdi*?"

Signora calls out the window, "*Via Isola delle Stinche*." All along the road there are posters stuck to the sides of buildings, advertising Les Ballets Jazz Europa. Before the girls have reached the main market only half a block away, they are surrounded by a gang of local kids, or '*ragazzi*.'

One little ragamuffin points to the poster advertising the ballet, "You want *Teatro Verdi*? *Vieni con me*." He signals for them to follow as he hops onto a dilapidated bicycle and pedals across the *Piazza Signoria*, disappearing down a side street.

"Wait up, you little snot!" The girls stagger precariously after him, navigating the uneven paving stones in their high heels. They have to be on stage that night, even if they break their ankles. Anna and Maggie gaze into the auditorium from the enormous thirty-foot stage.

"Goodness, this is plush, look at that Royal box and the gallery..." Anna's voice trails off, her eyes twinkling as she gazes in awe.

"Eight hundred people per night, sold out for the week, and Nikko decides to vanish into thin air. Bloody bastard! He has left everything to me to sort out. Look at the steep, raked stage."

Maggie is not listening, mesmerized by the sharp angle of the stage floor. She flings off her shoes, runs to the back wall, and with a joyous yelp, cartwheels all the way down to the footlights and leaps into the orchestra pit. As she disappears over the edge, Rudi arrives stage-left, already in practice clothes.

"Is Maggie with you?" he asks.

"She is off looking for ghosts and dead bodies in the dungeon," Anna replies.

Rudi claps his hands for attention, puts two fingers into his mouth and whistles loudly.

"Hurry up, we have to start this rehearsal. Where the fuck is Nikko?" He asks no one in particular. Xavier is standing by the tape recorder fiddling with wires and knobs. Suddenly, the rock music for the ballet 'The Leather Boys of London' erupts through the speakers, echoing around the century-old burgundy and gold walls.

"*Merde*! Turn that down." Frank hauls out the huge hemp pulleys, lowering the main curtain, hiding the stalls from view. Ronáld brings out the props for 'Leather Boys' and the rehearsal begins in earnest. The reputation of Les Ballets Jazz Europa depends on a brilliant opening night, with or without the Maestro Nikolaus Pávlos.

Just before curtain time, the door to the boys' dressing room opens and Nikko slips quietly inside. He has a very large drink in his hand and a nasty bruise spreading under his left eye. Rudi looks up, his eyes ringed in dark greasepaint, wearing his black leather motorcycle jacket and bad-boy pants.

He takes one look at Nikko and jokes: "I hope she was worth it." Nikko, looking more like a 'mod' than a 'rocker' in a sober business suit, ignores the remark and responds humbly.

"Thank you, *merci*, for carrying on without me. I was detained."

As the applause dies down at the end of 'The Leather Boys of London' and everyone takes their bows, they hurtle toward the dressing rooms backstage like a pack of hounds after a fox. Appearing from the wings, Ronáld saunters on stage as though he has all the time in the world. He is not wearing his trademark Fedora hat, instead modeling a new, Italian '*borsalino*' hat that makes him look like Harpo Marx in an adorable, curly wig.

Beginning his monologue banter, he throws his arms wide, embracing the whole audience, calling, "*Buonasera signore!* Are there any ladies present?" This brings a chuckle from the mainly masculine audience, as everyone knows no proper lady would be allowed to leave their homes after dark. "I went to Roma last week, to visit my dear friend, Pope Paul VI," he begins, in a credible local accent. "I asked him how many people work at the Vatican. The Pope paused, thinking for a moment, and replied, 'About half of them.'"

The audience roars their approval, shouting obscenely, "*Pigri maiali fornici*"*. After a few more remarks insulting the traditional enemies of *Firenze*, the folk from Pisa, Siena, and Montalcino, he breaks into an all-time favourite song, "Goodbye, *Firenze*, *ciao*," waving his hands about like an Italian politician. The orchestra plays with gusto, and without warning, the audience is on their feet singing and swaying in unison. Ronáld, grinning happily, ends up the conductor of an eight hundred voice male choir. The noise could have awoken the dead bodies who lie below the stage in the medieval dungeon. Meanwhile, the dancers are costumed in their spanking white fringe and ready to perform 'Mambo Diablo.' Maggie turns to Romeo and demands a translation.

"He just called the Pope a lazy, fornicating pig."

Maggie sighs, "I'm sorry I asked."

A bandaged toe sticks out the front of a wooden sandal made by Dr. William Scholl of Chicago, Illinois. Maggie has an excruciatingly ingrown toenail that has become infected, staining the gauze bandage a pinkish, ochre colour. It is not yet 7:30 a.m., but she sits in the airy *Loggia dei Lanzi* on one side of the *Piazza della Signoria*, in the heart of Florence. She is curled up, hugging her knees, at the foot of the marble statue of Perseus holding the gory, decapitated head of Medusa. He is stark naked, except for a sash around his hips and a pair of sandals with wings attached. Perseus stares downward at the headless body with cold, marble eyes. Maggie stares up in astonishment at his immense black testicles and penis. Besides pigeons, other scavenging birds, and a lone figure of a garbage collector, the piazza is empty at this hour. Maggie watches the trash man as he stands near the replica of Michelangelo's statue of 'David' who is wearing a modest fig leaf. He continues to empty the bins into a rusty, green wagon attached to a motor scooter. He drives the revolting bags of *'rifiuti'* away down *via dei Magazzini* and the square is empty once more. Maggie opens "The Agony and the Ecstasy" where she left off on page 415, and reads…

"He went to David's face, carved it tenderly, with all the love and sympathy in his being: the strong, noble face of the youth who would, in one more moment, make the leap into manhood, but at this instant was still sad and uncertain over what he must do; the brows deeply knit, the eyes questioning, the full lips expectant… his face must convey the idea that his conflict with Goliath was a parable of good and evil."

Somewhere nearby, a church tower chimes the hour, and Maggie slaps her book shut. She peers around the corner to face the main door of the *Uffizi* Museum of Art.* It is an L-shaped stone building, standing on the banks of the Arno River. She takes a small card from her purse: a student's pass. Pushing the door open, she runs smack into the ticket taker.

"You are an eager one, are you not?" he says, in flawless English. Flustered, she's rendered speechless. He has the most sensual but sensitive face she has ever seen in all her twenty years on earth. Blushing, she hands him her student's pass. He looks at her intently.

"Are you an art student at the American Academy?"

"Ahhh, yes. I mean no! I am studying at the University of British Columbia in Canada," she lies. She doesn't want him to know that she is in show business. Somehow, everyone changes when they find out.

"I'm a student, too," he responds while gazing at her, taking in as many details as possible. He smiles at the freckles on her nose, her thick red hair, and huge hazel eyes.

"You look like a ticket collector to me," she jokes. "Are you going to let me in or not?" He steps aside.

"I am studying engineering at the *Università degli Studi di Firenze*." Maggie is limping painfully up the long marble staircase and calls over her shoulder, "*Ciao*," then disappears into the first exhibition room of 15th century masterpieces by Fathers Lippio Lippi, Giotto, and Fra Angelico; mostly portraits of pasty-faced prelates, painted on gilded wood.

Downstairs, the young man whistles softly, "*Ciao bella*," and blows her an unseen kiss.

For the third day in a row, Maggie is lounging in the Botticelli room on a leather bench, her favourite place in the *Uffizi*, without a soul in sight. There are two sensational paintings that make her nostalgic. One is the "*Primavera*," a Medici bed-hanging of three red-headed sylphs in filmy robes. Maggie imagines herself and sisters; 'Geri' and Alleycat, dancing in their bare feet in the fields of wildflowers at home in North Oyster. The other painting on the left, also by the Florentine master Alessandro Botticelli, is the Goddess Venus arising out of the sea as she balances gracefully on a clam shell*. Venus is pale, exquisitely fragile and vulnerable, yet unashamed by her nakedness. *She* doesn't have a pimple on her face and certainly not a swollen, pus-filled toenail. Venus has the face of an angel.

After days of reading "The Agony and the Ecstasy," Maggie is a bit fed up with Michaelangelo. *He is always bellyaching about money, despite being the best paid artist of all time. Money, money, money...my own mother, too! She keeps writing letters asking to explain why, if we are so famous and successful, are we not paid enough to live on. I do wish she would shut up about all my high school friends who are getting married, having babies, making Nanaimo bars* and baby mush from their own flipping gardens. She implies that I am 'on-the-shelf,' an old maid at twenty, and must be lonely. Damn it! That's when she hits the nail smack on the head. I am lonely! Being in a ballet troupe sounds so glamorous and it is, I am loving it, but, after the final curtain comes down and we have our one meal of the day and stagger into a crummy hotel room, a great, big, silent parachute of emptiness drifts down and settles over my bed. Why am I doing this?*

Across the street from the *Teatro Verdi*, in a scruffy bar with a green, baize billiard table, the Maestro is leaning against the wall by the public telephone box. A half-dozen elderly men are hanging around, some playing nine pin skittles and others arguing. The lone bartender wipes his nose on a towel and then hangs it neatly on the back of a wooden chair. Amid the cracking of balls into pockets and shouts of encouragement, Nikko is listening intently into the receiver. He shakes his head violently.

"No, no, not a chance. They refuse to buy it. What do ya mean?" He listens, "The vase of flowers, Max," he groans. "It must be *given* back... with an apology! Ha ha ha! Not one lira, not for six hundred million lira. That damn thing was stolen, *a raubkunst!*" He is shouting into the mouthpiece to be heard. The room is suddenly silent. "Gotta go," he whispers, "there is no negotiation." The receiver goes quiet. The billiard players are warily watching, as he pulls out a wad of lira, slides a stack onto the bar and says *"Grappa* signors?"* The bartender lines up eight shot glasses, wipes each one carefully on a towel, and pours a generous slug into each one.

"Porco dio!" Ronáld is peering at Maggie's toe and hisses, "you need a doctor to lance that." She is in full stage make-up and false eyelashes, costumed for 'L'Atelier,' which has been a wild success the entire week. The local newspaper *La Nazione* writes that the BJE is the most inventive, modern ballet seen in the Teatro Verdi in years. She is preparing to dance her role in bare feet as she cannot get her pointe shoes on. The Maestro bangs the stage door closed with a *whoomp.* He hurries down the corridor, takes one look at Maggie, and hands her a 'grappa'* with two white pills.

"Swallow!' He orders her. "Don't argue." Then, more gently, "Stay in back, do the arms, and Xavier will adjust the lighting so you won't be seen." Maggie swallows. He lights a cigarette and disappears into a hazy cloud of nicotine. From the giant speakers, the music begins and she takes her place in the wings.

If you aren't on stage, you won't get paid. She clenches her teeth and makes her entrance.

While most residents of the city sleep, a trattoria at 56 *via Porta Rossa* is coming to life. A taxi races down a narrow cobbled street and screeches to a halt, unloads six passengers at *La Bussola* and disappears, belching a cloud of carbon monoxide. Liliane opens the heavy glass door of the restaurant and the aroma of garlic, warm olive oil, and bread baking in an open hearth brings groans of pleasure. *La Bussola* is well-known among theatre people; dancers, musicians, comedians, painters, and strippers. They arrive every night to unwind after work; a sort of clubhouse for eccentrics. Every inch of the blood-red walls is covered in autographed photos of smiling celebrities, slick-haired boys singing into microphones, and nearly naked chicks in feathers and furs. Maggie is half carried to a wooden armchair and propped up against a wall. The pills have taken effect and her head droops onto the table. No one notices as the chianti flows and platters of *calzone*, pizza, and *pappardelle* pasta fly by on metal trays. The noise and laughter gets louder and louder, but for the one asleep in the corner, all is silent.

It is nine o'clock in the morning. The shutters on the top floor of the *Pensione Tenti* are tightly closed against the cooing of pigeons, revving of scooter horns, and clanging of bicycle bells. Inside the bedroom, Maggie stirs and says with a groan, "What were those little white pills? I think I'm going to be sick." She leaps onto her sore foot, and stumbles into the bathroom. "I *am* going to be sick," and she retches loudly. Anna rolls over, puts a pillow over her head, and tries to go back to sleep. The other beds are empty.

Inside, the bathroom looks like wash day in a Singapore slum, with wet laundry hanging on every conceivable hook and handle. A makeshift clothesline is strung with bras, panties, g-strings, slips, garter belts, and 'smalls' according to Rosie. A jumble of toothbrushes lie on a small wooden shelf with an open tin of tooth powder. Maggie is desperately trying to force the window open for fresh air.

There is a knock on the door and Anna calls, "My turn." She opens it without waiting. "By the way," she says nonchalantly, "we are unemployed and Nikko has taken off, yet again."

Fifteen minutes later, the two girls climb the steps to the

marketplace and stop to look at a statue of a life-size wild boar made of brass, turned into a fountain. At the base is a small pool filled with coins, and the words, "*Il Porcellino*" etched on the rim.

"Rub his nose," the bystanders cry. "*Buona fortuna!*" Anna bends over in her white wrap skirt, bottom in the air, and shows off her legs up to the tops of her stockings. She puts a coin in the pig's wet mouth as the male onlookers hoot and whistle. There are no young Italian girls in the '*mercado*' this morning, unless escorted by their mothers. No boy would ever dare whistle without being swatted around the ears for impertinence. The elderly ladies wear only black; long black skirts, black cardigans, and black scarves covering their heads.

Anna speaks to one of them politely in Italian, "*Buongiorno signora*," and is pointedly ignored.

"She is probably in mourning," Maggie observes, "and doesn't like the sound of English voices. Too many painful war memories."

"Rubbish," says Anna, as she pauses to inspect the leather belts, purses, and bookmarks covered in intricate designs. Her manicured fingers glide over a soft, leather cigarette box dyed Royal blue with the symbol of the city of Florence; a lily called a '*Giglio*,' embossed in gold leaf.

Handing it to the salesman, "I'll give you fifty lira for it."

"Ha, ha, ha!" He clasps his hands in mock horror, appealing to his buddies, "*Signorina Inglese*, she tries to rob me," and so the bargaining begins. Maggie is watching the back and forth bickering in awe. A crowd has gathered, as Anna takes on the leather vendors of *Firenze*. A short time later, she pushes her way through the merry group and triumphantly holds up her trophy, like a Spanish matador displaying the severed ear of a bull.

"It helps to be half Jewish," she laughs and tosses her head provocatively. "Oh, don't look so disproving, Mags, they expect you to bargain. Did I ever tell you that my grandfather, Moisey

Belenitsky, was from St. Petersburg? It got changed to Bell and that was that," and she snaps her fingers, dismissing Grandpa Belenitsky forever into history.

For the first time in weeks there is time to meander. Anna and Maggie enter the sunlit piazza like two brightly-coloured canaries among the pigeons and crows. They are searching for a table in the outdoor café across the cobblestone square from the Uffizi Gallery.

Two priests get up to leave and Anna darts ahead into the seat, puts her bag on the other and takes out her Dunhill gold lighter and her cigarettes. In a flash, a waiter is beside her, looking like a puppy anxious to please. Anna can do that to people, Maggie observes. She is very sexy and when she looks at men with her bedroom eyes, they almost fall on their faces.

Maggie arrives a few seconds later, removes the handbag, and gently slides into the empty chair. "Did you order '*due expresso?*"

"*Expressi,*" corrects Anna, blowing a smoke ring in the air.

"Oh, don't be such a smart-ass," Maggie retorts, as she dives into her copious bag for a bottle of aspirin.

"The guy who takes the tickets at the Uffizi is very good-looking," Maggie blushes. "I wonder if he will be there today."

The jolt of caffeine brings everything back in focus: the brilliance of the sun, the magnificence of the crenellated *Palazzo Vecchio*, which is the old town hall built in 1314, and the incredible good fortune to be travelling free to the most famous sites in Europe, and all she has to do is dance.

"It's good to be alive!" She sighs with satisfaction. "Anna, I'll get the *expressi*, you go ahead and get your Uffizi ticket." She turns to call the waiter who is there in a flash helping Anna out of her chair as though she is Caterina de Medici.* Anna carefully crosses the square, dodging clouds of pigeons feasting on bits of pizza crust and puddles of melted gelato. Maggie takes her time paying the bill, reapplying her lipstick and wincing at the sight of a reddened pimple reflected in her compact mirror. She puts her huge, dark Audrey Hepburn sunglasses on and crosses the piazza, limping painfully.

Within a hundred yards of the Uffizi entrance, in the shade of the portico, she sees Anna and her ticket collector leaning together in a seductive way. Anna gently pushes his hair back off his brow with the tips of her fingers, while gazing at him with pursed lips and fluttering eyelashes. *She is flirting with him. That bitch, that horrible tease. She can have any man she wants and now she is throwing herself at the only interesting man I have met.* Maggie is jealous and turns away feeling friendless and incredibly alone. Half running, half dragging her foot down side streets into tiny passageways, she tries to disappear. She pushes people aside, tourists who are milling around the *Ponte Vecchio*, meanwhile dodging traffic as she turns left onto the next bridge, the *Ponte Trinità*. She finally stops, panting and gasping for breath, and stares down into the Arno River; that slimy, green, turgid water that meanders toward Pisa and ultimately, the sea. *I will not cry,* she thinks. Anna is stunning, sexy, and a beautiful dancer. She has everything I lack and I will never be able to compete with her. I should be glad just to be in this ballet company. As soon as her breathing becomes normal, she straightens her back and crosses to the other side. The south bank of the river looks like a rabbit warren of houses, but somewhere inside there is a palace. *That* is where she is going. The sun is noon high, but as soon as she enters *via Maggio* and turns left onto *Borgo Tegolaio*, the road becomes a gloomy passage, lined with tall apartment buildings visibly damaged by bombs and pocked by bullet holes. The street feels like a wind tunnel of blowing dust and torn newspaper; *La Nazione*, tossed aside as yesterday's news. She is going in circles, but it doesn't matter.

"*Via Guiccigridini, via Mazzetta, Tegolaio,*" the words sound mysterious and foreign as she tries pronouncing them out loud. Rounding a sharp corner, an unshaven man is sitting outside on a broken, wooden kitchen chair in frayed work pants with blue and red striped suspenders. His fly is undone.

As she passes, he spits at her feet. *"Tedesco,"* he says, coughing and spitting again.

Maggie doesn't understand and replies, "I am a Canadian."

The walls are covered in a celadon silk damask, and the floors; a quilt of exotic hardwood. The magnificent, domed ceiling is frescoed with flaxen-haired angels, puffy clouds, and bare-bottomed babies called *'cherubim,'* who are holding garlands of roses and tiny forget-me-nots. Maggie is walking around the Pitti Palace in a trance. *Holy cow,* she breathes, *wait till I tell Gran about this.*

There are only a few tourists lingering and silently looking, plus a few guards in bossy, blue suits saying, "Shush," to no one in particular. She hobbles through a twelve-foot door covered with golden curlicues, into the next gallery, covered in more Florentine lilies. This room is thickly padded with burgundy silk stripes and rows of enormous oil paintings that hang the entire length of the gallery. There are masterpieces by Perugino, Caravaggio, Raphael, and other unpronounceable geniuses of the Renaissance. It's all too much to take in at once, causing her to almost walk by a black and white newspaper photograph. The image is a painting of a vase of flowers with a butterfly by Dutch artist Jan van Huysum. She peers at it closely, and sees a sign written in three languages, clearly and boldly: German, Italian, and English. *"Gestohler—Rubato—Stolen."* Maggie takes a step back and stands on someone's foot.

"Scusi," she jumps, and Vincenzo, the ticket taker, steadies her.

"We waited for you," he whispers. "Why are you running away from me?" Maggie is embarrassed to answer so she changes the subject.

"Who," she whispers, "would steal this fantastic painting?"

With a sigh, he says, "Wartime makes thieves of a lot of people. It was a German corporal who thought his wife might like it hung in their house. When the war ended in 1945, the family said it belonged to them and refused to send it back to Florence. Later, the same German family tried to sell it to the Uffizi Gallery."

Suddenly, two guards swoop down upon them like hawks on a pair of rabbits hissing, "*Silenzio*" in full shattering volume. "Shh, shush!" They shake their heads in unison.

Large, round sunglasses disguise the faces of Maggie, Rosie, Talitha, and the others as they cross the *Ponte Vecchio*, spanning the Arno River in the early morning sunshine. The glasses do not fool anyone who happened to be watching, as the girls are almost six feet tall, wearing high, sling-back shoes, with hair pulled into tidy *chignons* and posture that would make a soldier straighten up. They are obviously the foreign dancers from the *Teatro Verdi*. No one knows that they are now the unemployed, former dancers who have not been paid, who are traipsing over the bridge toward a rehearsal hall to continue their classes so they do not lose their flexibility and stamina.

Freshly-shaven shopkeepers are unlocking and opening the heavy shutters on the stores along each side of the bridge, revealing a treasury of gold. Row upon row of twenty carats sparkle in the sun: crosses both large and small, hearts with tiny birthstones, lockets for babies and ladies, medallions of Saint John the Baptist, the patron saint of Florence dribbling water on the heads of men kneeling in supplication. There are rings, cufflinks, golden charms to hang on bracelets, and of course, the ubiquitous, bloody lily that pops up everywhere, even on tie tacks. Maggie is bug-eyed, having never seen such a display, not even in Switzerland.

"I can't afford anything," she moans. "Not even a teensy, weensy heart for my Granny."

A voice calls out, "Does anyone know where we are going?"

Liliane answers, "*Je ne sais pas*." She breaks into broken English and flips her hand in the direction of the South Bank, "Near zee San Niccolò, you know, Xavier, he finds a place."

In an alley somewhere near *Via de' Bardi*, Xavier is hollering "Allo, allo," and waving both hands over his head like a *carabinieri* directing traffic at rush hour. From the opposite direction, Ronáld is struggling along with the tape-to-tape recording device. He disappears through a door. The rubble-stone building is being held upright by a tangle of apricot-coloured roses and dark green ivy that is rooted in a cement trough. The glorious scent of minced basil drifts down from a window upstairs. Les Ballets has a rehearsal hall; battered, picturesque, and best of all, free. Xavier is pleased with his find and leans nonchalantly against the door jamb with an iron key on his finger and a smirk on his handsome, but annoying face. He is pushed aside. The dim interior looks like a storage room for church cast-offs. A hastily thrown tarpaulin covers stacks of religious paintings leaning against a far wall next to boxes of leather-bound Bibles and a haphazard pile of crucifixes and banners on poles. All along the sides are uncomfortable, ancient wooden pews, just the right size for a ballet barre. By the door is a marble Baptismal font split in two, and a headless cherub lying dead in a corner. Dust and soot is everywhere.

"*Dégueulasse*," Simone shudders with disgust as she grabs a broom and starts sweeping furiously. Ronáld plugs the tape recorder into an alarming electrical receptacle, and Maggie starts rummaging among the paintings with great interest.

Rudi, suddenly inspired, pulls his t-shirt off and wraps it around his head like a wimple.

With hands clasped together and eyes Heavenward, he sings in one long note, "Hail Mary full of Grace, please come and clean this place." Then, he grabs Simone by the waist and swings her and the broom in circles around the room. Everyone is in stitches, except Aneke. Maggie watches her out of the corner of her eye and wonders, *Why doesn't his wife Aneke enjoy his wacky sense of humour and joy of dancing?*

The majestic music of Mozart fills the room, and like Pavlov's salivating dogs, they grab hold of the makeshift *barre*, or rather, the edge of the pew, and begin the class.

"*Demi plié*! One, two, three, four, inhale, exhale. *Grand plié* and *un*, *deux*, *trois*, *quatre*, bend forward and stretch, tall-hold, hold and turn." Over and over until legs, arms and backs are warm and sweat streaks down their necks into their leotards. They are transcended to another place, far away from San Niccolò: a place between a dream and a destiny.

The door is abruptly kicked open and Anna steps over the sill carrying a heavy, metal tray of steaming pots of coffee, hot milk, a stack of thick, white porcelain cups, and an impressive pile of cream-filled pastries called *sfogliatelle*.

"The buns are on the house," she exclaims triumphantly.

"Who did you sin with, my child, to get those sweet treats?" Rudi snickers, behaving like a prissy priest, giving her a loud, obnoxious kiss on her cheek.

"Take it, you wanker. It's heavy. I'm going to drop it."

She is waiting near the statue of '*Primavera*,' meaning 'Springtime,' that stands on a pedestal anchoring the *Trinità* bridge to the north side of the Arno River. Maggie is wearing a green and white, full-skirted summer dress that is blowing in the wind, giving anyone nearby a glimpse of spectacular legs. A tangle of red hair reaches past her shoulder blades, and on her feet are Dr. Scholl's wooden 'klonkers.' From the south side a young man walks toward her, not quickly, but with purpose. He doesn't want her to run away again.

Maggie looks up at Vincenzo expectantly, with a small smile. They are standing just a few inches apart, saying nothing, oblivious to the passing bicycles and cars crossing the bridge. The silence is not awkward. Very calmly, their faces inch closer and closer, almost in slow motion. He lifts her chin with one finger, and gently, their lips touch.

Florence, Italy, August 3rd, 1944:

A satanic thunderbolt rocked the city of Florence at four o'clock in the morning of August 3rd, 1944, terrifying the four thousand evacuees taking refuge in the Pitti Palace, the cellars, and the churches of the city. The residents who live within one mile of the Arno are given three hours to pack a lifetime of family history, evacuate, and disappear. Within the palace the people are terrified and have no idea what is happening. It is forbidden to go outside. Some guess that "it's the bridges." Someone whimpers, hungry children snivel, and the elderly pray to the almighty. Others just listen. Minor explosions have been going on all night long. It takes not one, but three massive blasts of dynamite to dislodge the stones of the Ponte Trinità that was built in 1567. Three mighty explosions bring down the three elliptical arches, shaped like ship's prows, sending the statues representing spring, summer, fall, and winter shooting through the air like rockets before their final dive into the murky river bed. The houses on both sides of the river crumble into rubble like burnt cookies. Florence is essentially cut in two. And why? So the Nazi army has more time to loot and retreat to the north before the American, Canadian, and British forces can liberate the city.

Almost every nation in the world condemns this senseless destruction and finds it unforgivable. Only the bridge upstream, the Ponte Vecchio survived, probably because it was too fragile to carry the weight of the Allied tanks and trucks, and therefore deemed useless to the advancing army. However, more charitably, many believe that the German Commandant simply could not bring himself to blow it and defied the orders of Adolf Hitler.

Dear: Mom, Pop, and Granny:
We have been abandoned for the past three weeks. Don't worry

because the Maestro has paid for our hotel so I have a roof over my head. We have been living on bread and spaghetti so I am getting fat. Every day I have been exploring the city, every church, museum, palace, and park, guided by an engineering student who seems to know every detail of the history and gossip of Florence. Don't worry about me. Love, Mags. P.S. My gums are bleeding because I can't afford any fruit, I probably have scurvy by now. P.P.S. The naked statue on the front of this postcard is 'David,' not my tour guide. Ha ha ha. Your Mags xxx

Only two tiny tables fit under the white canvas awning outside of the bar *Volpa e l'Uva*. On the glass door leading to the interior tables is a silhouette of the wily fox, '*the volpa*,' with a bunch of grapes in his mouth. At one of the tables, Vincenzo relaxes as he sips a small glass of amber-coloured *Vin Santo**. An ice bucket and two glasses await. He checks his watch. As Maggie comes flying around the corner and across *Piazza dei Rossi*, he breaks into a bemused smile. Maggie seems to be in a perpetual state of frenzy; forever late, flustered and dishevelled, yet he finds her utterly charming.

She sits across from him, wriggling like a puppy, "*Scusi*, I'm late."

"Hey, hey, *calmo*," he responds, grabbing both her hands and pressing them to his lips for a second. He pours two glasses of chilled white wine from the bottle in the ice bucket. An onlooker would see two lovers, heads together, chattering animatedly, without a care in the world.

"I'm leaving tomorrow," Maggie blurts out without any preamble. "All of my friends want to go to Rome, but I…" and she hesitates.

Vincenzo softly replies, "I know."

She is immediately alert, "Know what?"

"Oh Mags, I've known all along that you are in the ballet and not a student." Her face reddens. He nods. "I have been watching you dance since your opening at the *Verdi*. I came back every night and watched you, only you. There is a long pause and she takes a large, unladylike gulp of wine. Suddenly, he jumps up.

"Oh, hell, let's get out of here," and he slaps some money on the table and slips her hand in his.

"Next on the tour, *signorina*, we go to a seventeen acre garden in the middle of Florence; not a public park, but a secret place, the largest private garden in any European city."

A sturdy, metal fence with bars, runs the length of *via dei Serragli*, holding in a forest of green from tumbling onto the ancient cobble stones, and keeping people out. "*Privato*. No Trespassing," reads a discreet, but completely unnecessary sign, as there is no entrance other than climbing over the top. The road is deserted, except for a mangy wolfhound urinating on the only flower growing between cracks in the pavement.

"Come," Vincenzo pulls her close to the fence and unhooks a hidden lever at the base of a support. A narrow panel, as wide as a garbage can swings open and the two slip inside. Winding through the trees, a gravel path leads onto a magnificent park of rolling green hills, manicured evergreens, wild deciduous giants, Roman sculptures and in the distance, a hillock, topped with a fairytale tower listing to one side, like the leaning tower of Pisa.

"Wow," is all Maggie can think to say. She kicks off her shoes and dances about, whirling and twirling as though she is in the meadow of her island home in North Oyster. Vincenzo follows her up the hill to the tower.

"Vincenzo, l love it here."

"Isn't it time you called me Enzo?" She is squinting in the afternoon sun, taking in the intricate pattern of the rocks, striped horizontally and then vertically with arches, niches, portholes, and crenellations. At the base, a plaque with three stars and a tower carved in stone. She leans back onto Enzo's chest and sighs. He continues kissing the top of her head.

"It's the arms of the Torrigiani Malaspina family* and this tower, called 'Anthanor' was built in 1824 for an eccentric uncle. He wanted to study the stars. Inside there is a chain and pulley operated chair lift." She swings around facing him.

"How do you know so much? Are you one of the family?" He shuts her up by kissing her roughly, then lets her go.

Suddenly, she spies a crypt with broken stairs going into a hole. Beside it is an ancient wall under the sprawling branches of a giant Maidenhair tree. Beside the wall, half hidden in the grass is a marble plaque etched with the words. COSMUS MED: FLORENTIE ET SENAR: DVX.H. She kneels down and runs her fingertips lightly over the ancient stone of Cosimo Medici, Duke of Florence and Siena, 1544. Enzo sinks to the ground beside her.

The next moment they are entwined in each other's arms; kissing, nibbling, and rolling about on the warm grass.

Suddenly, Enzo sits up and mutters, "I'd better take you back to your hotel."

"Oh no!" and she pulls him back down and slowly climbs on top of him. He looks at her intently.

"Are you sure?"

"Very, very sure," she whispers, and fumbles with the buttons on her blouse.

Long shadows of late afternoon stretch across *Via dei Serragli*. Maggie and Enzo shut the secret gate behind them and start down the road.

Maggie stops, "Please don't come back with me. I mean it." She shudders.

"I hate saying goodbye. It seems so final." Her eyes fill as she turns away, beginning to walk alone down the street.

"Mags, wait a second." She turns.

"Nothing, I just want to look at you one more time."

That night, most of the ballet get royally hammered across the street from the *pensione*. *La Bussola* rocks with music and laughter until dawn. After about two hours' sleep, Maggie wakes to a pounding on the door and in her head. Honking horns and shouting echo from below on *Via Porta Rossa*. Anna puts a pillow over her head and says, "Bugger off."

Talitha moans, "Is that Nikko? I thought he was in Rome?"

Bang, bang, bang on the door.

Nikko shouts, "We wait for you, but hurry! *Dépêchez-vous!*"

Rosie is looking out the window. *Crikey!* A bright, orange bus is in the street, holding up all the traffic—a giant cockup. Pandemonium, the five dancers leap to their feet, pull suitcases from under the iron bedsteads, and start flinging clothes, makeup, books, and everything else into any available bag. Liliane storms into the bathroom and rips all the laundry off the makeshift line, tosses everything into a knitted satchel, throws all the toothbrushes on top, steals the soap and with a final glance around, picks someone else's stockings up off the floor and flounces out.

Outside in the street, Maria Tenti, the owner, is in tears. She hugs and kisses everyone in turn and pushes them onto the bus. "*Buona fortuna!*" The noise is deafening. Ladies with prams cower in doorways and even the pigeons are trembling. Drivers in the cars behind, hang out of their windows, yelling obscenities and indicating fornication with their hands, as only the Italians can. The bus driver shouts at anyone who cares to listen, "*Porco miserio,*" which translates roughly as "my life is as miserable as that of a pig." Les Ballets Jazz Europa departs *Firenze* in a cacophony of horns and utter chaos, some in agony, and one in ecstasy.

CHAPTER VI

Picasso, The Pope, and The Pill

Rome, Italy 1917:

*In the early spring of 1917, Pablo Picasso took his first visit
to Italy. In the eternal city of Rome, he fell in with the theatre
crowd, and into the arms of the ballerinas of the famed 'Ballets
Russes.' Not long after, Pablo Picasso and the enigmatic, Russian
impresario and founder of the Ballets Russes, Sergei Diaghilev,
created a stunning, futuristic, avant-garde production. Their
performance brought the ballet beyond the predictable, as well
as invited surrealism onto the musical stage. While the dancers
of the ballet were onstage performing the usual Russian classics
in the Teatro dell' Opera di Roma, Picasso was behind the scene,
designing fantasy costumes and painting an enormous backdrop,
depicting a dizzy and distorted panorama of confusion. The ballet
was to be called, 'The Grand Parade.' Sergei Diaghilev enticed
Érik Satie, whose own piano teacher had described him as "The
worst student in the history of the Conservatory of Paris," to
compose the music. Jean Cocteau, an eccentric opium addict and
close friend of the mad Nijinsky was to write the scenario, and
Sergei's latest, bisexual lover, the magnificent Léonide Massine,
was to choreograph. The unlikely team was an artistic bombshell,
waiting to explode.*

Paris, France 1917:

On the night of the grand opening in Paris, the sophisticated and beautifully dressed elite are poised on plush chairs, sitting expectantly in the galleries of the *Théâtre du Châlelet*. The conductor ascends from the narrow staircase under the stage to a polite applause, turns his back, and lifts a small, wooden baton. In front of him, Picasso's gigantic canvas of black and white clowns and flying horses awaits. The overture begins. From the orchestra pit come strange sounds of a busy street at lunch time, with sirens, horns, and screams. The canvas painting slowly disappears into the 'fly galley,' the open attic of a stage, and the audience gasps in surprise at the disturbing backdrop of angular shapes falling down and disappearing into a black sewer hole of Paris.

Abruptly, the music changes and dancers enter in costumes so massive and constrained that they can hardly move. A cardboard and canvas horse struggles to clop across the stage, closely followed by a twelve-foot apparition with a long, white, phallic opium pipe swaying from side to side. From the other side of the stage, a heavy, cardboard monster in an oversized black coat makes an entrance while blowing a square horn. The audience wiggles nervously in their seats and someone has a violent fit of coughing. At that point, Miss Hilda Munnings of Surrey, who has wisely changed her moniker to Lydia Sokolova, Russian prima ballerina, clatters onstage in black 'Mary Jane' shoes, white knee socks, and a sailor's hat. She dances like a stiff-legged Charlie Chaplin to the sounds of a stenographer who is pounding the typewriter keys in the orchestra pit.

Four people in the front row get up from their seats, collect their coats, walking sticks, top hats and gloves, and push their way to the aisle. Madame Proust and her retinue flounce out snorting, "Vulgar, *absolument* rubbish," and "bunch of *nutters*." From behind there are cries of "Sit down!" and "*Asseyez-vous!*" Ladies in '*décolleté*' frocks lean out of the gilded boxes exposing their ample bosoms to the crowd.

From halfway up in the auditorium, newspaper music critic Jean Poueigh foolishly stands up and languidly pulls on his evening gloves, gesticulating that he too, has had enough. Like a tigress protecting her cub, Érik Satie leaps over the person next to him, storms down the aisle, and grabs the unfortunate critic, screaming, "Asshole, *cretin*, musical nitwit," and swings a punch. Érik, who is blind as a bat without his glasses, which are now splintered on the floor, begins to slap anyone within his arm's range. Meanwhile, the entire audience has taken sides. Some are shouting, "*Bravo, bravo, magnifique!*" while others cry "Boo, hiss, piece of *merde.*"

The uproar continues until the orchestra and typist stop and take refuge down the staircase in the pit, slam and lock the door, and the main curtain drops with a resounding thud. Meanwhile, four of the five artistic directors, Massine, Picasso, Diaghilev, and Cocteau, pour champagne into tumblers and rejoice. The fifth collaborator, Érik Satie, gets eight days in jail for assault and battery.

Art historians agree that this single stupendous performance in May of 1917 marks the birth of modern ballet.

Rome, 1964:

Forty-seven years later, Les Ballets Jazz Europa arrives on the outskirts of the eternal city, in a dilapidated Pullman, left over from WWII. It has been belching smoke all along the *Appian Way.* Everyone is in good spirits, laughing, joking, and ready to open at the *Teatro Sistina* near the Spanish Steps. Everyone, that is, except Simone, who is whining about her splitting *mal de tête* from the *fumée* of the horrible bus. The moment that the much maligned pullman arrives at 129 via Sistine, the door opens and she is the first one out. Simone dashes into the theatre dramatically crying "Nikko, Nikko, *j'arrive*," as though she is a lifeguard rescuing a drowning man. The Maestro has gone ahead by train, presumably to sort out the orchestra. Archaic rules include: paying for stagehands' 'work permits' whether they show up or not and 'up front' money for a full orchestra who are not expected to play a single note. All the ballet music is on a reel-to-reel tape. The main job of the orchestra is to look professional and sit on their duffs, doing nothing. Some of them can't even read music.

During the trip south, she sprawls across the back row with her square make-up case open. The lining of the case lid is a mirror.

"No!" she hisses to herself, noticing the worsening blister on her mouth.

"Oh, so you *did* have a good time in Florence, didn't you dearie?" Rosie cattily points out in front of the entire bus. Like a bunch of teenage monsters going off to summer camp, everyone erupts into laughter and teasing.

"Who is the tosser who kissed you? Oh, la la!" Maggie is the brunt of multilingual obscenities that she is fortunate enough not to fully understand.

Romeo swaggers back to the bus and in an exaggerated accent calls out, "Ah ha, Meez Canada, she just got laid." Maggie reddens and slams the beauty case shut.

"You are like my bratty cousins at a family reunion. Why don't you all take a hike?" She gives them the age-old Italian gesture *vaffanculo*, which needs no translation.

Ronáld quips, "Mags is learning international sign language." At that moment, Sophia Klemm, the beautiful German dancer, stands up and weaves her way to the back of the bus as it careens around a corner. She is flung into the seat beside Maggie.

"Ignore them, Mags, they do love you, we're just like *familie*. I'm a little worried about you. Are you on the pill?" Maggie is mystified.

"What pill?" she ventures.

"So you don't get how you say... '*schwanger werden*,' you know, '*enceinte*' in French, in English...knocked up?"

Maggie smiles, "Are you trying to say pregnant? As in have a baby? I never thought of that, but I doubt very much that Enzo is following me to Rome. He's a student. Anyway, once is enough. I'm not a virgin anymore, so everyone can just shut up about me." Sophia hugs Maggie hard. She is alarmingly close to tears.

"You're unique—a free spirit—and I'll never forget you." She rummages in her bag and brings out a cardboard card stuck with pills, one for every day of the month.

"Here, a farewell present for you." Maggie lifts her head.

"Farewell? What are you talking about?"

Sophia sighs, "I'm leaving the ballet in Rome."

She stands up and announces to all, "I have a '*beeg*' role in a movie called The Agony and the Ecstasy being filmed in Roma at *Cinecittà*." At that very moment, the bus swerves violently to avoid an oncoming car, and she lands in Romeo's lap.

"I am going to be a superstar!" He kisses her in a most unbrotherly way.

It is then that it dawns on Maggie that they really are a family.

"Sophia," she calls out. "You are right. We are a fabulously talented family, maybe just a little crazy. Good luck, I am going to miss you like a sister."

Cinecittà, near Rome, 1937:

The largest film studio in Europe was constructed in 1937 by Benito Mussolini, a man who knew that movies are a most powerful weapon for propaganda. Initially, he considered calling it 'Film Facisti Inc' but demurred to 'Cinecittà' or 'Cinema City Studios.' Bombed by the U.S. Air Force in 1944, it became a refugee camp in 1945, and by the 50's, American pictures came pouring out of 'Hollywood on the Tiber.' Notably, some included: Roman Holiday, Barefoot Contessa, and Ben Hur.

In 1964, The Agony and the Ecstasy is released with mixed reviews. In a small, but important scene, Sophia Klemm makes her acting debut. She holds a pot of wet cement for Michangelo to affix the egg tempera paint to the ceiling of the Sistine Chapel. Her acting is superb. Later, Sophia tells Maggie that the wet cement was really chocolate pudding. "I was very popular," she giggled with a wink.

Teatro Sistina, Rome, 1964:

In the center of the bare stage, the Maestro paces back and forth, doing little bits of dance movements and humming to himself. Everyone knows that this is not a moment to interrupt; he is creating or recreating a ballet. At that moment, it is in his head, but soon, he will erupt into a dynamo of creative movement. Maggie is wearing a soft, wool, hand-knitted leotard that Simone gives her. It fits her perfectly. Actually, Simone does not give it, but rather, flings it at her.

"I am sick of your horrible leotard," she says grumpily, but the expression on her face is hopeful that perhaps a bridge might be crossed. Maggie knows that Simone is complex and hides her true feelings, and knows about her history. She is fragile, having lost her entire family because of the British RAF, and lives only for the ballet and Nikko Pávlos the Maestro, who is her saviour. He has saved her from a life of mourning for what she has lost forever: a family.

The music for the ballet is ricocheting through the empty theatre and everyone is warming up; stretching, doing the splits, jumping, spinning, and doing push-ups and kicks. The Maestro claps his hands for attention.

"*Daahlinks*," he calls. "We make some changes, eh! With Sophia gone," he pauses a moment in quiet thought, then continues, "I will come on and improvise in her place. Then, everyone else continues as usual, with the drums in bar four, you know, *d'accord*?" He turns to Rudi and nods. The music begins with the trumpet solo. Rudi, with his back to the audience, mimes the trumpeter. His body begins to move slowly and lazily to the blues.

Curtain time. The *Teatro Sistina* is sold out and there has been no time for a full dress rehearsal of the entire ballet. Maggie is in heavy stage make-up, enormous false eyelashes, and little 'Clara Bow' lips hiding her red and swollen cold sore. She is wearing a matching sequin cloche hat and sparkling peach 'flapper' dress of the twenties. Peeking through the side curtain, she is waiting for the impromptu, unrehearsed fill-in. *Here it comes!* Her heart skips nervously. She has never really seen the Maestro dance full out, and he will have to hide the slight limp in his right leg.

The spotlight pinpoints a dot on the darkened stage. Footsteps can be heard, but not seen. Suddenly, the music pours out of the speakers, and a tall figure in a wide-brimmed fedora, baggy pinstripe suit, and white spats over his shoes, jumps into the circle of light. He is wearing gangster sunglasses and has a cigarette in his mouth. With a quick flick of his fingers, the smoking butt falls to the stage and is extinguished with a twist of a foot. In the next few minutes, the Maestro comes alive, as though filled with the energy of a tiger. He has the rhythm, the moves, the humour, the flexibility, and the soul. Like Gene Kelly and Fred Astaire, he becomes another instrument of the music. *Christ, he is as old as my father, but look at him go!* Maggie is elated. He can tap, spin like a top, do hand flips like a circus acrobat, and be as smooth as a ballroom champion. *Holy cow! That man really can dance,* she muses. She has renewed respect for the complicated stranger who is her boss.

Before the dance is even finished, the audience spontaneously bursts into applause and Maggie makes her entrance with the '*corps de ballet*,' bringing the 'The Twenties' to a roaring finale. One hour and fifty-six minutes with no intermission leaves the ballet emotionally exhausted, but still ready to party.

When in Rome, the only place where everyone in show business, including the paparazzi, T.V. crews, film directors, and those 'in the know' frolic until the early hours of the morning is called Piper Club. It is an underground 'go-go joint' on *Via Tagliamento*. The 'Go Go' dancers hired to entertain the wild crowd are nothing compared to Les Ballets Jazz letting their hair down. Maggie and Romeo, and the rest of the troupe dance themselves into a frenzy in the deafening noise and light show. It is almost dawn when Romeo drags Maggie outside, props her onto a stolen, red motor scooter and drives like an Italian: too fast and too cocky, down all the back roads, until he unceremoniously dumps her at a rooming house owned by a former Russian ballerina, 29 *Via Rasella*.

March 23rd 1944 Via Rasella, Roma:

It was a disastrous plan by the Italian partisans to plant a homemade bomb in a garbage can on Via Rasella just as the German 11th Company SS Police Regiment was to march down in a show of bravado. It backfired! The blast killed twenty-eight Nazis and the reprisal was vicious. Over three hundred innocent people; Jews, Christians, and prisoners, were ripped from their homes and jails, taken to an old quarry, and shot through the head by a few officers who were drunk on cognac. The bodies were hidden by a mound of earth over the hole and the next-of-kin were never notified. That massacre broke all the rules of international law. The final insult was that the wretched Pope Pius XII knew in advance what was planned and did nothing to intervene. To this day, it brings fury and condemnation of the Pope, and especially against those who gave the orders for the massacre of the three hundred innocents.

Number twenty-nine *Via Rasella* is written on a small piece of paper in Maggie's hand. When the taxi stops at the destination, she looks around, realizing there is no sign of a *pensione* or hotel in sight. She climbs out and drags her suitcase across the pavement, finally noticing a very small sign written in Russian with a childlike drawing of a bed. It doesn't look promising. She opens the door to a gloomy storage area for dustbins, bicycles, and mice, which exudes the smell of cooked cabbage.

Climbing part-way up the spiral staircase, she calls, "Hello? Hello?"

A voice from above replies, "*Dobro Pozhalova*, welcome. Come up, I speak a little English." With a sigh of relief, Maggie hauls her suitcase up the stairs.

"You may call me Madame Lebedinsky in Russian language, it means 'beautiful Swan.'"

"I'm sorry, I only know one word in Russian and that is '*babushka*,' a head scarf."

Madame Lebedinsky looks a little surprised and remarks, "*Babushka* means old woman."

Maggie blushes with embarrassment.

"Come in and have tea. Russian tea, *naturellement*, I know many languages," her eyes light up remembering.

It's easy to tell that Madame is a former ballerina. Although at this age, she appears as fragile as a little bird, rather than a swan. She sits regally, her hands gently resting in her lap while her tiny feet are unaffectedly pointed. As to her age, perhaps she was born in 1900, perhaps not. Her hair is still jet black, pulled back into a chignon at the nape of her neck, and huge, ornate earrings weigh her lobes down. Her make-up is outrageously theatrical. Maggie looks cautiously around the room. It is a magnificent clutter of memorabilia; stacks of theatre magazines litter the worn, Persian carpet, and the walls are a photographic history of the Russian Imperial Ballet and Diaghilev's Ballet Russes de Monte Carlo.

"Holy cow," breathes Maggie. "This is a museum. Wow." She

looks at the photographs, scanning the endless rows of famous faces and peering at the autographs. "I recognize Léonide Massine, because he played the shoemaker in the movie, 'The Red Shoes.' What was he like?" she asks. Madame rolls her eyes heavenward.

"A monster, a conceit, and a magnificent dancer."

"What about Aleksandra Danilova? I've seen her dance."

Madame stands very tall and poised and sniffs, "She is a bitch my dear, an absolute bitch."

Maggie starts to giggle. "I don't think much has changed in the ballet world. Maybe it's because dancing is so competitive. And who is this dancer? She is beautiful."

"Ah," Madame responds, "that is Olga Khokhlova, who married Pablo Picasso." She sighs, "I think all of us rather fancied him but, my friend Tamara, she was very foolish..." and her voice trails off to some distant memory.

Maggie's room for the next four nights is stark, compared with the plush sitting room. The floor is bare tile and the wallpaper faded to beige. It contains a slightly sagging double bed with a bleached linen spread that her mother would call 'old rose' but in this case more like 'dead rose,' a heavy, mahogany dresser on one wall, a shuttered window and a cupboard. As Maggie puts her suitcase out of sight at the back of the closet, she spots a parcel wrapped in a blanket. She stares at it for a moment, hesitates, but then curiosity wins out and she quickly pulls the blanket off, revealing an unsigned oil painting of a woman and child on a beach. Intrigued, she turns it over and gasps with recognition. The signature is unmistakable. Very, very carefully she rewraps the blanket snugly around it and slides it back exactly where it was. As she closes the door to her room she looks around for a key. *That painting must be worth a fortune, she thinks uneasily, why is it left so casually in my room?*

"Where is the key?" she calls out.

"My dear," Madame Lebedinsky replies, "I have nothing of real value to worry about."

On the third morning, Maggie wakes to an unexpected burst of hot weather. She hasn't seen anything of Rome and springs out of bed and into the communal bathroom, slams the door shut, and locks it. Madame is still sleeping, so she slips out the front door into the deserted street. Not even the pigeons are awake. She looks up and lets the sun warm her skin, before she takes off down *Via del Tritone* to the bottom of the hill, where a rabbit warren of streets should lead her to *Via del Gato*; Street of the Cat. From there she should find *Via della Pigna*; Pinecone Street, and the *Basilica di Santa Maria*. Meanwhile, she is going around in circles. She stops a street cleaner on a corner and he looks at her as if she is crazy. Lazily, he points up, and there it is, a perfectly smooth cement dome like a giant pudding bowl not fifty feet away.

"*Grazie Buonjourno*," Maggie replies, gazing at the building. There it is, Santa Maria, the largest non-supported domed structure in the world, built two thousand years ago. Amazingly, it is as high as it is in diameter, one hundred and seventy-two feet to be exact, and known by its former Roman name the *Pantheon*—a miracle of construction.

The doors are never closed as it is a place of worship, so Maggie walks right into the epicentre and looks up. A seven foot, perfectly round opening casts a beam of light indicating the hour on the floor below. Maggie's wooden sandals clatter on the marble breaking the spell. She takes them off and walks barefoot around the centuries old mosaic tiles in absolute silence. The air is cool and refreshing in the dome, despite the temperature outside climbing.

Suddenly, there is a honking of horns and the first busload of tourists arrive; English couples complaining about bitter Italian coffee and whiny brats wanting gelato for breakfast. Sitting in a coffee shop on the opposite side of the ancient square, in front of the Pantheon, the Maestro and Frank are absorbed in the local newspaper '*Il Messaggero*,' reading the review of the show and drinking coffee with small glasses of grappa. The mood changes without warning as Nikko translates the small police report next to Les Ballets Jazz review. "MASTERPIECE STOLEN IN MILAN." It describes a religious painting by Alessio Baldovinetti, stolen the previous week from a private home in the north of Milan. The small painting is one of forty pieces missing since 1944 and belongs to the Grand Duchess of Luxembourg. Police investigation continues.

Frank growls, "They know nothing, *niente*."

"This is too dangerous," murmurs Nikko. Snapping his fingers, he calls to the waiter, "*Por favore, due bicchiere di Grappa*," and drains his glass of brandy in one gulp.

"Jesus, it looks like a brothel." Anna, Rosie, and Maggie are staring in disbelief at the room assigned to them for a whole week. It is at the end of a corridor that lists like a sinking ship. A double bed, a single cot, and a sagging sofa line two walls that are papered in gaudy, red roses climbing up a trellis. Sewer and water pipes run in tandem through the floor to the ceiling above and are painted a leafy green. Every time a toilet is flushed the pipes gurgle. An enameled bidet sits in a corner with a large, wooden crucifix hanging above it, decorated with a painted Christ, bleeding profusely from his crown of thorns.

For the upcoming week, Les Ballets Jazz is performing two shows a night in a cabaret dinner theatre in a poor section of Rome. It is a joint called *Il Circolo 60's*. Maggie looks around the empty stage and thinks, *My father would have heart failure if he knew I was dancing in a nightclub and sleeping in a brothel!*

Opening night is unforgettable. The dancers perform 'The Twenties' which always goes well, followed by 'The Leather Boys of London,' a potentially unfortunate choice for the already fairly belligerent audience. During the fight scene between the 'mods and the rockers,' some twits try to get into the act and climb onto the stage shouting insults. From other tables, clients shout, "Shut up and sit down," "*Stai zitto e siediti!*" There is a scuffle in the front row of tables and someone throws a chair. That seems to be the signal. If this gang of thugs thought they were taking on some prissy theatrical lightweights, they made a big mistake. Rudi, the premier '*danseur*' of Les Ballets, spent his childhood in the Indonesian slums of Amsterdam fighting to survive the war, racism, and rationing. His fists are like a machine gun. Xavier, a veteran of the vaudeville circuit is quick witted and street savvy, Romeo is ex-army and even Ronáld is no stranger to handling homophobic harassment. No one should be foolish enough to get in Frank's way. The Maestro is calmly trying to get control of the situation before someone gets hurt. The uproar continues until one by one, Nikko picks up each troublemaker and tosses them, like flimsy rag dolls, into the auditorium before pulling the curtain. There is hissing and booing from the other side and sounds of breaking glass.

"Quickly, change into the *finale*," he orders, to no one in particular. Out comes the ugly, yellow, tail-feathered costumes with matching top hats and gloves. We haven't used them in months. What a mistake! The inebriated orchestra attempt, without any rehearsal, to play Stan Kenton's 'Artistry in Jump,' and it grinds to a discordant dirge. The girls, now without music, rush to take refuge in the dressing room. They slam the door and laugh uproariously. Meanwhile, there is a shouting match in Sicilian and Italian between the Maestro and management. Maggie hasn't witnessed a good brawl like this since her graduation dance at Ladysmith High.

"What is '*La Salle*?" Maggie asks the others.

Talitha is carefully filing her fingernails to a sharp point, and replies, "It's a sneaky little obligation written into the contract that means all entertainers must mix with the audience after the final show and ask for the most expensive champagne to pad the bar bills."

Maggie rolls her eyes, "I think it's time I went home."

Ladysmith High, Vancouver Island, B.C. June 1960:
Graduation Day

From the big, black speakers hanging high up on the rafters of the gymnasium of Ladysmith High blares the voice of Marty Robbins, singing 'A White Sports Coat and a Pink Carnation.' Maggie is in the arms of Fergus Dunsmuir, her so-called grad partner. The selection of 'grad dates' was thought up by the principal who wanted everyone to have a partner. Any girl who was too square or unpopular had to draw an available boy from a cardboard ice cream bucket and be their date until the end of the first dance. After that, it was every man for himself. Maggie is furious and humiliated that her neighbour Ronnie has not asked her. They have been playmates for years, but his "date" he announces with a smirk, is Samantha. No one has heard of her. It turns out that Samantha is actually his damn Siamese cat. Ronnie thinks he has been terribly clever. On the afternoon before the big day, Maggie's metal braces come off her teeth, leaving a big, white, smooth smile after three years of a whole lot of pain.

With her new smile, she models her graduation dress that really is a work of art, or at least a work of love. With limited materials in post-war Canada, her mother has found a beautiful piece of fabric and decorated it with small bunches of artificial violets taken from her grandmother's hat. Maggie put her hair up in a sophisticated 'french roll,' piled on lots of make-up and pinned a gardenia corsage from her graduation "date" on the top of her head with about fifty bobbi pins. A dab of Chanel #5 behind her ears and a sprinkle of Johnson and Johnson baby powder in her knickers and she is ready.

Arriving at the gym, Maggie takes off her shoes and puts on bobby sox, because the floor is freshly varnished. She glances around to see if Ronnie has actually brought his silly cat and he is staring at her as if he has never seen her before. Her date, Fergus Dunsmuir, dances with her non-stop and even tries to kiss her with his mouth open. *Yuck!* By midnight everyone is sloshed and are dancing themselves silly. The punch has been spiked with over-proof vodka, and some fool has set off the fire alarms and no one even notices. Suddenly the doors burst open and a busload of students from Nanaimo crash the party. Fights break out, Ronnie gets a bloody nose and Maggie's date, Fergus, hurls in the wastepaper basket in the corner. From the speakers, "'The Four Freshmen' harmonize *We'll Remember Always, Graduation Day."* The police arrive about midnight—the gymnasium is abandoned, there is no sign of a fire, and the varnished floor is awash in sugar syrup, orange peels, vodka, and broken glass. Maggie arrives home, her dress in tatters, and sleeps for ten hours straight.

Rome, Italy, Il Circolo 60's, 1964:

After the rather shaky start, the rest of the week at '*Il Circolo*' is an outstanding success, a full house every night. Somehow, word gets out that Les Ballets Jazz is the most avant garde troupe of dancers to be seen in years and the audience changes from local hoods to international film stars, television producers, and businessmen slumming for the night. After selling out their supply of the most expensive champagnes in the world, the nightclub has no need to pad the bills. Rome has been conquered and it is time to move on.

CHAPTER VII

The Grand Tour

With no regrets, Les Ballets Jazz leaves the sprawling capital and follows the ancient Roman Appian Way southeast, toward Terracina on the outskirts of Naples.

Rosie calls to the back row of the bus, asking "Did you see who was in the audience last night?" No one replies. "Marcello Mastroianni," she says haughtily. Maggie stops reading and puts down her book, 'The Leopard' by Giuseppe Tomasi di Lampedusa. She turns to Rosie.

"Are you kidding me? Marcello is my dream actor. I didn't see him?"

Sarcastically, Rosie replies, "Well, that's not surprising. You are always too busy showing off to notice if there is an audience there at all." An uneasy silence falls. No one breathes, no one comes to her defense.

Well, this is a giant step backwards, she thinks, *and just as I was feeling a part of this company. Why, only last week, the Maestro took Anna and me out to a fancy dinner. Do I really ignore the audience?* Maggie questions herself. *Certainly, the Maestro is continually complaining that I adulterate his choreography.* "You must be one with zee audience—most important not to dance for only you, but for people to love you, you must look at them and dance only for them. Let yourself go with zee music and zee love, *daahlink*." Often, he just stares with unreadable eyes and stays silent. *Lord knows that I am technically his strongest female dancer, well perhaps along with Anna because she has unshakable balance and soft, expressive arms, like willow branches in a breeze. I become fairly stiff and controlled when nervous and the Maestro has that effect on me. I realize that I will never get a solo, not even a tiny one, if everyone is against me.*

She unfolds a handful of letters from home and hunches back in her alarmingly vomit-smelling, ripped leather seat to gnaw her fingernails and re-read the distressing comments from home.

Father writes: *"Dearest Margaret Alice, Isn't it time you stopped this gallivanting around in foreign places and got a real job? It's not too late to register for teaching college, if you come home immediately. I think you owe us that."*

Mother writes: *"Dear Margaret, You do worry me my dear. Everyone in your graduation class from Ladysmith High is either happily married or has a diamond on the fourth finger, even our neighbour, Ronnie, has a steady girlfriend. Your sister Geri is expecting, as you know, and you could be a great help to her with a newborn. Perhaps, you should enroll in a finishing school, in Switzerland, and train to become a Nanny."*

In her ancient, scratchy, old-fashioned scrawl, Granny writes: *"Oh, to be in Italy at this time of the year, how delightful! I live for your letters describing all the beauty around you. It is almost like being on 'The Grand Tour.' I am enclosing forthwith a small bank draft so you are not caught short."* She concludes with several lines from Keats, who wrote the greatest odes in the English language, and died in Rome at the age of twenty-three. *"Beauty is truth—truth beauty, that is all ye know on earth, and all ye need to know. Fondest regards, Granny."*

She is not sure whether to laugh or cry as she pulls on her

hangnail until it bleeds. *Her grandmother is never judgmental, but her parents...she sighs. What is a real job, anyway, and how much does one owe one's parents? There are so many questions and no answers. One thing is sure, she is not going to any ridiculous 'finishing school,' and solo or no solo, she is not going home like a defeated hound dog with its tail between its legs.* "No siree, Bob!" She shouts out loud, "I'm not finished yet." No one is listening, as most are sound asleep or absorbed in silent solitaire.

Ristorante Alfredo alla Scrofa, Rome, 1964:

A light drizzle splatters off the windshield of a green and black Fiat taxi as it glides to a stop at *104 Via della Scrofa.* Before the taxi driver can get out to open the doors, Maggie, Anna, and Nikko Pávlos climb out and lira changes hands. The Maestro, carrying his usual, dark brown briefcase, opens the glass door etched with the words *Alfredo alla Scrofa dal 1914.* Anna and Maggie make their entrance, looking spectacular in flawless makeup, silk stockings, short, cotton sheath dresses, and sling-back heels. Heads turn. The room oozes charm, its butter yellow plaster walls lined with autographed photographs of celebrities all eating fettuccine and grinning like happy cats who got the cream.

Bustling from the back of the dining room, a florid, slightly moist gentleman with a bushy moustache flings his arms around the Maestro in a sweaty bear hug, shouting, "Nikolaos Pávlos! My friend, *mio amici, benvenuto*, welcome, come, sit right here." Then, he turns to the girls, bows to them, and waves them to seats. With the flick of his wrist, he signals a waiter who arrives with four crystal goblets of sparkling white wine from the hills north of Rome. "*Tchin, tchin,*" and he downs his in one gulp. Another waiter arrives with the legendary solid gold fork and spoon in a velvet frame. Engraved in the cutlery are the English words 'To Alfredo, King of the Noodles, July 1927.' On the spoon, 'from

Douglas Fairbanks, junior' and the fork is inscribed 'from Mary Pickford,' both stars of silent films who spent their honeymoon in Rome. "*Mele di luna*, honeymoon," the waiter intones gravely, as if marriage in Italy is something of a tragedy. In "The Leopard," the Sicilian author, Lampedusa, writes that marriage starts with "Flames for a year, ashes for thirty."

Nikko looks up sharply as the door to Alfredo's opens. A well-dressed gentleman of about forty-five surveys the room with a sweeping glance, strides over to the table, nods to the girls, and introduces himself as "Massimo Badalamenti." Putting his black briefcase down, he sits next to Nikko. They lean close and converse in Sicilian dialect with such little intonation, that it is impossible to follow one word.

Anna's eyes are sparkling as she whispers to Maggie, "I think Anita Ekberg and that director Fellini are sitting on the other side of the room."

"Who's Anita Ekberg? Never heard of her."

Anna gives her a withering look, "She's the star of *La Dolce Vita*, you know, it won the Cannes Film Festival?" Maggie stares blankly.

"I haven't seen many movies because there is no theatre in Ladysmith. There is an outdoor movie screen in North Oyster, but we only go there to drink beer."

From the kitchen, a mist laden with the aroma of roasting meat, garlic, and onion wafts across the dining room. Three large platters of steaming fettuccine are heading toward the table and Massimo smiles. "*Buon appetito*," he says, as he picks up the Maestro's brown briefcase and disappears. Maggie looks puzzled and raises an eyebrow to Nikko as if to say, "You must have noticed?" The Maestro's face betrays nothing. His eyes demand her silence.

He turns to the waiter and cries exuberantly, "*Benissimo, grazie.*

Fettuccine al triplo burro," and plunges his fork into the pile of noodles glistening with triple butter. The waiter returns with a bottle of very fine red wine and opens it with panache.

"Wow! This sure beats macaroni and cheese!" Maggie is ecstatic. "I've never tasted anything so delicious in all my life, *squisito*."

"Aah, Maggie," the Maestro is bemused, "you learn *italiano*, *brava*." A golden Dunlop lighter appears from nowhere and lights Anna's cigarette. She looks up at the waiter and puckers her lips. Two manicured fingernails remove a tiny speck of tobacco from the very tip of her tongue and the waiter almost swoons onto the red tiled floor. *Jesus, she is trying to seduce the poor waiter in front of the Maestro,* Maggie notices. Anna takes a long, seductive drag on her cigarette and gently blows it out her nose.

Region of Campania, 1964:

Everyone is asleep or in a trance as the old bus struggles along the Appian Way, turning east toward Capua and Casserta. A well-fingered map slides to the floor, wrinkled with use. It almost looks like a game of snakes and ladders, with inked-in dates and drawings scrawled on the borders. Les Ballets are performing in every village, town, and collection of houses that have any semblance of a theatre. The exotic sounding names are a blur of old opera houses; *Teatro della Popolo, Manzioni, Municipale, Citti di Fondi, Communale,* and *Remigio.* Most are savaged with bullet holes and falling down in disrepair. The once proud theatres are rat-infested burrows, crawling with cockroaches and full of broken seats, but to the dancers, *the opera houses are magical.*

The farther south they go, every village and city has a *Piazza Garibaldi* at its centre. Giuseppe Garibaldi was a rough and ready soldier who unified or became the symbol of the unification of Italy in 1860. He and a band of one thousand armed rebels who called themselves 'red shirts' managed to break the religious stranglehold over the lives of the poor, and defeated the power and privilege of a few landowning aristocrats.

Via Matteotti pops up too, in every town, and is a reminder of a socialist troublemaker who stood up to Benito Mussolini and was promptly tortured and murdered by the fascist secret police 'OVRA.' This stands for 'Organization for Vigilance and Repression of Anti-Fascism;' a nasty group of 50,000 thugs.

With a spine-shattering bump, the bus pulls into a dusty main square, engine steaming, ready to explode. The driver gets out and disappears into the nearest bar.

"Where are we?" The dancers stagger out into a noon heat wave as unruly crowds of urchins gather around, all squealing in an incomprehensible dialect. A few young girls, smiling shyly, come forward with pieces of paper for autographs. They long to escape the impossible life in a war torn, politically unstable city of the south. To them, Rosie, Talitha, Aneka, and the rest look like goddesses, and ballet: a way to escape poverty and sexual abuse in a system gone wrong yet again.

The girls of the ballet gather up their make-up cases and practice clothes and file through the '*entrada di artisti*,' the stage door, into the cool gloom of backstage. All are dog tired, but there is plenty of work to do. Like robots, everyone pitches in and sets up the stage, hanging up costumes from the skips.

Nikko's voice can be heard, "*Sur scene*; on stage, *daahlinks!*" The rehearsal begins. With each new stage, the choreography gets changed to fit: small, big, raked, and flat. Xavier fiddles with the sound system, Ronáld hauls the scenery to the wings and Frank, Rudi, and Romeo empty the truck. After a few minutes, the local orchestra staggers in to get paid before they retire for a few glasses of fortifying *grappa*, before the first performance.

"Are we staying the night here?" Someone calls out hopefully.

"No, we sleep on the bus," is the reply.

"A trattoria is staying open for us after the second show."

Maggie pulls leg warmers over her knees despite the heat, and begins class with slow, deep *plies*, trying to build up strength and control of her limbs. Perspiration runs through her heavy hair to her neck and down between her breasts which have grown considerably since she has been swallowing Sophia's "forbidden pills."

"They are a sin," Rosie comments.

"The Pope also banned lipstick," Maggie snaps, "and I don't see you dancing bare-faced and throwing away your pile of Max Factor!"

Les Ballets has been warned that the southern towns are poor, overpopulated, riddled with crime, and dangerous.

"Audiences," warns Nikko, "are infamous for being loud, booing and blowing raspberries. It is up to you, *daahlinks*, to see that they are entertained and happy to part with the price of a ticket." Few homes have anything resembling a television and their theatre is all they have. Nikko chooses the program with care, eliminating 'The Leather Boys' so there is no fuel for a fight up in the stalls. The houses are packed every night, with two shows, one at seven and the second at ten. That is two hours of non-stop dancing, followed by a short break, while the theatre empties and refills and the second show ends at twelve. By the time the scenery is dismantled and the dressing rooms emptied, it is well after midnight. Every member of the troupe is frantic for food and drink.

One hot and airless night in Naples, after an exhausting two shows, seven dancers are huddled in the square in front of the '*Teatro San Carlo*.' Their clothes, hair, and underarms sticky with perspiration, they are wondering how safe they are and where to forage for food—any food at all, and of course something to drink— preferably wine, and lots of it. Finally, Rudi takes the plunge.

"I'm going this way," as he spins around, goose-stepping* down the street as though he is in the German army. The seven of them laugh and follow his antics, kicking their legs in grand battements all the way down a hill. *"Eins, zwei, vier, fünf"* he bellows. Soon, they are completely lost.

All of a sudden, an enormous figure jumps out of a tunnel, with a shrill, Arabian war cry, and blocks their way. Rosie screams and throws herself into Xavier's arms. Out of the gloom appears Frank, grinning like an idiot.

Liliane slaps him across the face and shrieks rudely, "You scared us to the death, *va te faire foutie!*" Then, she turns on Rosie. *"Putin,* leave my man alone, you English *salope."* Maggie watches the scene with interest. *Hah! A catfight over Xavier, of all people. Now, if it were over Rudi, I would understand, but a sly little ferret like Xavier, hmm.*

Liliane is consumed with jealous rage, but she allows Anna to take her gently by the arm, cooing, "Let's go! We are all tired and hungry."

"Come," Frank says, as he waves at them to follow.

There is a single, dark, wrought-iron lantern placed high up on a corner. Its dim stream of light reveals a flight of steep, stone stairs descending into an ancient archway with a metal door partially corroded with rust. It is called '*Trattoria Caruso.*' Frank knocks and it opens immediately into a subterranean chamber, glowing with soft candlelight, smelling of the sea and a welcome by a smiling couple clapping their hands as though they are greeting their own family. Even Liliane turns on the charm, grateful that it has remained open so late.

A large, black and white framed photograph dominates the rock wall beside the kitchen alcove. It is, of course, a portrait of the most famous tenor of all time, Enrico Caruso, who was born in this neighbourhood in 1873, into a poor family of twenty-one children, one of whom survived. While waiting for the spaghetti to boil, the host tells the legend, which is translated into English, French, and

German around the linen clad tables. For once, Les Ballets Jazz is being entertained rather than entertaining, quaffing a robust wine from Aglianico grapes and hearing about Enrico.

"The Great Caruso began his career as a street singer and was booed during one of his first concerts because he couldn't afford to pay for a *claque*, or folk hired to applaud. Humiliated, he vowed never to sing in Naples as long as he lived. *'I will never come home except to eat spaghetti.'* And he kept his word. Enrico Caruso died on August 2nd 1921 at the local Vesuvio Hotel, having made over nine million dollars in recordings and performances worldwide but, never, ever again sang a note in Napoli."

Maggie is bubbling with enthusiasm and wine. She turns to Romeo, thinking of the letter from her mother.

"I will never go home to become a nanny, not ever!" He looks at her, mystified.

"What you talk about?" as his eyes drift down to her breasts.

"Eata lotsa pasta, it's good for you." The plate of the evening is *spaghetti alla puttanesca*, or in the Neapolitan's dialect, *aulive e chiappariell*; spicy olives and capers. An astonishing amount of it is consumed, empty bottles line the serving table like a guard of honour for the wine. Multiple nationalities who were once at war with one another dine in peace and sing in harmony.

The souls of 25,000 dead civilians must be wondering if there was any point to the bombing of 1943 for control of the Port of Naples. *

Ballet dancers all over the world complain that their careers are ridiculously short, usually only ten years, from the ages of seventeen until twenty-seven. Ten years of training for a ten-year professional career. Factoring in no money, no sleep, improper diet, injury and accidents, Maggie is surprised that anyone survives ten years. Certainly not doing one-night stands in an Italian heatwave in 1964. And yet, there is nothing more satisfying than the certain hush, the anticipation, arrhythmical fluttering of the heart just seconds before the music begins. It is a moment of pure ecstasy, and something magical happens: body and soul are lifted to another space.

It is almost dawn when the bus loudly backfires on the poor inhabitants of *Napoli* as it heads out of town. The sleepy driver rumbles through a maze of shuttered shop fronts, dilapidated apartment blocks, and cobbled piazzas searching for the seafront street, the *Amalfi Coast Road*—famous in all guidebooks as the scariest road in Europe.

Les Ballet are a sorry lot, curled up like pill bugs, mouths agape, snoring like West Coast lumberjacks after a night on the town. The magnificent sunrise goes unappreciated. Fortunately, they do not see the twisting, turning road that is cantilevered in places, dropping to jagged rocks below. Nor do they look with horror at the paint-scraping one-way tunnels and the ever-narrowing switchbacks. As the determined morning traffic comes alive, grinding teeth and gears, it joins the fray that darts from Sorrento to Amalfi, to Salerno and back. Everyone is jolted awake with sudden traffic jams, fender benders, and brawling and impossible snarl-ups. A trip to Ravello that should take two, or two and a half hours at most is not looking promising. Les Ballet must reach the posh *Gardens of the Villa Rufalo* in time to unpack, set up, and rehearse—this time, on an outdoor stage hanging over the cliff. For this performance they will have a real orchestra playing their complicated scores.

Back on the coast road, tempers flare as the heat rises. From a tunnel between the villages of Amalfi and Atrani the bus thunders out of the darkness into the blinding light of the sun and slams to a standstill. The road is blocked.

"*Che casino*," Romeo yelps as he is thrown from his seat, smashing his shoulder on a metal bar. Buses, trucks, scooters, and pedestrians jam the narrow stone bridge ahead that curves around the picturesque cliff-side village of Atrani. Too steep for roads, the villagers must climb staircases and paths the mere width of a mule, in order to go from their houses to their churches. From the black sand beach to the tower in the clouds, Atrani looks like a beautiful cluster of pastel barnacles joined by dollhouse steps.

Near the top of the cliff proudly stands the *Collegiata di Santa Maria Maddalena*, a sparkling dome covered in saffron yellow and acid green mosaic tiles. Next to it, a rectangular bell tower of brown, volcanic tuff tolls mournfully as it has done since the 16th century. *Bong, bong, bong!*

In sudden comprehension, the driver smacks his forehead with the palm of his hand, swearing, '*Porco madonna.*' A funeral procession. The Maestro buries his face in his hands and groans. A procession thrice around the village is the norm for the most important moment in a person's life, or more logically speaking, their death. Lying in a heavy, wooden coffin covered in an avalanche of red carnations, the corpse is carried three times around their community by road, staircase, and mule path. Leading, the '*corteo funebre,*' the bearer of incense, slowly creeps along, waving aromatic smoke to ward off evil and disguise the flatulence of the clergy. This procession could last an eternity. Every few yards the priest shuffles to a stop and raises his beringed hand. Everyone who is not crippled with arthritis kneels down, while the kids lie flat on the stones, kicking and biting their siblings.

Tour buses still stuck in the tunnel blast their horns, and cyclists in shiny, leather jackets try to sneak ahead only to be halted by armed police who look like trigger-happy teenagers begging for a brawl. Strangers, tourists, and locals jostle each other for a better view.

Anna jumps up and orders the door open. "Sod it! I'm going to the beach. We'll never get to Ravello tonight. I need some sun." She stomps across the bridge, down a metal staircase, and is last seen lying on a black sand beach in her push-up bra and pink lace bikini underpants.

Her defiance is seen as a signal. Ronáld slips into his carefully folded cream-coloured linen jacket, adjusts his ever-present fedora, and drifts off looking for action.

"A... telephone box?" queries Nikko as he steps carefully onto the bridge, hiding his eyes with enormous sunglasses. He looks like a film star. The bus empties and the *conducente di autobus* climbs out of the driver's seat, slides into a more comfortable one, and with a pop, pulls a cork out of a bottle of brandy. He smiles, settling down for a siesta in the sweltering heat.

Hours later, when traffic is beginning to come alive, the driver, disorientated and tipsy, struggles to his feet, opens the door and the dancers file back aboard. All except the Maestro appear to be present. Rudi stares at the driver.

"Hey Pops, you okay to drive?"

He mumbles, "Don't worry, *non preoccuparti amici*." So, they don't. Instead, they pray and pass the bottle around like a communion cup.

"*Ave Maria*, full of Grace, get us out of this place." With a head-snapping jerk, the bus takes off around the cantilevered curve of Santa Maria. The sozzled driver is determined to set a new record, honking and hollering out of the side window at the last of the mourners who are clinging to the rock face, the ruins of a medieval fortress. Old men shake their fists and ancient crones genuflect. With gathering speed, the bus hurtles past small settlements, roadside bathing beaches, and smart patios with umbrellas and spanking white chairs. The transparent blue waters, so inviting, are just a passing dream. After countless hair-raising twists and turns, Les Ballets Jazz Europa burst into Salerno by the Sea and are dumped unceremoniously at the stage door of the opera house. Yet again, it is a *Teatro Verdi*. As in so many Italian towns, the theatre is named after it's most famous composer Giuseppi Verdi. But, the redemption is across the piazza, the old-fashioned Hotel Diana, a *pensione* with actual rooms, hot water, bathtubs and soft beds.

"Hang the cost, give the cat a goldfish!" cries Rosie, as she darts across the square, abandoning her belongings at the side of the road.

Salerno, Italy 1964:

After a long and luxurious soak in the tub and a naked nap on her bed with sea breezes caressing her body, Maggie feels seductive and is longing for a night on the town. Humming a tune from the musical show 'Gypsy' she slips into a pale green cotton sundress, leaves her mop of damp hair loose, and joins Talitha in the vast, marble lobby of the Hotel Diana. Full of high spirits, the two tall dancers, one blonde and one red-headed, hurry down the street to an open air seaside fish house, *Osteria sul Mare.* Shaded by tall palm trees and scented with lemon trees, the *osteria* resembles an aviary of exotic, colourful birds screeching and babbling in foreign tongues. At night, lights twinkle overhead, giving the effect of a jewelled ceiling sparkling on the happy diners below.

"Aah, *ballerini,* you come with me," a tall, swarthy waiter, looking more like a pirate than a Calabrian native, guides them to a long table where most of the others are already seated in a closed circle. Talitha squeezes in beside Frank and gives him a kiss, obviously not the first. Xavier and Liliane are holding hands, and for once, looking content. Anna and Romeo are deep in conversation with Rudi and Aneka. In a blur of couples, jabbering in French, Italian and German, the world starts spinning. *Am I the only one here that has no one special?* She thinks. *I seem to be the odd one out. I feel rejected, and like an outcast. How can I meet anyone to love when we work all night and travel by day?* Maggie presses her fingers to her eyes to stop them from burning.

Without warning, Nikko arrives, and everyone shuffles around

116 | No Intermission

making room. He takes a place between Rosie and Simone who passes him a full bottle of wine.

"*Ce vin est incroyable*," announces Simone.

"*Brilliant*," finishes Rosie with a faint flush to her cheeks.

He laughs, "I've just come from the vineyard of the Caruso brothers." He leans in and starts telling an amusing story en francais of his adventurous trip up to the hilltop castle the Villa Rufalo where Les Ballets were to perform. Mags misses a lot in translation but she does hear him mention the name "Peggy Goldenstein."

"What about her?" She asks.

"Peggy is going to sponsor the ballet in Venice as soon as this tour is over."

"Venice," Maggie is jubilant. This would make her grand tour complete. She has been longing to visit the famous floating city held together by one hundred and eighteen islands and wooden pylons. Her favourite movie, *Summertime* was filmed there, starring Rossano Brazzi, who is the most gorgeous Italian actor she has ever seen. She wept at the final scene as the train carrying a lovesick Katherine Hepburn steamed out of the *stazione centrale*, leaving her lover on the platform holding a gardenia—pure Hollywood schmaltz, but so romantic.

Perhaps that should be my final scene, as well, she is thinking. Leave by train from Venice and return home to Canada. No one, of course, would be standing on the platform with a flower. Her career seems to be at a standstill and on her next birthday she will be turning twenty-one, for heaven's sake. She is already a spinster as her mother keeps reminding her. *Yes!* Her mind is made up. After Venice, it will be the perfect time to say goodbye, pack her bags for good, knowing that she will hardly be missed. Sadly, she reflects, *There are always dancers younger, prettier, and better waiting in the wings. Nothing lasts forever.* Maggie drains her glass and it is topped up by the hovering waiter.

Giant platters of fried fish, shellfish, squid, winkles, and *frittura pesce* arrive at the table, along with baskets of fresh semolina bread called *pane di padula* with local olive oil. Let the party begin! Somewhere in the darkness, an accordion begins to play a haunting song of the sea; '*Tango del Mare.*' As the accordion player draws near, Ronáld, the consummate performer, climbs unsteadily on top of one of the lemon tree barrels with a large glass of Caruso in one hand, a cigarette in the other, and of course, begins to sing in Italian.

"Mare perché questo notte il mio perduto amor..."

"Why do you beckon to me—oh sea of sadness, why do you beckon me to dream and suffer? I can't forget my lost lover."

There is a loud scraping of chairs on the other side of the *osteria* and a heavy-set man with boyish good looks weaves his way between the tables toward the swaying Ronáld who has paused for a good glug of *vino*.

"Claudio," he yells in astonishment, jumping off the lemon tree. The two throw their arms around each other like wrestlers.

"Signore e signori," he announces.

"Claudio Villa!"

"Who is he?" Maggie whispers. Before anyone can answer, the two tenors start again, both trying to top the other in the high notes. *"Mare perché, questo notte il mio perduto amor."* Perspiration runs down their faces, they fling their arms dramatically and are enjoying themselves as only two performers with huge egos and enormous respect for one another can. Rudi has found a guitar, a band from a different venue arrives, and the fish house in Salerno swings all night long.

This would never happen in Ladysmith by the Sea. Not in a million years!

Teatro Francesco Cilea, Reggio Calabria, 1964:

Mirrors surrounded by bright, bare bulbs reflect the row of

dancers in an unforgiving light. Freckles, pimples, bags under the eyes, and cold sores—everything shows. There is a knock on the dressing room door and the bored voice of a stagehand drawls, *venti minuti* as though he were half asleep.

"It's full-on war paint tonight," remarks Maggie, as she takes false eyelashes out of a match box. "Why are such tiny lashes so expensive?"

"I make my own out of thick paper. "Here, try them," and Talitha hands her a pair of homemade paper eyelashes and a pot of spirit gum.* From the grand orchestra pit, muted sounds of instruments, piano trills, a violin sliding down the scale, and a trumpet blasting anticipate the start. Excitement mounts. A final dab of Max Factor foundation is placed and the sharp arch of an eyebrow is painted on, heavy lips are outlined and giant, fake eyelashes are glued onto swollen eyelids. The effect is thrilling.

The Maestro opens the door, and hisses, "Two minutes, *deux minutes, daahlinks*…break a leg." Maggie slips into her costume, adjusts her hair, and is ready to make her entrance. Her heart quickens, and like a rolling surf, the familiar anticipation begins to drown out all other senses.

She remembers the Maestro's words: *"Only the music matters… listen only to the music…dance for your audience."* With a hush, lights dim, stage hands stop jabbering, they adjust their testicles, blow their noses into large squares of cloth, and take their places. The ancient, thread-bare velvet curtains part in the middle and stop dead on their tracks.

"*Godverdomme,* Goddamnit!" Rudi is center stage a with fake trumpet in hand, waiting for the first note of the blues. Two grunting stagehands yank on the ropes one more time to free the curtain. Successfully, it whips back into the wings like laundry on a windy day, sending up a storm cloud of dust. Sneezing violently, Rudi wipes his face on his sleeve, and puts the instrument to his lips just as the sound of the trumpet erupts from the speakers. Simone is apoplectic over the snot-smeared costume.

"Dirty boy, *dégoûtant*," she hisses at him. He winks and then disappears into his stage character, dancing with the grace of a matador. Boxes, stalls, and the gallery are jammed with Reggio Calabrians who have not yet emigrated to America. Another performance begins.

Seven nights, seven cities, it must be the quickest grand tour of Sicily on record. Les Ballets Jazz pack, unpack, dance and eat '*arancini*,' rice balls, for breakfast, lunch, and dinner. Somehow, the bus holds together and rumbles along from Catania in the north to Taormina, south to Siracusa, Noto, Avolo, and west to Agrigento, ending up in the historic center of Palermo at the Teatro Bellini near the dockyard.

Palermo, Sicily, 1964:

The heat is unbearable. It seems to bounce off the buildings onto the empty *Piazza Bellini* as the dancers tumble out of the smelly bus, stretching and grumbling. The rest of the world is having a siesta. At the stage door, the Maestro is arguing with a short but muscular dark-haired guard who is armed and barring the entrance. Both wave their arms about and it is easy to see that tempers are flaring. The costume truck and all the skips, scenery, and recording equipment has been stolen and will not be returned until a large sum of money changes hands. Simone rushes up protectively and screams *en francais* at the uncomprehending fellow who flicks her away as if she were a mosquito, implying that females belong at home making ravioli and washing diapers. She stamps her feet and bursts into tears of frustration.

Maggie is peering at a city map looking for *Via Butera*, and the address of the palace from her book 'The Leopard.'

"Come with me Anna, let's go exploring."

"I need a cold drink," Anna retorts, as the two wander off down the deserted *Via Alloro* completely unmoved by the drama of the disappearing costumes.

"Oh, Nikko will find the money somewhere. He always does."

Via Alloro resembles a faded black and white photograph left out in the sun. The houses on both sides, the pavement, bare earth and dust-covered rubble are an unhealthy, yellowish ochre. Although the bombing of the shipyards and port of Palermo by Allied and Axis air forces ended twenty-one years ago, the destruction in the surrounding neighbourhood is untouched.* Wires hang out of masonry walls, staircases end in a jagged drop, roofs are missing, and plumbing exposed. Stray dogs waffle among the broken glass, splintered beams, and debris. Anna and Maggie look like bright, summer flowers among the devastation. Through half lowered shutters, they are being watched by dark eyes. The occasional child cries out, but besides the momentary interruption, all is still, like a town from the 'Twilight Zone.'

"This is creepy." Anna is uneasy and hurries on. Around the corner, the *Chiesa di Santa Maria della Pietà* stands tall. Bells are ringing and a happy bride in a parachute of white silk satin is posing on the church steps with a small army of family members, including dozens of infants, babies, and toddlers in expensive, lacy, white frocks or miniature white linen suits.

"At last," cries Anna as she spies a bar across from the church on *Via Butera. "Agua frizzante por favore."* A cold bottle of sparkling water appears and is downed in record time. Maggie is practicing blowing smoke rings when Anna drops the bombshell. "Rosie is pregnant again." Maggie gags.

"How did that happen?"

Anna smiles sadly, "Well, obviously she doesn't take any precautions, does she."

"Rosie would be much happier if she went back to England, married a nice English boy and had a family."

She pauses, whispering, "Me too. I could be happy..." At that moment, the bridal cavalcade drives by amid cheering, hooting and blowing of kisses. The groom looks glum and is sweating in his starched white collar, but the bouncing bride beams with satisfaction. She has got her man.

Venice, Italy 1625 - 1789:

Of all cities on 'The Grand Tour,' Venice is the jewel in the crown for the young British aristocracy in the seventeenth and eighteenth centuries. From 1625 until the beginning of the French revolution, all gentlemen born to privilege and their tutors called cicerone who had unlimited lines of credit, were encouraged to broaden their horizons and have life altering experiences. Young men descended upon unsuspecting relatives and other well-born families in Florence, Rome and Naples, ending up in Venice, and behaving very badly. Letters and poetry sent home describe art, architecture, beauty and free spirits but fail to mention, drunkenness, whoring, bisexual liaisons, gambling, and incest. Women too, if married or suitably accompanied by a retinue of servants took the high road in the name of education or inspiration. In 1758, a poetess, Lady Mary Wortley Montagu, arrived in Venice and was less than charmed by "An old place stinking of ditches, having a square decorated with the worst architecture I ever yet saw." One must assume that Lady M had just found out that her teenaged, bisexual lover had vanished into the arms of a Prussian prince and was peeved. English poet Percy Bysshe Shelley, the 'Mad Shelley' wrote of Venice... "Its temples and palaces did seem like fabrics of enchantment piled to heaven." He suffered from gonorrhea, hepatitis, and kidney disease, and drowned in Viareggio, near Florence at the age of twenty-nine. Centuries later, he is remembered only as a brilliant poet. His forgotten wife, Mary Shelley, wrote the first horror novel, "Frankenstein," which is far better known than any poem. The Shelleys' friend, Lord Byron, *born George Gordon Noel Byron the 6th Baron of Rochdale, is perhaps the only one whose reputation is better known than any of his poetry. He is infamous for squandering not one, but two fortunes, fathering his half-sister's child, swimming the Hellespont, and dying at age thirty-six of an epileptic fit caused by alcoholism and syphilis. One of his many mistresses, the scandalous Lady Caroline Lamb* is often quoted, "Lord B. was mad, bad and dangerous to know." Those that survived the debaucheries of 'La grand tour' went home with crates of paintings, sculptures, and precious coins for country house collections and private museums. Artists such as Canaletto, Titian, Bellini, and Bassano became renowned throughout Europe and America. Italy was launched as a tourist destination, a place to broaden horizons, admire art and architecture, drink wine, and fall in love.*

Excelsior Palace, Lungomare Guglielmo
Marconi 41 Lido Venice, 1964:

Dear Mom, Pop, and Granny:
I've survived the not-so-grand-tour from Milan to the southernmost tip of Sicily and back up the east coast, Brindisi, Bari, Taranto, Pescara, Ancona, to Venice. It was exhausting, exhilarating, and a never-to-be-forgotten experience. I didn't behave as badly as Lord Byron but saw great wealth as well as poverty. By chance, I met the Duke of Palma. He gave Anna and me a tour of a ruined palazzo that he is renovating. I loved the hand-painted walls, and mom—you would have gone crazy in the library with the thousands of books it held. Even the worn-out herringbone floors were spectacular. Anna wasn't as impressed as I was, but then again, she can be such a snob. Every small town has an opera house and a church or two. Religion and entertainment keep the people's spirits up. Our

show goes over like gangbusters, partly because there is no other entertainment. Very few, if any families have a television set and their small living rooms are so crammed with enormous families from grandma down to newborns that there is no space. Some bars have television but it is 'snowy' because there is only faint reception. Anyway, most men play billiards for fun or just sit in the main piazza, argue politics and swear. I am exhausted with the one-nighters and so glad to be in Venice for ten whole days. We are living on an island away from the main centre at a very fancy hotel/casino/outdoor theatre called 'The Excelsior Palace.' It looks like a palace, too, but we are not allowed inside. The stage door leads to basement dressing rooms. But, we are permitted on the private sandy beach which is raked every night into perfectly even stripes with no footprints. You won't believe this but...some people lie there, buck naked. I'm NOT kidding! At first I didn't know where to look and was very embarrassed—all that blubber for the world to see. But, then I saw that no one paid any attention. Everyone was busy oiling themselves thoroughly like plump chickens ready for roasting. I am under a sun umbrella as I write. Love from your skinny, white, and freckled daughter, Margaret Alice xx
P.S. Happy Birthday Granny. Ninety-three years old. I'll be home soon and that's a promise. Love, Mags xxx

"My balls are on fire." Rudi is naked, except for a dance belt, standing in front of a mirror in the boys' dressing room. He is scarlet, and already, baby blisters are erupting on his raw shoulders. "*Goddammit*. Eyeeeee!" he squeals as his wife Aneke slaps lotion on his back. Her face is grim.

"You fool, *een idioot*, serves you right."

"Oh, there you are," Nikko comes through the door with an icy drink in his hand. He stops, "You're late. On stage in ten minutes."

He fixes his eyes on Rudi. "What the hell did you do?" He shakes his head, "Fall asleep?"

"Ja, slaap gevallen? I'm burning up, dammit." Rudi pulls up his trousers, gritting his teeth, and slips the suspenders onto his shoulders as Aneke dashes from the room to get into her costume for her first entrance. She is white with fury.

The Excelsior Palace has an enormous, outdoor night club that is very elegant and ridiculously expensive. It costs more to get in than the dancers make in a week. The stage is a miracle of hydraulics. It is a checkerboard of opaque glass that rises from the ground with sides that hide a complicated, modern lighting system. As the dancers make their entrance, the squares light up in different colours to the beat of the drums. Opening night, the drummer starts quietly. Maggie creeps like a panther after prey, snapping her fingers to the off-beat of the drums. Then, *bam!* As she takes her pose, the square beneath shoots a blue light, startling her off balance. *Wow,* she thinks, *this is so groovy, so mod,* she feels like cheering out loud. As Rudi might have said "Outta sight man," if he hadn't been perched delicately on a stool in front of the drums, nursing a burnt bum.

The audience must think the same, because the ballet is a hit. Each night the crowd gets bigger, with more chairs and linen-clad tables jammed into the garden. Of course, it could have been for the star attraction: '*Monsieur 100,000 Volts,*' Gilbert Bécaud, singer, composer, actor from France. No one could possibly guess that his real name is Silly, Léopold Silly. One night, Maggie and several others went out on the town and he confessed his unforgettable baptismal moniker. *I wonder,* thinks Maggie, *what the Maestro's real name is, and who he is? That is the unsolved mystery. I would bet my last lira that he's not Greek, even though Pávlos is a Greek name.*

Other than Nikko and the pregnant Rosie, Les Ballets Jazz

spend the last night on the fancy private beach lolling in the sand, eating pizza and olives, while making a grand mess of the finely raked pattern. There will be a price to pay in the morning. The moon is high, lifting away their thoughts as bottles of Amorone get passed from hand to lips. Without warning, they all take off their clothes and go skinny dipping. On this sublime night, with the stars dancing over the Adriatic and phosphorescence trailing from fingertips, a dozen naked bodies twirl and slither like eels with hair plastered to scalps, bare buttocks, balls, breasts and legs entangled, they feel deliciously decadent.

Their time in Venice is over too quickly. Maggie has seen nothing at all except one trip down the Grand Canal on the way to the Lido, and one afternoon with the Maestro seeing the collection of Picasso drawings and paintings in Peggy Goldenstein's private art collection. Between rehearsing, taking classes, and performing, there is simply no time to be a tourist.

All thoughts of going home dissolve when the Maestro strides into the dressing room and announces that he has signed a new contract. We are invited by the government of Egypt as 'the most modern ballet in Europe' to perform for the Arab leaders. Maggie is torn. *I miss my home, my mom and pop and especially my granny. But, this is my one chance in a lifetime to perform in front of the kings and presidents of eighty-five countries. Holy cow, I can't miss this opportunity,* she argues to herself.

She turns to the Maestro, "I'm coming too. From the Grand Canal to the Suez Canal, how cool is that?"

Les Ballets Jazz Europa gather at the Stazione Venezia Santa Lucia, the main train station in Venice. It's not the usual departure, because Rudi, Aneka, and Romeo are not going.

"Aneke refuses to leave Europe," Rudi apologizes, looking down at his feet as if to say, 'it is not my choice.'

Maggie is standing on the platform wearing enormous

sunglasses and staring forlornly after the three of them. They barely say goodbye, after performing together for almost two years.

Rudi whispers in her ear, "I'll be back," as he kisses her goodbye. Romeo just casually waves his hand, and Aneka picks up her neat and tidy suitcase and stalks to the other end of the station to the Paris-bound train. And that is that! Then, Frank and Ronáld help Maggie toss her suitcase through the window of the southbound train. With a sigh, she climbs aboard, pulls out her tattered map and writes the date on the edge of the Adriatic Sea. Talitha sits next to her on the soft leather bench and takes out her knitting. Anna, Liliane, and Rosie start a game of 'hearts.' Maggie makes a note to pick up a postcard in Naples to send to her parents regarding the change of plans. Scrabbling in her enormous handbag, she pulls out 'Death on the Nile' by Agatha Christie and settles back for a long, long read.

Just as the southbound train is pulling out of the station, a pretty blonde girl with a pixie haircut flings herself into the carriage gasping, *"Allo, je m'appelle Nicoletta."* She whips out a cigarette, lights it, and blows smoke out of her nostrils. With sublime confidence, she crosses her legs, letting her tight skirt ride up to her crotch. *Here comes trouble.*

CHAPTER VIII

Alexandrian Rhapsody

"Life is like a cucumber. One minute it is in your hand, the next it's up your ass."
—Lawrence Durrell, 'The Alexandrian Quartet'

Naples, Italy 1964:

Maggie staggers up the gangplank of the SS *Media*, bound for Egypt. The port of Naples is oppressive and stifling hot, as hordes of humanity mill about selling goods, loading the ship, pushing and shoving toward the edge of the wharf. There is a hot smell of tar, dead fish, sweat, and halitosis.

Rosie turns to her and whimpers, "I'm going to be sick."

"Breathe deeply and think of England," Maggie says. Rosie rolls her eyes in dismay. Feeling a rush of sympathy, Maggie puts a comforting arm around her shoulder, and the two lean against the rail, watching sharp-eyed seagulls circling around searching for fragments of food to feed their young. After all this time with the ballet, Maggie doesn't know a thing about Rosie's life, except that her mother makes toothbrushes and is about to become a grandmother.

The old SS *Media*, a rust bucket, carries tons of freight and fifty-six unsuspecting passengers across the Mediterranean Sea, famous for its unpredictable and savage turbulence. Les Ballets

Jazz comprises fourteen dancers, including Nicoletta from a small village near the Italian French border, and a newcomer, Daniel Warren from Gloucestershire, who is eighteen years old. They have both been booked with third-class tickets. Much to their horror, the girls' stateroom is a dormitory of a dozen bunk beds with a narrow corridor down the middle. The aroma of composting carpet is overwhelming.

"I'd rather sleep on deck than in the bilges," raged Anna.

"*Dégoûtant*, impossible," voices echo.

The new girl, Nicoletta, lights another evil-smelling Egyptian cigarette, '*Kyriazi frères*,' and flings herself on the bottom bunk nearest the door, growling, "*Je m'en fous*, I don't give a fuck!" This expression becomes her favourite French expletive and is soon understood by all, even those who do not speak a word of French.

Three days out and only Maggie and the newbie Daniel are still on their feet. Pitching and thrusting, the SS *Media* is pounded relentlessly by the waves. As the wind picks up, it hurls salt spray on the windward deck, drenching anyone foolish enough to be there. From the bowels of the ship, disturbing noises send all passengers to their berths in terror. First, second, or steerage class, it makes no difference. If the *Media* goes down like the *Titanic*, class won't matter at all.

What *does* matter is the food in steerage. Huge copper vats of soupy stew swimming in rancid olive oil is ladled out at both lunch and dinner. It never varies, except in name; '*Stifatho*,' '*Psito Katsarolas*,' or '*Fricassee*,' it all looks the same; greenish lumps in gooey gravy. It takes courage and a cast iron stomach to eat. If it wasn't for the freshly baked torpedoes of bread called '*psomi*,' most would have starved. Maggie stuffs her pockets with *psomi* and prays that the stew will be finished soon.

"I should give the chef a recipe for mother's Rice Krispie chicken."

The sea has calmed considerably as the *Media* steams closer to the coast of Africa. Sitting in a canvas lounge chair in the third-class section of the deck, Maggie is devouring the words of Lawrence Durrell's *The Alexandrian Quartet*. His descriptions of his beloved Alexandria are like poetry and his sexual adventures inexplicably arousing. A shadow causes her to look up and she locks eyes with an extraordinarily good-looking boy about her age. She slaps her book closed and tosses it casually into her handbag next to her stolen bread rolls, hiding it from the stranger's beautiful eyes.

"May I?" he enquires, as he pulls another canvas chair closer and sits down. His accent is impeccably upper crust.

"You speak English?" Maggie is enunciating each syllable as though speaking to a deaf child. He laughs out loud, displaying perfect white teeth. *Oh hell,* she thinks, *perfect lips, mouth, bedroom eyes, this guy has the works.*

"Yes, I speak English, Arabic, French, Farsi, German, Italian..." His eyes twinkle at her and he moves closer. After a barrage of questions about Cairo, shopping, pyramids, museums, the Nile, where to buy henna dye for red hair and English bookstores, Maggie is longing to kiss him.

Suddenly, he pulls his chair back into the shadows, half out of sight, and murmurs intimately, "I shouldn't be seen with you."

She replies, "Don't you mean the reverse, I shouldn't be seen talking to you?" The minute the words are out of her mouth she blushes with embarrassment. He looks disappointed.

"I was speaking about the Hellenic Cruise rules; first-class passengers are not to mix with third-class." He pauses. "You are referring to the colour of my skin." He gets up with dignity, gives her a slight bow and formally wishes her a pleasant visit. Maggie has a lot to learn.

Later, as the *Media* inches toward the harbours of Alexandria, the oldest in the ancient world, built around 1900 B.C., everyone on board is hanging over the rails tingling with excitement, anticipation, and awe. Even the Maestro has abandoned his first-class chums and is hopping about giving orders.

"Stick together, *daahlinks*. Remember, not a word about Jews..." Looking at Maggie, he adds, "Not even in a letter." *Now why*, wonders Maggie, *would anyone write about Jews in a letter?* Her mother would wonder if she had sunstroke or food poisoning if she discussed religion. Her parents were 'E and C Christians,' meaning Easter and Christmas churchgoers. Sunday was the day she and her sisters were tossed out the door and sent on a three mile walk along Cedar Road to attend Sunday school at St. Phillip's in the woods. Rid of the kids for a couple of hours, the parents could go back to bed for some undisturbed time together. She had no idea what Jewish children do on a Sunday morning.

The Maestro is collecting their passports to give to the secret police, '*El Mukahabout*.'

"You will get them back when we leave the country." Maggie is on high alert. Without her passport she feels naked.

Ronáld, standing close, says "Watch for pick-pocketers. They are pros, especially the women and homeless children." A wave of apprehension rushes over her. He bumps her elbow as if by accident, and from his jacket pocket takes out her wallet.

"See how easy it is?" He laughs at her shocked face. SS *Media* gives three deep blasts on the ship's whistle, indicating she is entering the harbour, *hoot-hoot-hoot*, Les Ballets Jazz is welcomed to the pearl of the Mediterranean.

Alexandria, Egypt 1964:

The gardens of the Méditerranée Hotel and Cabaret on the seafront in '*Saba Pasha Ramleh*' are lush with giant oleanders, smelling of ripe apricots but deadly poisonous—a sweet-scented killer that in ancient times was used as a treatment for cancer. Palm trees cast shade from the relentless sun, urns spill over with exotic foliage, and ponds sprout tall, fuzzy-headed Egyptian papyrus. It is a secret garden locked in a dust-laden city of poverty.

A long, narrow balcony runs the length of the hotel rooms on the second floor. It overlooks the stage and into the shrubbery below. Nicoletta, Talitha, and Maggie are an unusual threesome, observing the stark, white room with a trio of wood-slatted beds lined up like a hospital ward. The balcony is the savior, its cool breeze a welcomed relief from the heat. The three are sprawled on the beds, semi-naked, and grumbling. An ancient, overhead fan lazily circles around, batting flies out of its way but making no change in the oppressive heat of mid-afternoon.

"We should be taking a class." Talitha yawns, not making a move. Nicoletta opens a bottle of overly sweet soda and gags.

"*Yetch!* There is a dead fly inside the cap. Inside! How did it get there?" Maggie grabs the can of Piff Paff and sprays the room with its deadly poison. Flies drop down on their wings waving their spindly legs in the air for a brief second before they die. Only the sounds of setting up tables and chairs and the arrival of an orchestra, rouse the three from their inertia.

The final rehearsal, with a full orchestra, fills everyone with misgivings. The music is a disaster—quite unrecognizable. With Rudi gone, the Egyptian drummer is to start the performance with a slow solo on the brush sticks. The mood is set with snapping fingers to the off-beat of the drum. Over and over, the dancers make their entrance to the first eight bars of music, and each time the drummer falters and the orchestra comes crashing in on the wrong beat. Xavier plays the recorded music again and the Egyptian orchestra listens intently. Then, they go right ahead and play their own version like boisterous children at rhythm band.

In the midst of the confusion, a fussy, little man minces across the garden and dumps a large basket of brown, cotton body suits on the stage. He waves in the general direction of the dancers and announces that they are to be worn under the costumes.

"*Non, pas de tout*," snaps Simone.

Smoothing his moustache in a gesture of importance, he recites in several languages, "It is the law. Women do not show their skin."

Liliane picks up one pair of the offending long johns, holds it up with two fingers as though it is a soiled diaper, and replies, "*Mon dieu, absolument ridicule*, we will look ridiculous." She is right. That hot and sultry night, Maggie stands in front of a mirror wearing the lumpy brown jumpsuit under black tights, elastic briefs, thigh-high boots, and a stiff leather shirt. Beads of sweat appear on her forehead, mascara pools under her eyes and slowly rolls like black tears down her cheeks, dripping onto her clothes and staining it in dirty blotches. She looks like an albino turtle.

Later, they discover that professional belly dancers do not wear the ugly suits, they just pay a fine when they are arrested. That is a rare occurrence, as everyone, including the secret police, love to see the writhing flesh and undulating belly buttons of the *raqs sharqi*; the traditional dances of their untamed land.

Montaza Palace, Alexandria, September 11, 1964:
Arab League Summit

Opening night at the Méditerranée is surprisingly cohesive, with the orchestra in fine form. Although the applause is lukewarm, the management seems satisfied—no infractions of the navel law occurred and no one got assassinated. Many in the audience are well-armed bodyguards of the Royal guests and Heads of State in town for the Arab League Summit. Watching for trouble, the guards ignore Les Ballets Jazz, with their weird music and lumpy costumes. From the stage, all that the dancers can see is an audience of dark glasses. Behind them are the cunning eyes of the leaders of the Arab states, plotting a united strategy against the State of Israel; a battle royale. The world is waiting.

Maggie is reminded of childhood battles in the branches of an ancient Gravenstein apple tree she and her sisters had built—a treehouse of rotting boards, blankets, and a cast-off Chinese tea chest. Halfway up the rickety ladder was a provocative sign painted in bold letters, demanding "**NO BOYS.**" Her buddy Ronnie and his snotty-nosed baby brother would hurl wormy windfalls through the branches while the chosen ones ate the perfect, sweet, juicy fruit. She can't remember why they were so cruel and so unkind, because there were plenty of apples to go around.

Backstage, Simone gathers up the sodden bodysuits and hangs them on the costume racks. She is in a filthy mood, kicking at cockroaches and snarling at Nicoletta who she knows is flirting with her beloved Nikko. She turns on Daniel, berating him for sweating so profusely.

"*Sale Anglais, Dégoûtant!*" Remembering the advice Rosie gave her so long ago, Maggie whispers to him, "She barks worse than she bites. Actually she likes you, or she would be silent as a sphinx."

A small, concealed walkway leads from the dressing room through a side garden to the hotel. Les Ballets Jazz is high with energy, strutting and dancing along the pebble path, chattering about the show when Maggie stops and yelps, "I forgot my book. I'll be right back," and she returns to the dressing rooms. The light above the stage door is off. Maggie feels around for the doorknob, turns it, and starts to push the heavy, wooden door open. A feeling of foreboding makes her shudder involuntarily. From down the dark corridor, low rumbling voices can be heard. *Nonsense,* she thinks, and boldly steps inside, half closing the door behind. The voices stop! Hardly daring to breathe, she flattens herself against the wall and listens. A light is on in one of the dressing rooms. As her eyes adjust to the low light, she makes out the shape of the Maestro, beside the man he was sitting with earlier. His companion is a dangerously sexy looking stranger with a strong, aquiline nose. Neither are wearing sunglasses, but are gazing at a painting that the Maestro has pulled from the bottom of the costume basket. They are bent over it and are studying every detail.

"Nikko, you are sure this is not a forgery?" Maggie inches backwards trying to get to the door before she is discovered. Her foot hits something on the floor and she freezes. Both men look up and listen.

"Rats?" There is a long pause.

"Well, Nikko, it looks like a Van Gogh, but…" he hesitates, sucking air between his teeth.

"Take it or leave it, Nassim. I am the courier, not a fucking art critic." Meanwhile, Maggie can feel the draft of the open door, so she reaches behind and silently slips out into the night. Without a sound, she pulls the door closed and races like a white-tail jackrabbit, down the garden path and through the door to the hotel. Running through her head are Nassim's final words, "…lots of buyers for *stolen* art, no questions asked!" He laughs, but nothing at all is funny.

Classes begin very early in the morning, long before the heat sucks all strength, initiative, and discipline away. The curtains blow lazily back and forth in room eleven, and from the garden below - olive tree warblers, chiffchaffs, and babblers begin a morning song. Dragging themselves from their damp beds, Talitha, Nicoletta, and Maggie dress in their mismatched practice clothes, slightly hungover from copious amounts of *Cru des Ptolémées*. They groggily head downstairs for coffee. It's just another day in a dancer's life—or is it?

Talitha is standing on stage with her back to the garden, now swarming with workers, clipping shrubs, watering urns with large water jugs, dead-heading roses, and raking spent blooms off the immaculate grass.

"Belly dancing," she intones as though she just discovered the connection, "is very much like modern dance; the isolations, the taut inner core versus the relaxed, almost weightless arms and shoulders." She places the needle on a record and the troupe begins the warm-up exercises known to all dancers worldwide; *plié, battement tendu, developé, et retiré.*

From her knitting bag, Talitha removes a parcel wrapped in white cotton and tied with hemp.

"I found these at the street market called the *Souk el Attarine* near the beach."

"*Qu' est- ce que c'est*, what is it?" Simone is immediately suspicious, as she alone is responsible for buying everything needed for the ballet; ribbons, elastic, new inner soles, and snappers. She needs her job to be indispensable.

"*Zills*," and she hands everyone in the ballet two pairs of metal finger cymbals. Xavier sniffs haughtily, as only a Belgian can, storms off lighting a cigarette, and tosses the match at the bare feet of the gardeners.

"It's not as easy as it looks," Talitha warns, and places the cymbals on her thumbs and third fingers. *Ting, ting, ting,* a tiny high sound like the ringing of chimes or the sound of a cricket comes from her graceful fingers. "The basic rhythm is three beats and an infinitesimal pause," she lifts her arms high and plays *ting, ting, ting.* "Then, we play the *zills* to the music while we dance, at the same time."

The gardeners are slack-jawed in amazement as music from West Side Story fills the air, scattering the birds into the papyrus fronds. The dancers ungulate, shimmy, and leap about, completely out of control, playing the zills like they are Spanish castanets. "I like to be in America, *ting, ting, ting.* Okay by me in America, *ting, ting, clang.* Life is all bright in America... *ting, ting, clap*...if you're all white in A-mer-ri-ca!" There is applause from the pathway.

"*Bravo, brava* my *daahlinks*," and the Maestro wanders in with a small cup of strong, Turkish coffee, all smiles, looking relaxed and supremely content. Maggie stares in amazement. *Was last night just my imagination?* She ponders.

By mid-day, the Egyptian sun God 'Ra,' that half-man, half-eagle deity, sends bolts of fire down upon the streets of Alexandria, scorching the pavements and blistering the paint off the walls. The intensity does not seem to affect the armies of flies who grow bolder by the minute. They love to gather in the blobs of fresh camel dung littering the pavement before flying onto bare, white arms and sunburnt ears. Maggie is deeply perturbed by them, even dreaming about their dirty, crawly legs on her face at night. A can of aerosol poison filled with a toxic mist is sprayed before bedtime; a carcinogenic cloud hovering above their sleeping heads.

"*Manashataldhujbab*," she announces proudly.

"What's that?" Daniel is waiting for her outside the main entrance to the Méditerranée.

"An Egyptian fly swatter." Daniel grabs her hand and they set off on a quest to obtain a flyswatter. He has become her soulmate and confidant since arriving from England. *Wasn't it only a few weeks ago?* At first, Daniel was painfully shy, barely speaking to anyone, but one day that all changed. In the middle of a particularly exhausting rehearsal with everyone slowly fading, he executed several perfect *grande jetés* in quick succession followed by a difficult combination of steps. He was on fire. The Maestro looked up, impressed, and nodded. "That is perfect." Those three little words pumped life and confidence into the new arrival.

On board the SS *Media* weeks ago, he had blurted out in a moment of confession, that he was an orphan, speaking almost as if it was somehow his fault. Two spinster ladies of the parish in

Stowe-on-the-Wold had raised him until he could be shunted off to a boarding school and cut out of their lives.

"Don't worry about it, you're not alone," Maggie replies. "I might possibly be the only one in this company who actually has a mother and a father—alive, that is." With a small sigh, "No one discusses their past, as if the war blotted out a whole generation." Daniel looks relieved.

"In my case, you are right."

"Well, I'll be your big sister."

So, it was understood, and they spoke no more about it.

The two set off down the sun-baked street into a labyrinth of alleys, tunnels, and canvas awnings, the underbelly of the city where few tourists dare to explore—the *real* Alexandria. The narrow, clay road seems endless. On both sides, rickety houses in peeling earth tones prop each other up like an abstract painting. A sudden burst of flowers in primary colours; red, yellow, and blue tumble from rusting flowerpots and old buckets. They decorate the front of tiny shops selling cooking pots, brooms, sacks of wheat, and bolts of cotton cloth. There is not a sound. All places of work are deserted in the noon-day sun. A few sleepy people shamble silently along the dusty road, but most take the *qailulah*, an afternoon nap, in the shade of their homes until the immense heat and blowing sand retreats.

"I think we're lost, Daniel." Maggie stops as a gust of wind throws dust in her face. "Maybe we should turn back." From behind, a jumble of broken bricks and canvas, a small boy of about seven or eight appears; dressed in nothing more than rags, a pair of filthy shorts, and a faded shirt with no buttons. He has a beautiful, mischievous smile and grimy, brown hands.

"Cigarette, lady?"

"You're too young to smoke." He tilts his head like a puppy, not understanding a word. "Here, take this," Maggie says as she pulls a few coins from the pocket in her dirndl skirt and drops them into his dirty little palm.

Like magic, a few miserable coins, or *piastras*, bring a stampede of bodies from doorways, hidden alleys, and stairways. The deathly stillness of siesta hour erupts into a shrieking, jabbering crescendo of sound, accompanied by begging hands. Daniel empties his pockets and Maggie does the same with her change purse. There seems to be more and more pleading fingers.

"All gone," she cries, "I haven't any more money." A plague of urchins arrive from nowhere. All poor, all needy, some with pus oozing wounds, infections, and runny noses. Maggie is frantic. "I have no more money," she whispers desperately as she is being pushed backward and forward like a game of tug of war. "Daniel, Danny, where are you?" A hundred voices taunt, "Dani, Dani, where's Dani?" Her ears throb with the beat of her heart and she feels woozy. Fingers claw at her skirt, scratching her arms and face. "Please don't hurt me," she whimpers, pressing her back flat against a door jamb for support.

From a nearby shop there comes a sharp whistle. Daniel and the shopkeeper, who is dressed in a flowing cotton tunic called a *jilabîyah*, dash into the street, and the ragged mob of children vanish like cockroaches within seconds. "I'm okay." Maggie is shaken but no longer terrified. "I just ran out of *piastras*. These poor kids, they need so much more than I can ever give."

"Look at this," Daniel says as he holds up a fifteen-inch horse tail that looks like a theatrical hair piece.

"It's a flyswatter." They both laugh more with relief than amusement.

"It couldn't hurt a fly."

"Thank you, thank you," but the shopkeeper has already disappeared behind a beaded, clickedly curtain into the shady interior of his den to fidget with his *misbaha*, his worry beads, and to nod off in the heat. Far away in another quarter of the city, the sweet cry of the *Mu'sezzin* calls men to stop what they are doing, prostate themselves on the ground facing east, and pray to Allah, the one true God.

Backstage at the Méditerranée Cabaret:

Half-hidden among the jumble of make-up brushes, grease pencils, and lipsticks scattered on the long dressing table at the Méditerranée lies the ponytail flyswatter with a decorative hammered-tin baton.

"It's my good luck charm," Maggie tells Anna, who is bronzed from a day on the beach. "It doesn't actually kill the flies, but pushes them onto someone else."

"I like Piff Paff," retorts Anna, as she dabs a little behind each ear as though it were the finest fragrance from Paris. Maggie slaps a heavy layer of Max Factor make-up paste onto the scratches on her neck and face, peering at her reflection to see if any bruises show. She is singing, *"I like the island Manhattan, so smoke on your pipe and put that in."*

"Vingt minutes, twenty minutes until showtime!" Someone calls from behind a closed door, reminding the dancers. The hum of activity in the dressing room climbs a notch as hair is brushed, eyelashes glued on, and plain, scrubbed faces are turned into feline goddesses. Without knowing it, the dancers morph, like pupae into butterflies, into their onstage personalities. The magic begins. A light tap on the door startles Maggie out of a trance.

"Two minutes, *deux minutes, daahlinks!*" En masse, Les Ballets file out and take their places in the wings, breathing heavily, like stallions snorting before a steeplechase. Above the ringing in the ears, one can hear the faint *tap, tap, tap* of the conductor's baton on the lectern, and Maestro's hushed directions:

"Main curtain, *ACTION.*" And another show begins, full of hope and promise of a flawless performance.

Hotel Méditerranée, Alexandria, Egypt:

Dear Mom, Pop, and Granny:

I hope this reaches you well, because all our mail is opened and censored. We are leaving for Cairo in a few hours so I am hoping to catch the last mail boat. I have been up all night at a wedding reception and now really feel like a spinster because the bride was a child. We were all invited to a ritzy party in a government mansion, really a manor-house, in the middle of a lush green park not too far away. A fleet of taxis and one limousine for the Maestro took us there, speeding across the desert sand in the moonlight. Just breathtaking! Actually, I'm not sure why we were invited, but suspect that we look madly modern and good for press photographs. I wore my green and blue sundress with matching stole so I could cover up whatever was supposed to be covered. But, I digress. Mom, the bride was truly no more than twelve years old. Sitting forlornly on a stiff, wooden chair, she looked like a plaster-faced doll, with unblinking, painted eyes, weighed down in a heavily embroidered robe and a stunning, turquoise necklace. Beside her sat an old man with a bushy Santa Claus beard and a disgusting, life-sized beetle, a scarab, carved on the ring adorning his pudgy fingers. I wondered if he was the Governor or her grandfather until Ronáld translated that he was the groom. I almost threw up. It might have been the overwhelming smell of hundreds of flower arrangements; scented jasmine, roses, lilies, and blossoms. The mansion was enormous, stinking of money. Every salon had a different orchestra playing; in a library, a ballroom, an art gallery, and a long, arched corridor lit by a thousand twinkling candles. Drinks were served by household servants dressed in white with red sashes, a regiment of them offering everything from a sour berry juice to champagne. They must be Christians, called 'coptic'* here, or there would not have been alcohol. Food was not served until the bride left, so we were up all night eating and dancing and watching belly dancers. At dawn, we danced in the courtyard with all the women shimmying and shaking. Don't worry about me, never a boring moment. Love, Mags xxx

Countryside near Alexandria, 1964:

Threading her way through a roomful of strangers gabbling in foreign languages, Maggie turns into a peaceful gallery filled with ancient tapestries, wall carpets, sculptures, and European paintings. Fascinated, she slowly tours the room and inspects the treasures. Behind dozens of enormous, pungent flower arrangements, she spies some familiar works. She presses close, astonished at the signature of one piece, peeking around a bundle of lilies.

"Holy cow," she breathes, "this is a Degas original."

"A forgery," a voice behind her replies. She spins around to find herself gazing into the stern, unreadable eyes of the Maestro. *Is he teasing me?* He looks slightly tipsy, so she sniffs haughtily and jokes, "Well, how would you know?"

"Shh," he moves closer to the painting and whispers, "look closely at zee brush work in the background—is not the same as zee horses," he muses. "I leeved with an art dealer in Switzerland when I vas a boy," he mumbles, seeming as if he is regretting having opened his mouth. A large gulp of whiskey halts further conversation, just as a man with some authority comes up and takes the Maestro by the arm, completely ignoring Maggie as though she is a pretty but poisonous oleander.

"Nikko, my friend, I want to show you my newest find, a Vincent van Gogh." The Maestro turns to Maggie and gives her the slightest suggestion of a wink and then walks toward the other end of the gallery. Hot on his heels, a servant pursues them like an obedient hound, but not before she manages to snatch a full glass of wine from his tray. *He knows!* Despite the sweltering heat of the evening, Maggie finds herself shivering.

CHAPTER IX

Dancing on the Nile

*In the summer of 1943, during the latter years of WWII, a grand
cabaret of dubious respectability opened on Pyramid Road in Cairo.
One of its most enthusiastic patrons was the corpulent, young King
Farouk of Egypt until he was forced to abdicate and leave the country
forever. He was only thirty-six years old when he lost his other title
as 'King of the Nightclubs.' The cabaret Auberge des Pyramids is
famous throughout the Middle East, and hires the best belly dancers
in all of Egypt. As well as performing on stage, it is expected that the
dancers will descend into the private "Gold Room," in the cellar,
and drink with the international patrons until dawn. By 1954, the
activities in the Salle D'Or at the Auberge des Pyramids were closely
monitored by President Gamal Abdel Nasser and his notorious secret
police, El Mukhabaret. It was their job to see that belly dancers wore
costumes that covered their bodies and that performances did not
'arouse excitement' in the audience. Egyptian dancers needed signed
government permits to perform traditional Egyptian folk dances, but
not to 'entertain' clients below the stairs.*

Cairo, Egypt 1964:

Dodging the afternoon chaos of overloaded trucks, honking
horns, pedestrians in Western dress or flowing cotton *yelek*, three-

wheeled bicycles, and donkey-carts loaded with everything from cement bags to vegetables, a black and white taxicab with its radio blaring screeches to a halt. The door opens to the front entrance of the Hôtel Windsor, a once fine, old colonial building that housed the British Officers Club, but now, an aging grimy, mid-priced rooming house. It is home to Les Ballets Jazz for the next few weeks. According to the taxi driver, its one claim to fame is having the oldest manual wooden elevator in the entire world. *"C'est vachement génial,* bloody marvelous," Simone mutters with typical vulgar sarcasm. Clutching her enormous sewing basket, Simone, Maggie, and Rosie pile out and claim the rest of the luggage from the roof rack, squinting in the dazzling sun. A second taxi squeals to a stop and unloads a wide-eyed Daniel and Frank, who now goes by his Algerian name of 'Fahad,' with a carload of baggage. There is no sign of Anna or the Maestro.

"Probably at the Hilton," sniffs a voice. Everyone is hungover, bad-tempered, and being bitten by mosquitos which swarm around feasting on our fresh, young skin.

"I think I prefer the flies in Alexandria," says Maggie, slapping her ankles, arms, and neck as she staggers, dragging her battered suitcase across the floor and through the iron gates of the Hôtel Windsor. In awe, she gapes at the ancient elevator, a contraption not unlike a torture box hanging from rusty chains.

Room 201 is the size of a horse stall, but at least has a very high ceiling with fancy, plaster mouldings and a central fan which sends hot air from one side of the room to the other. Maggie is reclined on one of the two metal beds, reading a guidebook. Her headboard, once painted a clotted-cream colour, is now chipped and smudged in graffiti. *Kilroy was here, Mr. Chad loves Fifi, B 29, Luke the Snook,* and other slang from World War II. At least the sheets and coverlet look fresh, and the excitement of being in one of the most fascinating cities of the world is almost more than she can bear. Even the street noise outside, an ear-splitting din, is exhilarating. Without saying a word, Rosie lays on the other twin bed, and stares at the ceiling. There is a knock at the door, followed by an immediate entry by someone who wasn't waiting for an answer. Talitha pokes her head in.

"We have five minutes before we go to the photo shoot— Shepheard's Hotel. Dress up, look pretty like a tourist, head-scarves..." and she continues down the corridor, knocking on doors.

The lowering sun sparkles over the great Nile River as a slight breeze fills the canvas sails of a picturesque skiff, a *felucca*, hired for the photo shoot. Waving happily at the cameras, Maggie, Anna, Talitha, Rosie, and Nicoletta exude health and vitality: perfect Western tourists with pearly teeth, freshly shaved underarms, and smelling of English roses.

"Why isn't Shirel here?"

"They want only white girls in the photos," is the reply. In the background, the rebuilt Shepheard's Hotel gleams, the old one having been torched on Black Saturday in retaliation of fifty Egyptian police slaughtered by British troops. Next to it, President Nasser's pride and joy, the brand-new Egyptian Nile Hilton. The hotel stands tall, where there were once sprawling Egyptian-Turkish army barracks, *Kasr el Nil* which were taken over by the British army for sixty-six years.

"I'm going to throw up," Rosie moans as she leans over the side and empties her stomach down the side of the *felucca* and into the black waters of the Nile.

Shaking with suppressed laughter, Maggie snorts, "I wonder if the press got a good shot of that." Anna turns to Rosie, accusing her.

"You're still pregnant, you fool. Why did you come with us without...?"

Maggie looks astonished, but Nicoletta reaches for a cigarette, sighing "*Je m'en fous!*" The press swings their boat around again to get more shots.

"Smile girls, having fun?" The five wave happily, like delightful young ladies sailing down the river.

A black, battered Mercedes taxi streaks along Pyramids Road, spewing dust, sand, and soot. It sends the cloud of debris into the exhausted faces of mothers, carrying babies swaddled in their shawls, mangy dogs scratching fleas, drowsy camels with their heavy loads, and poor workmen coughing and spitting into the sand. The car radio is turned full volume to the ear-splitting rhythm of rattles, double-pipes, tambourines, and the Egyptian lyre, the '*simsimiyya*.' Sucking on a 'Craven A' cigarette, the driver blasts his horn at anything moving within his vision. Anna, Rosie, and Maggie clutch the back of the seats as they sway and bump one another. A short while later, with a squeal of brakes, the Mercedes lurches to a standstill in front of 229 Pyramid Road or '*al ahram*,' the address of the infamous *Auberge des Pyramids*. Directly across the way is a bald cluster of miserable fly-blown huts, half buried in a sand dune. This comprises a village called *Kom al Akhdar*. The driver points and smiles, proudly thumping himself on his chest.

"*Beiti*," he says, "my home."

Looking around the Auberge, Maggie can feel her parents' disapproval as if they were standing beside her. Thank God they're four thousand miles away. The hotel looks like a pharaonic whorehouse filled to the rafters with gaudy lashings of gold curlicues, serpents, flowers, and eagles, that are chipped and layered with years of nicotine residue. It stinks of perfume, old sweat, cigars, and brandy. The ornate room has tasseled alcoves, corridors lined with paintings leading to other salons, and mysterious doors behind velvet drapes that would be the perfect setting for an Agatha Christie murder. One wall opens onto an even larger inner terrace shaded by flowering date palm trees, statues, and splashing fountains.

"Where is the stage?" she asks, bewildered. "Surely we're not dancing on the tables."

"Well, perhaps you are," Anna sniffs in her haughty British accent, "but not me. There must be a theatre here, somewhere," she says, as they climb a carpeted staircase to the next level.

The Maestro's decision to open with 'The Leather Boys of London' comes as a surprise. Anna tries to convince him that a ballet depicting British mods and rockers is a rotten choice.

"Nikko, Arabs hate us, and the music from *West Side Story* was composed by Leonard Bernstein, a Jewish-Ukranian American.* What are you thinking?"

"They *vaant* modern dance so modern dance is *vaaat* they get."

Congress of Non-Aligned Countries:

There is more excitement backstage than in the audience for the command performance. All of the girls are clustered around the small gap in the curtain trying to get a glimpse of Jordan's young and sexy King. The Maestro, wearing his opening-night Italian suit, is standing in the wings arguing furiously with the owner of the nightclub, who has earned the nickname Mr. Grabi because he can't keep his hands to himself unless he is fondling his testicles.

"I forbid the taking of photographs during the performance— of any of my dancers." Nikko is roaring, in English, French, and Arabic. "Not for newspaper, not for advertising, no, *non, la, la, la*."

Mr. Grabi is equally adamant that the dignitaries, press, and bodyguards can do what they damn well please, "Anytime, anywhere," and he hisses like a snake, saying "*al yahûdî*', I know who you are," before storming off to his office.

There is a familiar hush from the grand room. The resident orchestra takes their place and play a circus 'oompa pa' fanfare before sitting down on their backsides until it is time to play the finale. Backstage, Maggie glances at Rosie, who makes the sign of the cross. Even if she is dying, she must get onstage or no one will get paid.

Quietly, Les Ballets take their places. The Maestro softly

murmurs, "Break a leg *daahlinks*," turns on the recorder, gives the signal, and with a slight rush of cool air, the curtains part and all is forgotten except the addictive euphoria of the music.

Sitting with their noses a few feet from the edge of the stage, Presidents Abdel Gamal Nasser of Egypt, Josip Tito of Yugoslavia, Ahmed Ben Bella of Algeria, Sukarno of Indonesia, and the King of Jordan wait. Behind, in parallel rows, the Heads of State from eighty-five non-aligned nations perch on gilded tapestry chairs, expecting to be dazzled by leggy blondes in stiletto heels, large glittering breasts, and feathers stuck to their asses. As the curtain opens, they, and the armed bodyguards, are struck dumb with disappointment. Before them is a scene from the slums of London; leather-jacketed thugs brandishing switchblades and clubs, and mascaraed girls in black leather boots and turtleneck sweaters, brawling in a gang war—the world of the mods and rockers of the sixties.

Suddenly, a barrage of flash bulbs light up the room. From a small, side door the Maestro tries to force his way over to a gang of press photographers, but is roughly shoved aside with a gun pressed against his neck. Ambassadors, dignitaries, and presidents snap away with their Brownie Bakelite flash cameras, having no idea that 'The Leather Boys' was inspired by Rudyard Kipling's famous ballad about equality, respect, and integrity between nations and individuals with conflicting religious beliefs.

> *East is East, and West is West,*
> *and never the twain shall meet,*
> *Till Earth and Sky stand presently at God's*
> *great Judgment Seat;*
> *But there is neither East nor West, Border,*
> *nor Breed, nor Birth,*
> *Till two strong men stand face to face, tho'*
> *they come from the ends of the earth!*

In the dressing room, Maggie, Anna, and the others are struggling into the ill-fitting bodysuits for the finale. They fasten hooks and eyes on the yellow, sequined, and feathered bikinis, and anchor plumed tophats with handfuls of bobbi-pins. Ronáld is just finishing his act, tipping back his trademark fedora and lighting a cigarette.

"*En scene*" someone calls in French. Nikko blocks their way.

"Take off those ugly, brown bodysuits," and he flips his hand to make them disappear like a conjuror in a magic show. "Bare skin tonight. I will pay the fucking fine to the police."

Suddenly, the orchestra is nudged awake, quite unprepared to play Stan Kenton's 'Artistry in Rhythm.' But, with enthusiastic determination, they see how quickly they can get it over with. The dancers gallop through their steps like frantic racehorses, spooked by plumes, feathers, and flying rhinestone earrings. Everyone keeps up as best they can for the full, ten-minute steeple-chase. Exhausted but defiant, the dancers step forward for their final bows as though they are in the Paris Opera House, not a pathetic, worn-out cabaret, three miles from the most majestic monuments in the history of mankind; the pyramids.*

Perspiration runs down necks, into cleavages, and bare stomachs glisten with sweat. Fahad, Daniel, Xavier, and Ronáld mop their brows with white handkerchiefs before returning them to the breast pockets of their threadbare tuxedos. At first, the response is polite, and then clapping gets louder and stronger. Les Ballets Jazz Europa have struck a chord. But, only Ronáld receives a standing ovation because he sang the Arabic songs, '*Shaabi,*' accompanied by an Egyptian folk band. *If they had known that the singer was a Jew from Western Europe, would the enthusiastic applause have been as heartfelt?*

It is well after two in the morning when Maggie tiptoes into the room on the second floor of the Hôtel Windsor. Rosie is asleep.

In the dim light from the window she quickly undresses and lies sweating on the top of the bed. Her suitcase is open on the chair by the window. "That's odd," she murmurs, before burping and dreaming of '*kashari*,' an Egyptian version of macaroni with spices, raisins, lentils, and nuts and a spectacular grilled pigeon stuffed with kidneys, liver, and sweet spice. *They probably just grab the little birdies off the streets and wring their necks,* she thinks, before nodding off.

At the first light of dawn, while Maggie lies on her back, snoring like a Beaver Cove lumberjack, her roommate Rosie slips out of the door, avoiding the noisy, manual wooden elevator, and takes the staircase to the main floor before disappearing into the early morning traffic. A hand-drawn map is referred to from time to time when she pauses for breath. No one notices her turning into a grubby alley, anxiously looking up at the numbers for some form of identification. She presses on, dodging animal filth and washing water thrown in the dusty path. In front of a small hovel, not really a shop at all, but, selling brooms, a half-dozen cans of Piff Paff, and some baskets of hand-made brown soap, she stops. Next to the shop front is a stone arch stained dark with urine, its keystone chinked in the ancient Roman numeral 'IV.' Beyond, a small door is ajar. With a deep sigh, almost a whimper, the tips of her beautifully manicured fingers hesitate. Before she can change her mind, the door is flung open, and a middle-aged woman pulls her inside. They walk up to a sparse, but tidy apartment on the first floor. Madam is not Egyptian, but looks to be central European, Polish, or Russian. She is wearing a long, faded blue skirt and a clean white apron with a pocket. Rosie is terrified. She slips a handful of Egyptian banknotes into the outstretched hand. Smiling with satisfaction, the midwife nods toward a bed, half-hidden behind a yellowing curtain. Rosie, white as an ancient marble statue, is similarly frozen in time, dreading the next few minutes of her life and the choice she has made. Silently, Madam indicates that she should remove her underpants.

Maggie has overslept. She leaps up, has a quick swish of the armpits in the tiny basin, sprinkles J & J talcum powder between her legs and dresses in a hurry. "I'm late for class, again," she growls. "Why didn't Rosie wake me up?" She suddenly remembers the open suitcase, and hardly daring to breathe, she walks across the room. Scrambling through her clothes, she pulls out a red leather picture frame that opens like a diary. Inside, behind the photograph of her idol, the beautiful ballerina Moira Shearer dancing the lead in The Red Shoes, is a secret pouch in the black taffeta lining. With trembling fingers, she searches for the wad of bills; her savings account, her security, her emergency money to buy a ticket home. *Empty!* Unwanted tears are wiped with the back of her hand and she bites her lip until it bleeds. "Oh, God," she whimpers, "I've been robbed."

A make-shift ballet *barre* diagonally crosses the stage at L' Auberge des Pyramids. Ten dancers start with the very basic ballet exercise, a *demi plié*, stretch, full *plié* straighten, bend forward like a scissor until the forehead touches the knee and backwards into an arch.

Maggie looks around, "Where's Rosie?" No one answers. "Rise on the *demi pointe*, arms in fifth position, and hold in balance—to the count of twenty." The Maestro stalks up and down the *barre* making small corrections and murmuring encouragement. He is a shepherd guiding his flock, counting *"un, deux, trois, quatre, cinq."* He glares at Abdul Grabi, who has come out of his den and is leaning against the door jamb, eyeing the young, agile bodies like a sly fox.

Two hours later, hot and perspiring, Maggie wraps herself into a cotton robe and boldly knocks on the office door.

"Enter," booms Mr. Grabi. She steps just inside the door, leaving it wide open—a quick escape. Without being coy or intimidated, she asks for her passport for twenty-four hours.

"I promised my grandmother I would take a trip to the Valley of the Kings before it is flooded by the new dam." She adds unnecessarily, "I cannot leave Cairo without my passport." To her horror, the boss agrees with a wink, but only on the condition that he escorts her on a private tour. Sucking on his cigar, he awaits her reply, purposely fondling his testicles with his left hand. He leans back on his chair and blows smoke rings in the air.

"Well?" Seething with rage, Maggie roars that she would sooner cut off her right hand and starve to death than get into his car. He laughs but his eyes betray his fury as she marches out of the office, head held high.

The moment the Congress of Non-Aligned Countries was over and dignitaries and world press left Cairo, Les Ballets Jazz Europa is fired—thrown out without warning and without pay unless all the girls of the ballet entertain special 'clients' downstairs in the infamous Gold room the 'Salle d'Or' after their performances. It is expected as part of his policy.

"Out of the question!" retorts the Maestro. "We are a respected, modern ballet company and my dancers are professional artists, they are my family." He adds "We were invited to Cairo by President Nasser himself, to prove to the world how modern Egypt has become. We have a contract," his voice is barely audible, holding in seething anger. "Read it! If you can read," and hands over the papers. Slowly and deliberately, Mr. Grabi takes the contract, rips it to shreds, and lets the bits drop to the floor.

"You will regret this" he glares, and with the dignity of a wise man, the Maestro turns on his heel and leaves, politely uttering the salutation, "*salaam aleikum*, peace be with you."

It was Daniel's idea, a brilliant derring-do, to climb the biggest, tallest pyramid on the day before the ballet is to leave this exotic, dangerous, corrupt but enchanting city of a thousand minarets.

"I'm going to climb ol' man '*Khafre*' tomorrow at sunset," he brags. "It's all arranged and I even have a guide."

"Me too," pipes up Maggie, before she has given it any thought whatsoever. Anna, not to be left out, adds, "Jolly good Daniel, let's have a toast to that." They are sitting in the Barrel Bar of the Hôtel Windsor drinking cold beer and swatting mosquitoes.

"*Tchin Tchin*, here's to the top!"

"*Mon dieu*," mutters Simone, "*vraiment stupides, les Anglais.*" Rosie just sits there saying nothing and gazes out the window at the seething mass of humanity, dogs, donkeys, and toddlers covered in rags playing in the refuse on Alfi Bey Street.

A taxi hurtles across town and out onto Pyramid Road as the sun begins to set. It spews a cloud of desert sand and dust in its wake as it gets nearer to the great pyramid of Giza, known as the Pyramid of Cheops or '*Khafre*,' built 2500 years before the birth of Christ. The enormity of this ancient triangle is sobering. Hand-hewn blocks of rock piled to a height of four hundred, eighty-one feet, comparable to a forty storied building. Screeching around the southwestern corner, the taxi halts within a few feet of the guide, whose name is also Abdul. Maggie, Anna, and Daniel pile out, pay the driver, and elicit a promise to come back for them in two hours.

"If he doesn't come back…"

Abdul chimes in. "*Salaam*, my friends, he come back, yes."

The guide is a tall, long-legged man with jet-black skin, flashing eyes, a wide smile that reveals large gaps where there should have been teeth, and very large hands. He hitches his rusty brown robes into a sash, after pocketing the money into a fold.

"My friends," he shakes his forefinger at them as a warning. *"You stay close, me climb, you climb, no stop, no look down."* His advice is followed and the four start up the rock face like monkeys up a tree. After a lifetime of balletic exercise and hour upon hour of dancing non-stop, the ascent is challenging but not impossible. About halfway up, the boulders begin to appear larger and not quite square, but worn on the edges. Loose rocks from above tumble dangerously close and soft hands start to bleed. Abdul's strong, dark hands grasp Anna's wrist as she suddenly cries out, blinded by dirt and pebbles.

Like an army sergeant Abdul gives orders, "No look down, climb with me," and counts, "one, two, three four, *wahid*, *itnan*, *taleta*, *arba'a*." Up and up they climb. Maggie takes a peek down the side and gives an involuntary squeal as pebbles careen down the side into the gloom below. The sun is beginning to set. With a final heave, they are at the summit, which is not a point at all but a worn platform buffeted flat by time, wind, sand, and rain. The three dancers stand together, hugging each other, laughing, crying, hysterically whooping and hollering into the wind. Abdul squats on his haunches, enjoying the spectacle. They are on top of the world, flinging their arms about, blowing kisses to the silent applause of the empty desert.

They burst into the high-pitched howl of joy, the Arabic ululation: *"La la la la lalalaleeeeesh,"* trilling from the uvula and the tip of the tongue. The majestic sky changes from a pinkish blue to a gentle orange, as the artist's brush dissolves it into purple. Suddenly silent, they listen to the lonely melody of the desert; the echoes of the Arab world.

"We go now," Abdul is watching the darkening sky and points to the headlights of a taxi still far off to the east. "Stay close please, I go down, you go down too." He disappears over the side and they hear the crashing of displaced rocks and pebbles like the erratic rhythm of a belly dancer's "zills," and the clatter of coins and bells of the hip girdle.

"I'll remember this moment as long as I live," and Maggie, taking one last look, vanishes over the edge.

CHAPTER X

Phoenix on Fire

Al-Ahram Weekly News. Issue 548:
"INFAMOUS NIGHTCLUB TORCHED"
"The Auberge des Pyramids, with its controversial downstairs
Salle D'Or, was burned to the ground late last night by
unidentified individuals. Fire trucks arrived minutes after the
alarm, but it was too late to save the twenty-year-old building.
Nasserite security forces have tried, without success, to close
the cabaret linking it to institutionalized prostitution. Auberge
des Pyramids was a conspicuous symbol of Western decadence
and affluence and thought to encourage the consumption
of alcohol and show indecent acts onstage. The owner is
unavailable for comment."

Middle East, 1964:
    The Sinai Desert, some twenty-three thousand square miles of sand dunes, sporadic waterholes called *wadis*, and jutting rocks, has been a hotbed of Egyptian-Israeli tension since May 14th, 1948, but a desert of despair for centuries longer. In the sky above, an aging Vickers Viscount* emblazoned with 'Middle East Airlines—Air Liban' transports Les Ballets Jazz and all their paraphernalia toward Beirut, capital of Lebanon, a former French protectorate. Maggie's

nose is pressed against the round, porthole window and she is mad with excitement.

"Oh, wow! I wish my grandmother was beside me. She has never flown before."

"I haven't either," replies Daniel, "so don't hog the window."

As far as the eye can see, the undulating plateau of fine sand glitters like a vast lake of gold and silver sequins.*

"Look, Daniel, on the horizon, three lone figures, riding camels. They look like the three wise men, heading for Bethlehem."

"Well," he laughs, "they must be lost. They're heading in the wrong direction." The noise and vibration inside the early Viscount is shattering and everyone has to shout to be heard.

"I should be heading for the Valley of the Kings, but that fat bastard wouldn't give me my passport."

"I can't hear you," shouts Daniel, as the plane bounces on the thermals over the scorching hot sands. She slumps back in her seat, brooding. *Granny's money went for an abortion. Damn, damn, damn! Why didn't she confide in me? Did Rosie think I would refuse?* She lights a cigarette, makes a face, and then stubs it out in the metal ashtray built into the arm rest.

Several rows ahead, the Maestro is reading the newspaper, 'Al-Ahram' with a slow, wicked smile. He passes it silently over to Fahad who, scanning the headline, throws back his head and laughs out loud. He fails to notice an item at the bottom of the page almost lost between the advertisements for cigarettes. *'Mohamed Mahmoud Khalil Museum robbed for a second time.' A painting believed to be by Vincent Van Gogh appears to be missing. Some experts believe it is a forgery. Security guards have been taken in for questioning.*

"What time are we due to arrive?" Nikko murmurs. "I have an appointment at the Phoenicia Hotel with an impresario. We need another contract after this fiasco in Cairo."

Beirut, Lebanon, 1964:

Known as the 'Jewel of the Mediterranean' and a playground for sheiks, kings, the Shah of Iran, Aristotle Onassis, diplomats, and the richest of European and Arabian elite, Beirut, or *Beyrouth* in French, is the centre of wealth and power at the end of WWII. Its port rivalles that of Marseille's in the South of France. If there is a deal to be made, it is made here on the famous, palm tree lined promenade called the *Corniche*, poolside at the Phoenicia Hotel, or in their posh nightclub, *Le Paon Rouge*; The Red Peacock. Sailors, petty gangsters, and other riff-raff head to a sleazy strip-joint on the seaside, called the Kitt Katt Club, used for the same purposes, plus satisfying sexual fantasies.

A Mercedes taxi, its radio blaring French hit songs by Sylvie Vartan, pulls up to a nondescript, white apartment block, just around the corner from the Kitt Katt Club, and drops off five passengers and their luggage. The driver unceremoniously grabs their money and leaves them standing at Baalbeck Street, named after an old cinema that is no longer there.

"He thinks we are kitty cats," Shirel giggles to Mimi.

"Welcome to the Paris of the Middle East," Maggie remarks flippantly and picks up her suitcase, brown beauty box, massive handbag and a hubbly-bubbly: a last-minute purchase in the Cairo market of *Khan El Khalili*.

"What a piece of junk," snaps Rosie, obviously recovering from her ordeal at the hands of the midwife.

"I would have bought some beautiful gold jewellery, if I hadn't been robbed."

"That's enough!" warns Anna. "We have to live together for a week, so let's try to get along."

The third-floor apartment, although cramped and smelling of leaking gas from a two-burner stove, has a view, or rather, a glimpse of the sea between two buildings across the street. The only single bedroom is immediately claimed by Anna, and the double bed in the second bedroom is taken by Mimi and Shirel, who Maggie calls 'The Bobbsey Twins' because they're always together. Rosie has an alcove with a curtain for privacy, and Mags ends up on an army cot in the sitting area.

"Well, ain't this cozy?" she comments sarcastically. Minutes later, the door to the hall opens and Talitha tosses bundles of letters and postcards onto the oilcloth table.

"Mail from the American Express office, from Egypt." Maggie picks up those addressed to her.

"Ah, from my mother, suggesting—no doubt—that I come home and get a job as a secretary in a coroner's office as my social life is irrefutably dead." She tosses the letters into her bag and announces that she is going to the posh Phoenicia Hotel to read in luxurious surroundings. "Who's coming with me?"

Anyone watching Anna and Maggie tripping down the 'Corniche' in slingback high heels would figure they were either movie stars or heiresses. Tanned from the Egyptian sun, hidden behind huge, dark sunglasses, they look like a pair of exotic birds: one in white with a stunning turquoise necklace, and the other in a very short, celadon green mini-skirt. "I hope I have enough money for a lemonade or a 'jallāb,' a sweet date syrup, or I'll look like such a fool." Maggie peeks inside her wallet. They pass luxury shops filled with French perfumes and silk lingerie that would never be seen in Egypt. "It is so modern and civilized here—like the United Nations, every religion, every nationality lives in harmony—at least on the surface."

Anna, hurrying toward the famous watering hole hisses, "Don't be naïve! Catholics, Muslims, and Jews can't stand each other. It's all about money."

A blast of cool air welcomes the two into the bar downstairs, forcing their eyes to adjust to the dim lighting, after the blinding

glare on the promenade. Maggie stops dead and stares at the see-
through wall behind the bar. A thick, glass window runs the whole
length of the swimming pool on the first floor, giving the patrons
who are sipping drinks a voyeuristic view of swimmers in fancy
bathing costumes propelling through the water.

Anna has taken a seat at the bar and whispers, "Keep your
glasses on, and don't turn around." To the barman she calls, "*Deux
coupes s'il vous plaît.*"

Maggie wails, "I can't afford champagne, for crying out loud."

"*Shhh!* He can damn well pay for our drinks," and she nods
across the room as though in a spy movie. Maggie spins around,
and in a dark corner, she sees the Maestro in huge, dark glasses,
with Nicoletta draped intimately over his shoulder. They are with
the man she met in Rome at Alfredo's; the trattoria with the gold
spoon and fork from Douglas Fairbanks Jr.

"What was his name?"

"Massimo," says Maggie. On the soft, padded bench beside him
is a large, gift-wrapped package.

"That French bitch is having it off with Nikko." Anna is glaring
at the table with fire in her eyes. "That is why he gave me this damn
turquoise necklace," and she unclasps it and tosses it into her purse
as though it is a string of cheap beads.

Maggie is opening letters one after another and reading intently.
"Same old news," she mutters. "Everyone having babies, yeh, yeh,
rummage sales, bridge parties, tuna fish casserole, why don't I come
home, sister Geraldine is a happy housewife, picking blackberries
for jam, piano needs tuning, etc." The last letter is from her father,
written in his English style handwriting, unlike the McLean method
she had to perfect at North Oyster Elementary school. She notices
the postmark, stamped three weeks ago. Dear Margaret Alice: *Regret
to tell you that Grandmother died last Wednesday, quite suddenly
after catching a chill while waiting for a bus to the library.* That was

it! She slowly crushes the thin, aerogram paper and it slips from her fingers onto the floor; a soiled paper napkin.

The Phoenicia bar spins like a merry-go-round, and the sudden squealing in her ears turns into a thump, thump, thump, of her heart. Her body temperature soars as if on fire and sweat runs down her back and armpits but she does not cry out. Anna is trying to appear cool and chatting to the bartender as Maggie rushes out of the room, up the stairs to the first floor by the pool.

"Are you a registered guest, *Mademoiselle*?" enquires a *tarbouch*-clad waiter.

"Go away!" She rips off her halter top, unzips the mini and stands poised for a second in her tiny lace bikini. Into the cool, green water, down, down, down to the bottom, she glides and rolls about like a wounded harbour seal until she runs out of air. Taking a gulp, she plunges again and drifts about, trying to remember her Granny's last words: "Margaret Alice, you have only one short life, you must go, explore, learn, see everything, good and bad, and finally you will be ready to come home. I may not be here, but I will always be with you in spirit."

She inhales a precious breath and slowly spirals through the water, arches her back and lazily corkscrews to the floor before a *'grande jete'* propels her up, up, up, to the surface. She can hear music, her mother playing the piano, longing for the career she was denied. Closing her eyes, she is transported to the small, sandy cove at Yellow Point, home to minnows, dungeness crabs, oysters, and geoducks. *I'll cry tomorrow,* she thinks. *Today is for happy memories of that remarkable woman, who, more than anyone else in my life, encouraged me to follow my dream.*

In the bar below the pool, some of the voyeurs, the Maestro, Nicoletta and the bartenders are watching the underwater performance.

"Now, she is dancing from her heart," the Maestro is fascinated. "I knew she could do it."

"*She ees bloody* show-off," Nicoletta says furiously.

"*Mais non*," he replies, "she is at one with her body and with zee music coming from within. If I can get her to dance like that in my new ballet, she'll be *formidable*."

"*Tu m'avais promis*...you promised *me* the lead role," Nicoletta argues in a loud voice. The maestro pushes her arms away and continues to speak in hushed tones to Massimo. They nod in agreement, Massimo stands, embraces Nikko, and walks out of the bar with a parcel under his arm. Nicolette's eyes narrow suspiciously.

Meanwhile, Anna has rushed upstairs to the edge of the pool with a large, luxurious towel in her hands, hand-embroidered in gold and red threads. It boasts the hotel logo of the famous mythological bird, the phoenix, who is consumed by fire and from the ashes, is reborn to fly again.

Rehearsal begins in a derelict warehouse near the Arab quarter. The BJE have days to wait before sailing back to Europe by ship, and time is precious. The Maestro is on fire with new ideas for a new ballet, his best yet, he promises. The ballet will be in two acts, representing Picasso's blue and rose periods, with no intermission. The characters and costumes are based on Pablo Picasso's harlequins; his many paintings and drawings created when he arrived in Paris in 1900, penniless and lonely. His models in the Rose Period dating 1904 to 1906 were acrobats, clowns, and trapeze artists who worked in the Cirque Medrano near Montmartre.

Everyone is gathered around a small worktable near the only window in the airless, cement room, looking at a sketchbook of harlequins.

"These are superb." Maggie is flabbergasted that the drawings are so brilliantly executed—almost forgeries of Picasso's originals. "You are an artist," she exclaims. He turns the page.

"This is for you, Maggie," and with a few quick lines of a

pencil, Nikko recreates from memory the famous 'Circus Family with Monkey:' a thin sad clown, a seated mother in a flowing dress with a baby in her arms, and a monkey sitting at her feet. "You will play Olympia, the mother who longs for a life beyond an itinerant troupe of poor gypsies."

"She'd make a better monkey, *un meilleur singe*," snips Nicoletta, scowling. "Nikko, *tu m'avais promis*. She can't have my role."

Maggie, enraged, replies, "I'd rather dance the role of a baboon than have to screw the boss to get a solo. Anyway, I'm leaving, as soon as I have enough money to get home."

"*Je m'en fous de toi!*" Nicoletta snorts rudely, her face contorted in fury.

Maggie takes a deep breath, grabs her bag, and heads for the door, fighting the urge to turn around and punch Nicoletta in the nose. The Maestro calmly lights a cigarette.

"*Daahlinks*," he closes his sketchbook carefully, "shall we begin? A famous photographer, Garo Nalbandian, will be here in a few minutes for a magazine photo shoot. Let's calm ourselves." He slowly wanders over to the recorder, and the room fills with music. "Please, we start with the entrance of Daniel and Xavier. *Un, deux, trois*, okay."

For the next week, Maggie eats alone in the small apartment on a diet of fried eggs and Lebanese flatbread called manakeesh, smeared with olive oil and *za'atar*, a spice mixture of sumac and sesame. She is convinced she is the only one who is not being paid anything while out of work and she is down to her last few coins.

"Go on ahead," she tells the other girls, "I am saving money." One night, she overhears Nicoletta speaking to the French Bobbsey Twins, raving about a dinner she had at the '*Casino du Liban*' a few miles out of town. While Maggie's French is not perfect, she knows the word '*jouissant:*' orgasmic. She smiles to herself. *At least my fried egg doesn't come with any obligation for sexual favours.* Her day usually ends curled on the cot reading—her latest find, 'Zorba the Greek' by Nikos Kazantzakis, a book she discovered at the *Librarie Antoine.* Friday, before the ballet leaves Lebanon, she takes a solitary walk along the tree-lined *Corniche* with the prevailing wind blowing wildly through her long, tangled red hair. Fingers absent-mindedly fondle the tiny medallion of St. Christopher, patron saint of travellers, hanging on a fine gold chain and she sadly ponders her future with Les Ballets Jazz Europa. Salt spray mingles with tears as she stares into the water pushing away suicidal thoughts. She leans far over the breakwater wall, staring at the waves and thinking about the undertow. Letters float in front of her eyes, wavy headings from a far-off newspaper, so very tired... She imagines her obituary in the Ladysmith Chronicle:

Ladysmith Chronicle
Here lies Margaret Alice, spinster daughter of pioneering Dinsdale
family of North Oyster—unsuccessful and unpopular dancer in
the corps de ballet of a bankrupt jazz troupe suspected of being
involved in an international smuggling organization. Ms. Dinsdale
drowned at age 23 in front of a sleazy clip joint on the waterfront
in Beirut. She will not be mourned by anybody at all.
R.I.P.

"*Mademoiselle*, are you alright?" An elderly gentleman with a clipped moustache stained with nicotine touches her lightly on the shoulder with his walking stick. "You should not lean out so far, very dangerous." He looks at her tear-stained face. "*Trop jeune pour les larmes, la vie ne fait que commencer.*" Too young for tears, life is just beginning. He smiles sadly, turns away and gamely totters on, heaving one leg after the other.

Beirut, Lebanon:

Dear Family:

The days of packing, unpacking, endless classes, rehearsals, performances, bleeding toes, sprained tendons, trains, taxis, and buses, are coming to a close. I can't live like this. I can't dance with joy in my heart, knowing that outside the theatre, in the street, children with running sores have no clothes and beg for a piece of bread, where politicians live like kings and anyone who complains is tossed into jail, where a country has to rely on secret police to keep order, where flies lay eggs on innocent blind eyes. I can't entertain brothers who would stab each other over political differences. I refuse to share my digs with cockroaches and my bed with anyone who will buy me dinner. This is not the life I envisioned while training daily for ten years to be good enough to be a professional ballet dancer, and then to be treated like a dim-witted street-walker. Miss Thelma Wynne was right when she said, "You have to be tough to survive in this profession—both morally and physically." I'm not strong enough to continue and I am ready to come home as soon as I can be replaced. I miss Granny more than I can say. She gave me confidence and I seem to have lost it.

Love, from your very discouraged and lonely Mags, xxx

From the exterior, the Greek Hellenic cruiser MS Lydia looks both inviting and seaworthy, with stewards in stiff, white uniforms welcoming passengers aboard. Below deck, it is a different story, an airless, iron dungeon awaits the unwary third-class dormitory passengers. Rather than suffocate below deck, the dancers start a continuous game of hearts on a makeshift table as Lydia plows her way westward. Maggie, in her usual scrunched up, barefoot position on a deck chair, is wrapped up in a navy-blue wool blanket with the logo of the Greek Hellenic Lines stitched into the corner. Clutching a battered edition of Zorba the Greek, her thoughts are miles away, on Vancouver Island, and the hopeless position she finds herself in. *What a confusing book! What is the story really about? Isn't it really about leading a sensual, fulfilling life, dancing to the music in your heart, or is the author mocking himself and others, who just observe and analyse life rather than being on its stage? Am I that uptight person? Do I avoid friendships and intimacy because I'm only half here and the other half is on the other side of the world?* She opens her handbag and puts the book away, closing her eyes and letting the sun calm her thoughts. Is the Maestro like Zorba who lives, loves and answers to no one?

"I wonder if it is too late for me to change my attitude?" she says out loud.

A voice from behind answers, "*Daahlink*, it's never too late."

Twinkling lights of Piraeus, the large port of Athens, appear on the horizon. It is Sunday night in Greece. A sudden flurry of activity begins as the BJE prepare to go ashore for a night on the town.

"We depart at dawn," warns Nikko, as they fly down the gangplank and climb aboard a bus to the capital. The Maestro disappears to his cabin as Maggie watches the others, feeling no desire to go dancing, drinking, and flirting, fearing no one else will pay her bill. As the bus disappears, she pulls a cigarette out of her leather cigarette box embossed with the coat of arms of Florence. It is a gift from Anna, from the marketplace with the brass pig. Their friendship is hampered by jealousy and ambition. It seems so long ago that she had a beautiful romance with Enzo in the Torrigiani Malaspina Gardens in Florence. She had not even given him her address in case her mother disapproved of him. Motionless, she stares at the empty road, wondering if she should have joined in the fun. She's missing her one chance to see the city of Athens, one of the oldest cities in the world; its recorded history spanning 3,400 years. Instead, she chooses to wallow in misery, aboard a stinking ship.

The flick of a lighter causes her to jump, but she finds herself looking directly into the Maestro's dark, piercing eyes. He really is an extraordinarily handsome man, even if he is as old as her father. He turns and leans against the railing, his back to her.

"When I was your age, maybe a year younger, I was hiding out in Greece—a place called Thessaloniki."

"Why were you hiding?"

"I am Jewish, and it was July 11, 1942, after the Nazi invaded Greece. Thessaloniki had a large population of Jews— more than fifty thousand. On that Saturday, Black Shabbat, all Jewish men between the ages of fifteen and fifty were rounded up in Freedom Square." Nikko drops his cigarette to the deck of Lydia and steps on it angrily, twisting it into powder. He continues. "It was blazing hot and we were wearing our Shabbat clothes; heavy jackets and long trousers, and told to squat as though we were shitting. We had to hold our arms out and then the beating began. If older men fell over in a faint, a bucket of water was thrown at them and they were revived and beaten again." Maggie is trembling in horror. "Hour after hour we were beaten, many died, and the spectators, German men and women, laughed and clapped, and took photos as men soiled themselves and fell bleeding to the pavement."

"How did you escape?"

"My fiancé managed to make a diversion and I rolled under a cart, my ankle fractured and hip smashed. Seconds later, someone tossed me on top like a sack of garbage." He pauses, staring at the land in front of him. "That is why I have a slight limp. It didn't heal properly. I never saw her again, my Olympia. By the end of the war, ninety-eight percent of all Jewish Greeks died or fled." He turns and stares at Maggie. "My dancers are my family, you understand, *daahlink*. They are all I have, and I will do anything to keep us together." Maggie bites her lip as he continues. "You must not sit in judgment over me, about things you do not understand. You have a family who write to you and send you money, but the others have only me." He pauses. "Come now, we go ashore, we drink cups of *ouzo*, yes and I will tell you about my new ballet. You will dance for me in Cannes, and if we are successful we will open in Paris. That has always been my dream—to create a ballet for the Opéra de Paris, and I need you."

The twenty-seven hundred tonne passenger ship, with a top speed of twelve and a half knots, took several more days to reach the coast of Sicily and past the island of Stromboli, closer and closer to the port of Napoli. With growing excitement, the dancers' spirits rise, the horrible food becomes more palatable, and everyone begins to tell jokes. It is a bizarre homecoming considering most are from northern Europe and England, not the Mediterranean coast. Anna and Maggie are leaning over the prow with the wind blowing through their hair.

Maggie asks Anna, "You know the Maestro better than the others. Has he ever told you where he was born? He is so secretive." Anna laughs.

"He is really a bastard, you know. His mother was a Russian ballerina with the Ballet Russes de Paris when she got pregnant. I don't know where he was born, Rome maybe, but she died and he was sent to an orphanage in Switzerland." Suddenly, the MS *Lydia*'s horn blasts the 'entering harbour' signal, *hoot, hoot, hoot.* They are approaching the port of Naples. Everyone is cheering and any more questions are drowned out.

The Maestro appears, shouting, "Tomorrow morning we will be in Genoa. We open at the Teatro Margherita." And so it all begins again. Down goes the gangplank, as some passengers are disembarking. They call greetings in Italian, Slovakian, and Greek. The clang of metal on metal as cargo is unloaded is jarring. Seabirds, seeking floating garbage, call and circle around Lydia. Small boats chug past, wafting the stench of dead fish, bilge water, and diesel fumes. Ronáld, in a fit of euphoria, hops on top of the lifejacket cupboard, and sings the Napoletani's favourite song, '*Funiciuli, funiculal*,' while waving his fedora to the departing passengers. Anna nudges Maggie and points toward Rosie and Daniel, who are holding hands and looking very much like young lovers.

Cinema Teatro Margherita, Via XX Settembre, Genoa:

On a large, battered tackboard, a hand-written sheet of paper announces the program. It has been crossed out and changed so many times that it is almost impossible to decipher; Jazz Blues, The Twenties, *Le Résistance*, a new comic ballet called *Pigalle*, from the red-light district in Paris. The leading role is to be danced by Nicoletta, which infuriates Anna, who pretends she doesn't care, yet still comments.

"No acting ability necessary, she already is a *putin*."

"*Wheew*, that's a long program, no intermission," someone groans.

"*Merde*, not the bloody *Résistance* again."

"En scene," calls a voice from the stage. Wearing favourite old practice tights, knitted knee warmers, old shirts, and cardigans tied around tiny waistlines, the dancers drift onto the stage. Many wear sweatbands, preventing perspiration from running into their eyes. The main curtain is tied up in the wings. Music pours from the recorder speakers as they warm up, with stretches of the legs, arms, and fingers. Some are jumping up and down. Higher, higher, toes pointed, land with *demi plié*, *ballon*—which means to hover in the air like a hummingbird. The dancers are all doing something different; working on problem steps, rubbing swollen arches, and humming nervously. The Maestro lights a *Gauloises*, leaves it in the corner of his mouth, and claps his hands.

Nikko is a man with a vision. He has a ballet bursting to get out, and he creates new lifts, entrances crawling like cats, and wild leaps in grotesque positions.

"No, no, *non daahlinks*." He changes his mind every ten minutes and jumps from one language to another without pause. "*Encore, une, deux, trois*. Stage left, Maggie, enter now, make *arabesque*," he stubs his cigarette into a coffee cup. "No! Stop, *arrêtez!*" And they start again. The choreography is fantastic. There is really no story, yet, there is a feeling that clowns are hiding their true feelings behind a mask of bright, funny faces, jocular hand movements, and a tangle of bodies. Abruptly, the Maestro stops, and saying nothing, leaves the theatre to wander around the town. He is lost in thought, dancing little steps in the middle of the street or the piazza, oblivious to anyone who may be watching.

"I need Rudi back," he decides. "We must have a strong male lead for Maggie, and at least three more dancers."

His mind made up, he searches for a public telephone booth. Amid the sounds of traffic, trucks hooting, trains, and horns, he speaks into the telephone. "Max, can you hear me? Find Rudi and ask him to come to Cannes." He sighs deeply. "*In the South of France*, the Riviera, near Marseille." The telephone crackles. "He is in Amsterdam or Brussels, somewhere, phone around to some television stations, ask around." Smoke billows around his head and fills the telephone booth with its unmistakable odor. "When you speak to Rudi, tell him we need girls, of course. Dancers—strong, classical dancers—at least three." Abruptly, he hangs up. Taking a handful of coins from his pocket, he places another call. This one is not an international call, but a private line to the Casa d'Agua Oro in Venice. "*Daahlink!*" he coos into the phone. "I need your expert advice for costuming my new ballet." He leans back in the telephone booth and listens, murmuring encouragement and slowly sighing with relief. "You will not regret this, Peggy." Slowly, he puts the receiver back on the hook, opens the door, and walks back to the

Teatro Santa Margherita, swinging his arms with confidence. His master plan is falling into place.

He imagines a poster in front of his eyes. *"L'Opéra de Paris présente ARLEQUINS chorégraphié Maestro Nikolaus Pávlos."* Still dreaming, he wonders if his famous father will be well enough or curious enough to attend.

Days fly by in a blur of classes, exercises, rehearsals, new music, late nights, endless cups of coffee, cigarettes, costume fittings, newspaper reviews, olives and cheese, and lots of wine. At the end of the week, Les Ballets board the train for San Remo, where the ornate casino built in 1905 has a magnificent stage on the roof and a theatre under the stars. Moments are snatched from rehearsals to sprawl or sleep in the flower-filled park or wander the seafront. Nice and Juan les Pins become faint memories of backstage dressing rooms covered in graffiti, shabby hotel rooms, and cafés on cobblestone alleyways where the locals eat fried fish and *frites* washed down with shot glasses of *pastis*.

Late afternoon, on the last day in Antibes—an ancient Roman harbour, the dancers stroll along the outdoor market eating *socca*, a chickpea flatbread dripping in olive oil, before returning to the Théâtre Antibéa. It is muggy, as though a storm is brewing, and Maggie climbs a winding roadway toward the museum Chateau Grimaldi.* Wiping the perspiration off her forehead with the back of her hand, she steps through the door of the civic museum to cool off. The breeze from the open windows is inviting, and since no one is around to collect tickets, she wanders from room to room. Most are empty, white-washed chambers exhibiting a few statues and ancient Roman pottery. Climbing another flight of stairs, Maggie pauses to look at some small drawings and collages that look to have the signature of Pablo Picasso, that unmistakable 'P.' There are no guards and no sounds except the wind off the ocean and the occasional hoot of a luxury yacht. At the far end of the room is an arched alcove with a brilliant stream of light, pouring out of an open window. She is drawn to it like a magnet. There is a framed painting of a woman on a beach with a child in her arms. Her hair is light brown, almost flaxen. Her dress is a natural wheat colour, rather than soft blue, but otherwise, it is identical to the painting she saw in Rome at Madame Lebedinsky's eccentric guesthouse. Maggie creeps closer, inspecting it inch by inch.

Suddenly, a voice right behind her barks, "Vat are you doing here? Do you follow me?" Maggie turns and her eyes widen as she recognizes the Maestro.

"I could ask you the same thing," she snaps. "I happen to love modern art, and grab every opportunity to see it. Picasso painted this one in 1921, three years after his son was born to the Russian ballerina, Olga," and her voice trails off to a whisper. She thinks, *That child would be forty-three years old now, about the same age as her father and the Maestro.*

He is examining the painting, absorbing every minute detail, with his back to Maggie.

"Is, is…" she stutters, unsure of if she should say anything. "Was your mother's name Tamara, a friend of Madame Lebedinsky, the dancer with the Ballet Russes?"

"What are you saying?" He asks so quietly that it is almost inaudible.

"If your mother was Tamara, she has left you a legacy—a very valuable legacy. It is a painting almost exactly like this one, except that the mother's hair is dark red, her dress has a hint of blue in it, and it is signed on the back, not the front. The signature is unmistakable and written in Greek. Pávlos, Pablo in Spanish, Paul in English," she finishes lamely. "Nikko, I saw it with my own eyes. It was wrapped in a blanket in a cupboard, and I begged Madame Lebedinsky to hide it. Go to her apartment on via Rasella, number 29, in Rome. There is a huge, ugly Russian lump of furniture in her sitting room that we pulled from the wall and hid the painting behind it. I asked her who it belonged to and she told me that when the time was right, Tamara's son would come for it, if he survived the war." She pauses, not knowing what else to say. "I think that time has probably come, don't you?"

Seconds pass without a sound except the lapping of the waves on the beach below and the far-off whistle of the coastal train running westward from Nice to Cannes. Slowly, he lifts his head as though struggling to remember something, and abruptly changes his mind. "That is the first time you have ever called me Nikko," he answers as though he has not heard any other word. The Maestro glances at his watch and grabs her roughly by the arm. "Go back to the theatre, you're late." He turns on his heel and disappears into the maze of whitewashed rooms that make up the former castle. She can hear the *click, click, click,* of his shoes on the marble floor getting fainter and fainter.

He doesn't believe me. Maggie is crushed.

Chapter XI

The Man Behind the Mask

Until the end of WWII, Cannes was a typical French fishing
village built on a rough, pebbly beach stretching east to west
in a gentle curve on the Mediterranean Sea. A half mile off-
shore, four islands, the Lérins, stand guard. The largest, Isle
Sainte-Marguerite, a penal fortress, was home for eleven years
to a mysterious prisoner known only as 'The Man in the Iron
Mask.' High up in the hills above Cannes, where the pine trees
thrive and all is silent but for the songs of the birds, lives the
most controversial artist of the twentieth century. In 1961, Pablo
Picasso found "the home of his dreams" in the Villa Notre-Dame-
de Vie, on the outskirts of the medieval village of Mougins. There,
he lives quietly with his child-bride, Jacqueline Rogue. Like many
artists, he hides behind a canvas mask, famous, but reclusive.

Cannes, France 1965:

At twelve o'clock noon, the movement of the railway carriage
slows, the rhythm changes from a gallop to a canter and Simone,
Anna, Rosie, and Maggie gather their belongings from the upper
racks in the compartment, extinguish their cigarettes, and open the
glass door to the corridor. They are arriving in Cannes, the most
famous resort on the French Riviera. Maggie is lost in thought. She

folds up the letter from home and crushes it into the white holdall, snapping the fastener with an angry *click*. Anna looks up.

"Well?"

"Father has never heard of Cannes and says if I don't come home now, he is going to come and get me. He won't, of course, but he is *threatening* me. I miss my grandmother." She takes a big breath and tries to get control of her emotions. "My granny was the only one who was truly proud of me and now, she is gone." Maggie feels defeated. *I have been a big disappointment to my family—a complete failure.* The train has stopped and Simone pushes past, knocking the bag onto the floor of the train. She is not about to listen to Maggie whine when she has lost her entire family in an air raid. "What's eating her?" Anna picks up her own precious make-up box and handbag.

"Oh, she's in a filthy mood because Nikko didn't get on the train in Antibes, but left late last night for Rome." She pauses, wondering if she should say any more. "He has a business appointment. Probably, he's making arrangements for another bloody tour of Italy." Anna sounds exasperated.

"Sometimes, I wish that my life was different, that someone would come and fetch me and take me home."

Stepping down onto the platform, Maggie, blinded by the dazzling light, pauses and puts on her sunglasses. Then, she spots him. There on the platform stands Rudi, waving his arms like an enthusiastic traffic controller. He is looking straight at her with his cheeky grin and cocked eyebrow. Beside him, Sophia is bouncing up and down with excitement, hardly the behaviour of a film star. She has flown in from 'Cinecittà' in Rome to dance with the company. She waves and blows a kiss. Sitting quietly on a bench is a beautiful Chinese girl; shy, angelic, and ethereal. "This is Zhu Li." With cries of welcome, they are engulfed with hugs and kisses of reunion. Maggie stands immobile, remembering Rudi's farewell kiss at the train station in Venice, so many months ago. She could feel his lips tickling her ear as he whispered intimately, "I'll be back." She has not forgotten how delicious that made her feel. *But, where is Aneke, his wife, and who the Hell is Zhu Li?*

You're not falling for him, are you? Maggie is horrified at the excitement she is feeling as he walks slowly toward her. Suddenly, the train lurches and the porter blows a warning whistle. "Crikey," Rudi and Daniel scramble aboard, open the window and start flinging everyone's belongings onto the platform below. The costume trunks, scenery, and sound equipment roll up from the freight cars. With seconds to spare, the porter pushes past, slams the doors and calls, "*D'abord.*" There is a final belch and the train slowly picks up speed and disappears down the track on its way toward Saint-Tropez and other fabled stops along the Azure Coast. *Clickety clack, clickety click,* and with one long *hoot* announces Les Ballets Jazz Europa has come to town.

Palm Beach Casino, Cannes:

The stage door is half-hidden on the rear wall of the sprawling Casino complex, which hosts an Olympic-sized saltwater pool, acres of manicured gardens, an outdoor nightclub called '*Masque de Fer,*' or 'The Iron Mask,' and a long stretch of palm-lined, private beach of the purest white sand. Beside the stage door, a few trestle tables have been casually set up as a semi-private, outdoor café, '*Le Pigeon d'Argile*' or 'The Clay Pigeon,' because the casino was built over a former shooting range. The casino staff, entertainers, and a few disenchanted drifters gather here for meals that don't cost a fortune. At one of the tables, Maggie sits with her aching feet buried in the soft sand. She has thrown a cotton shift over her sweat-drenched leotard, braided her hair into two 'pigtails' and looks like a school girl sneaking a cigarette. Peering over her dark sunglasses, she scans the menu that is hand-written on a tripod blackboard. The smudged chalk letters list: two salads, several different omelets, a cheese platter, or the catch of the day. She glances at the prices in French francs, and sighs "A plain omelet, no cheese, and a glass of tap water," and then quickly adds, "*Merci garçon,*" to the waiter, who raises one eyebrow in disgust and retreats into the kitchen.

Cannes is the most expensive and fashionable town on the Riviera. Only the very rich and famous can afford to shop along the elegant palm-lined promenade, buy fabulous clothes from designers such as Geoffrey Beene, Pierre Cardin, and Hubert de Givenchy, and drench themselves in the perfumes of Cristobal Balenciaga and Nina Ricci. Only jet-setters sleep in the grand palaces that line the '*Croisette*' and slip quietly through the underground tunnels from the hotels to private beaches, avoiding the riff raff. *Oh Man! The luxury of it all!* It had come as a rude shock to Maggie that she could not afford to dine out on local delicacies from the sea, nor sip *demi-tasse* coffees on the flower-filled terraces of the posh *Hôtel Martinez* nor the Carlton Hotel where Hollywood movie star, Grace Kelly, met her Prince Charming. He was Prince Rainier Louis Henri Maxence Bertrand Grimaldi, the monarch of the Principality of Monaco. *Rich and royal, what more could a girl ask for?* she muses. *A simple cup of coffee costs me half a night's pay in this seaside paradise.* She glances up at the snobby waiters wearing sparkling white aprons over rotund waistlines. *They might as well post notices to keep the punters out.* Money is not going to stop her from enjoying the view across the water and gazing in the forbidden shop windows. The first time she saw photos of the ballet featured on magazine covers, newspapers, and on posters plastered all over town, Maggie had wanted to shout out loud, "Hey guys, that's me, from North Oyster, B.C."

The beautiful white sand beach in front of the Palm Beach casino is forbidden territory. No one from the ballet is permitted to step foot on the beach, nor swim in the pool. "It is as if we all have dysentery or some disgusting disease."

"We're good enough to entertain the buggers, but not to swim with them," remarks Daniel, who is sitting at the next table.

While waiting for her eggs to appear, Maggie buries her head in the first English newspaper that she has seen in weeks—THE TIMES INTERNATIONAL. She reads out loud, "From Vienna, Austria: the *Jeunesses Musicale* organizers have cancelled a performance of a rock group called, The Beatles, due to lack of interest. From Frankfurt, Germany: the second Auschwitz Trial ended today and seventeen people were found guilty of mass murder. From Los Angeles, California: a race riot broke out that caused damage to Watts County, leaving thirty-four people dead and four thousand in custody. From Ottawa, Ontario: the Queen issued a proclamation making a little red maple leaf the national flag of Canada." Maggie throws back her head and laughs out loud.

"What's so funny about that?" Daniel is mystified. Maggie just shakes her head.

From the kitchen door of *Le Pigeon*, the waiter emerges with a tray balanced on his fingertips and shoulder and rushes over to Maggie. "One plain omelette, without cheese, one glass of tap water" he murmurs as the plate is carefully placed in front of her. She looks up sharply to see if he is being sarcastic with his exaggerated politeness, treating her as though she was dining at the Carlton on oysters and champagne. But, he is smiling. *Whoa, there's a change in attitude.* From under his arm he unrolls a poster advertising the ballet with her face in full stage makeup, half-hidden by a mask of red hair, draped seductively over one eye. Her jade-green floor length costume is slit to her waist. He winks knowingly, moves closer and asks for her autograph. *He thinks I am a floozy. Oh Boy, is he mistaken. I am just a dancer from a small town wearing phoney eyelashes, rubber falsies, and playing a vamp.* She giggles, *How do I translate that into French?*

"*En scene,*" a voice calls from the stage door, and she stuffs the rest of the omelette into her mouth, takes a large gulp of water, and follows the parade down the long, dark tunnel toward the metal stairs. The door to the girls' dressing room is ajar and she fumbles for the light switch. A piercing shriek echoes down the corridor. The dressing room floor is awash in bugs. As an army of beetles march over Maggie's bare feet and between her toes, she screams, "Cockroaches! *Disguuuusssting!*" and they scatter down the drain holes, under the piles of shoes, and disappear into the crevices and cracks in the cement dungeon. She snatches her shoes from a table, and charges up the stairs onto the stage. "Cockroaches," she spits out, "bloody thousands of them, horrible *scarabée*, running everywhere like a moving carpet, *un tapis*." She looks around at the casino with its gleaming glass windows shaped like cathedral arches, its polished brass railings, its dozens of Grecian urns filled with bright tropical flowers that spill onto the terrace, and glares at the stacks of gilded chairs that are waiting to be set up for the night's grand gala featuring the famous Roy Karls and his loyal back-up singers the 'Roylettes.' Leaflets announce that it costs one hundred French francs, the equivalent of two hundred and fifty bucks, per plate. "This Palm Beach is a sham, a smelly dump, a façade. Even the washroom stinks like an outhouse, no windows, no air..." Maggie rages. *"Elegant, my arse!"*

Rudi, who has been practising *pirouettes*, stops spinning and starts to laugh out loud. "You are funny, lady. Cockroaches and rats live in theatres—gotta learn to love 'em. We are all just a fantasy? *Ja?* Music and magic live on one side of the curtain, and cockroaches on the other. This is our world! Don't you see that?" He is standing so close to her she feels the heat of his skin and smells his perspiration. She trembles, but it is no longer with rage. Cupping her face with the tips of his fingers, he whispers, "Maggie, you can't live on both sides." Ignoring everyone, he kisses her on the mouth. "I've missed you, crazy *Canadienne*." The rehearsal begins.

Villa Marlene, #4 Chemin des Rosiers, Cannes:

Rosie, Daniel, and Maggie are standing in an overgrown garden in front of a very tall, but crumbling townhouse on a dead-end street. "Is this our hotel for the next month?" They have come directly from the Cannes train station to this address, *La Villa Marlene*. The others are billeted mid-way up a hill, in the old part of town called, '*Le Suquet.*'

"This can't be it."

"Oh for God's sake! It looks deserted."

"Wow! I don't believe this, straight out of a horror film." They all speak at once, words tumbling over each other.

"It looks like it is going to fall over," snaps Rosie as she snatches up her suitcase, "I'll be damned if I'm staying in this tip," and she is gone.

Fifty years ago, the cream and yellow mansion must have been a showcase for the *art nouveau* movement in architecture. The windows are a series of equal arches framed with elaborate carved garlands of fruit and flowers in the style of the Florentine artist *Luca Della Robbia*, but now, bruised by wind and weather. On the central windows of three levels, the remains of curved iron balconies wrought in the shape of butterflies and soft scrolling leaves are held in place by a tangled mass of blue wisteria intertwined by soft pink climbing roses. Dancing across the façade, carved statues of curvaceous ladies with bare boobs and buttocks are covered in bird droppings—some minus their toes and naked, naughty bits.

Quietly, the heavy, arched door opens. An elderly man is leaning on a walking stick, watching them from the threshold. If he wasn't so tall he could be a dead-ringer for Charlie Chaplin, with his clipped moustache, dark-rimmed eyes and a nest of messy, salt and pepper hair. From somewhere in the house, a distant piano is playing Beethoven's music. Maggie stifles a gasp of recognition. It is one of her mother's favourite sonatas. In a surprisingly loud voice, he welcomes them in German. *"Willkommen in der Villa Marlene."*

Daniel and Maggie look blank and finally she splutters, "Th-th-thank you."

"Ah, English!" He pauses, glaring at them for a few seconds, and then opens the door wider, muttering, "Come in, there is only one room. *Ein Zimmer.*" The old man adds sarcastically, "You are close friends, *ja?*" *He assumes that because we are dancers we have morals of alley cats.* She guffaws, "Not, that close, Buster. I'll take the attic."

La Villa Marlene, Cannes, France:

Dear Mom and Pop:

You won't believe this but I am living in a garret under the eaves of a haunted villa. Well, maybe not haunted, but there are a lot of strange noises in the middle of the night as though someone is moving furniture. My room must have been built for a chamber-maid. There is no running water, and it is furnished with a cot, a chair, one table, one lamp, and a jug that I fill with water downstairs in a communal washroom. The faint odor of mice is ever present, but my little hideaway has the charm of bygone days. Really, I am lucky to have a room at all, as Cannes is chocker-block full with rich tourists who flock south for the season like migratory ducks and geese, except that no one shoots at them like we do at home. These Parisian birds spend their days laying spread-eagle, naked in the sun in order to get an all-over dark tan in every crease and hollow. By the way, my landlord, Herr Hildebrand Görlott, (we call him Hans) is in love with Marlene Dietrich, and even named his villa after her. He claims he has gone to each and every performance at the casino just to hear her sing in German. Herr Görlott must have a lot of money hidden away somewhere.

Love, your Mags xxx P.S. European ladies have black, hairy armpits and never shave. Weird, eh?!

Sitting in the shade of an ancient apple tree, Maggie is reading her latest find, "Up the Down Staircase," by Bel Kaufman. It's a book about the struggles of a young woman who's trying to fit into a foreign environment and is torn between her career and the universal desire for a normal life—a husband, babies, and that sort of thing. She closes the book and considers her own life, her own future. She loves dancing and adores the wild, almost crazy choreography of the Maestro, but often, she is unbearably lonely and feels like such a misfit. Miss Wynne, her ballet teacher back home, tried to warn her that the life of a professional dancer is very, very difficult.

The villa is slumbering in the afternoon heat, its faded shutters half-closed like the drooping eyelids of a pansy-faced puppy. The garden, in the dappled light looks idyllic, so picturesque that she pulls her Brownie camera from her bag and focuses on a clump of blue delphiniums, faded wicker chairs, and a charming bird bath filled with stagnant green water. *Snap, snap, snap!* On the third snapshot, she notices a man sitting nearby reading the Paris news, *Le Parisien Libéré.* He jumps to his feet, shakes his fist at her and bellows in Italian, "Give me that camera, you bitch; *Dammi quella camera, Puttana!*" In a flash she recognizes him. "Massimo." He lunges at her and tries to grab the camera but she is too quick and tears across the garden, around the side of the villa and through the kitchen door that leads to the servant's staircase to the attic. Once inside, she bolts the door and flies up the three flights and locks herself in. "Now what?" She is late for the final dress rehearsal, has taken a photo of the man who switched briefcases with the Maestro in Rome, then turned up in Beirut for a clandestine meeting, and now he's here in Cannes and wants to throttle her.

Panic-stricken, she searches for a hiding place, but there is really nowhere. Eventually, she stuffs it into her pillow case and carefully makes the bed, pulling the flowered coverlet over the pillow. 'Bold is best' she decides, and very quietly slips down to the third floor landing and down the elegant main staircase as if she were Marlene Dietrich herself. Once out on the street, she's off like a white-tailed deer.

The main salon of *La Villa Marlene* is a shambles; an art collector's nightmare of confusion. The once exquisite silk damask walls depicting exotic birds and vines are covered with paintings, sketches, photographs, and war memorabilia. Black-out curtains cover the beautiful arched windows that soar fifteen feet up to an ornate, frescoed ceiling of angels and masked devils with grotesque appendages. Five crystal chandeliers cast shadows onto stacks and stacks of canvases, gilt-framed oil paintings, water-coloured landscapes, and life-sized portraits, all strewn about the herringbone floor. A mosaic table with ebony legs carved into serpents is piled with sculptured heads and broken body parts. Even in the heat of the afternoon sun, the room is cold.

In the far corner, Herr Görlott and Massimo Badalamenti are huddled around a painting. They are closely examining the signature. "It has been missing for a long time," begins Herr Görlott. Massimo remains noncommittal, as Görlott continues. "Perhaps it is from the collection of Baron Herzog, *ja?*" He pauses, but no response comes. He turns it over very carefully and examines the back of the canvas. "No date?" He laughs, "Forgery, perhaps?" Massimo plucks a cigarette from a gold case and lights it with a matching lighter, blowing smoke from the side of his mouth.

"Three hundred thousand francs, old man. You want it or no? I don't give a fuck, *Non me nè frega un cazzo*. Lots of buyers out there for an original Degas." * The old man turns it around and places it back on the easel smiling at *'Five Ballerinas'* who are sponsored by gentlemen who pay for their survival. Shuffling over to a leather pouch on the table, he unclasps it and fumbles around for a wad of French francs. Painfully, he counts out the money as though reluctant to part with it, turns and hands it to the Italian. "And now my friend, a little unfinished business." The old man looks up sharply. "Give me the key to that dancer's room, the red-head. She has taken a photo that links me with this villa and you; *molto pericoloso*." Herr Görlott nods in agreement. "*Ja*, very dangerous. Wait here," and he shuffles off, leaning heavily on his cane. The moment he is out of sight, Massimo tours the room looking over Hildebrand Görlott's collection, whistling softly to himself. Suddenly, he spots a small impressionist street scene by Camille Pissarro, leaning carelessly against the wall like a Parisian *putain* on the Rue St. Honoré.* It is no more than twenty-five by thirty inches and would easily fit into a nondescript suitcase. Footsteps and the *tap, tap* of a walking stick cause Massimo to jump back and feign interest in a small sculpture of a broken foot, perhaps Egyptian?

Masque de Fer, Casino Palm Beach, Cannes.

Dress rehearsal has begun for the Maestro's opening ballet titled *Les Petits Rats de Paris*, but it is not about little rats at all. It is about big rats in top hats and tails who frequent the Paris Opera and prey on the poor young dancers, most of whom are from the slums. The ballet is a thinly veiled condemnation of the artist named Edgar Degas and his fascination with semi-naked children.

"You're late," the Maestro says in a monotone voice as Maggie runs to take her place with the other four: Anna, Rosie, Nicoletta, and the new girl, Zhu Li. The music begins and they dance full-out to see if the costumes cause any problems or need adjustment. Simone is standing to one side, watching like a hawk.

Two hours later, they stagger back to the dressing rooms, and Simone snatches the costumes from them to examine any imperfection. Anna and all the French girls strip naked, squeeze into tiny bikinis, and head to *la plage privée*. After the opening night, the management decided they should loll about the private beach like ripe plums. *I guess it looks good for business to have girls and boys looking fit rather than blubber bellies baking on the sand.* Maggie changes into a man's white oversized shirt covering her shoulders and chest. She is already burnt and has a zillion new freckles. Padding up the stairs to the stage, she searches for the Maestro. She must warn him that she has seen Massimo and has inadvertently taken his photo on her Brownie camera. The *Masque de Feu* is deserted. Suddenly, she feels afraid, that everyone: the waiters, the orchestra, and the Maestro have scattered like cockroaches into cracks, and corners, watching and waiting. She senses that she is not quite alone and shivers

Crossing the marble terrace, she slips through a glass door into the cool shade of an empty banquet room that is poised and waiting for fairytale guests to arrive. Silver walls, covered with antique mirrors from floor to ceiling reflect an army of crystal goblets, French *Lalique* glass sculptures of mermaids, masses of polished English silver knives, forks and spoons, and the finest German Rosenthal porcelain rimmed in gold—a United Nations of luxury. A warm breeze from the windows that overlook the sea fill the curtains like a spinnaker billowing over the bow of a sailboat. The effect is magical, like a stage set without any actors.

Very faintly, Maggie can hear music coming from the next room. She pauses, alert, listening and slowly, with growing certainty, realizes that it's the music that has been created for the Maestro's new ballet. Without making a sound, she crosses the room between the tables and listens at the door. *Why was I not called to this extra rehearsal?* Her hand grasps the ornate door knob, and she turns it, hearing a small *click*, and opens it wide enough to peep in and not be seen. "Bloody Hell!" She is staring at Rudi who is teaching Zhu

Li *her* role in the ballet. He is teaching Zhu the romantic *pas de deux* that was choreographed especially for her. She watches in stunned silence as they dance together so beautifully, so lyrically, as though they have been dancing together a lifetime. The lifts that Maggie struggled to perfect seem effortless to Zhu, and she is a fragile bird in his arms. As the music ends, Rudi, sweating and filling his lungs with air, does not let her go. His hands slowly caress down her back and gently, he lifts her to his hips. Zhu moans in ecstasy and wraps her legs around him.

Bam! Maggie slams the door shut and in a fit of frustration, grabs the nearest thing, a *Lalique* crystal mermaid, and hurls it at the door, smashing it into a thousand shards of glass. Tears burn her eyes as she runs from the room, across the terrace and down into the gloom of the empty dressing room.

Mougins, Alpes-Maritimes, France.

Slipping into low gear, the sleek, black Citroën DS taxicab begins the steep climb into the hills behind Cannes, winding up and up through the wild sage, fennel, lavender and wind-whipped maritime pines. The scent of the scrubland, the *garrigue*, is distinctively spicy, wild, and unforgettable. Sitting in the backseat, his hand resting protectively on a large, flat, leather binder, Nikolaus Pávlos is lost in thought, ignoring the incessant chatter of the *chauffeur de taxi*. As soon as the medieval town of Mougins can be glimpsed between the branches of the pine forest, the driver slows down and casually lights a cigarette.

"The address, monsieur?"

"La Villa Notre-Dame-de-Vie." The taxi slows down to a crawl.

"Are you expected? You might not get a warm welcome if you do not have an appointment."

The Maestro remains silent as the taxi pulls up to a pair of stone pillars with an imposing two-story villa in the distance. An iron balcony runs the length of the second floor. He climbs out of the Citroën silently and hands the driver a wad of bills without a word. Just as he reaches the gate, he turns and smiles. "Yes, I am expected," and with the grace of a dancer, turns and strides down the cobbled pathway to the main door. If anyone were watching from the upper windows, they would not have noticed the slight limp in his right leg. Before he can knock, the door opens and the two men face each other for the first time—one is eighty-four and the other, forty-three, but the similarity between them is unmistakable.

By eight in the evening the casino is alive with excitement as the beautiful starlets arrive in their fine jewels and furs. Business tycoons, movie directors, and playboys stroll about in spotless white dinner jackets posing for photographs, feeling very important. Even the elegant and wealthy Begum Khan, widow of the Aga Khan III, former Miss France of 1930, is rumored to be present for the grand gala night. The entire casino complex is surrounded by armed security guards stuffed into tuxedos and looking constipated, like lumpy penguins, waiting to use the mens' room.

Deep in the bowels, below the stage, Simone explodes in a rage as Les Ballets have to vacate their rooms for the American singer Roy Karls and his backup girls 'The Roylettes.' "*Sale Américains… les salopes.*" 'Filthy trollops,' she splutters, as she lugs all the costumes from one room to another smaller one.

Rudi comes in and blows exaggerated kisses to everyone. "Did you see those Roylettes? *Woweee!* Holy shit! After the show, we swing at the "Whiskey-A-Go-Go. Ja?" Smiling happily, he dances off, singing to himself, "Hit zee road Jack." Maggie shrugs, *He will never change and Zhu will have her heart broken, just like Aneke— but, he won't break mine.*

The Maestro appears to be slightly agitated this evening, chain-smoking free Peter Stuyvesant cigarettes that litter the casino. On every available table there is a sign with their slogan 'The Taste of the Whole Wide World' and a heap of gift packages for the guests. Peter Stuyvesant is one of the sponsors of tonight's gala in honour of the veterans of WWII, along with Nina Ricci perfumes. "I don't see any free bottles of perfume about."

"Ha ha, cheap punters."

"Dahlinks," Nikko, finally gets their attention. Tonight is very important for me... for us." He takes a swig of scotch and continues. "The biggest impresario in France will be in the audience for the gala. He *vants* fresh, new, modern ballet to open the winter season at the *Opéra de Paris*." His voice drops conspiratorially as he adds, "This is our moment." He is about to say something else, but changes his mind and goes to the door, calling over his shoulder, "*Cinq minutes.*" Abruptly, the room is silent as everyone concentrates; some on make-up, applying it like the finishing touches on a portrait; others are warming up in the corner, arching their feet, pulling leg warmers over their knees. Tonight, they will be pushing themselves to their limits of endurance and as always, there is risk of injury that could end careers.

The costumes for 'Les Rats' are wild, quite unlike anything seen at the *Masque de Fer* before. There are no sequins and spike heels, instead, paint-splattered dresses of old-fashioned gauze, men in top hats and lopsided tails with no shirts and naked bodysuits, smeared in pigment. Nikko is taking a gamble that this frivolous audience will be sophisticated enough to appreciate his art. "*En scene,*" calls a voice through the tunnel. Silently, they file out, hearts are beating faster, ears are ringing, and they climb the stairs and take places in the wings. Maggie pulls at the tight velvet band around her throat and swallows nervously. From behind, someone takes her hand and whispers in her ear.

"Zhu means nothing to me." She pulls away, absorbed in the moment.

With perfect timing, house lights are turned off. All is dark except for the stars above. Maggie takes her position onstage. Seconds pass in total silence, and then with theatrical flair, spotlights explode in her face, the music begins, and the audience sees a replica of a painting by Edgar Degas. A spontaneous burst of applause erupts, although only one person, an elderly man with a cane, knows that the ballet was inspired by a painting that disappeared in 1944 and has never been seen since.*

La Villa Marlene, Cannes, France:

"I have been robbed." Maggie is sitting cross-legged on the bare mattress in her attic cell. The room is in an upheaval. Every item in her suitcase is strewn on the floor, the bed stripped bare, with a tangle of sheets and coverlet heaped over the foot board. Her precious books are tossed into corners, the water jug broken and the camera and film gone. The only thing untouched is her leather case with the photo of Moira Shearer in 'The Red Shoes.' She still has her money tucked in the secret fold in the back of the picture. "Well, Massimo, you win." She hiccups drunkenly. *What a day this has been!* With exaggerated care, she tiptoes around the room looking for her nightgown and attempts to make the bed. But, too much red wine and not enough to eat is a poor combination. Clad in only her bikini panties, she curls up like a kitten and passes out.

In her dreams she can still feel the beat of the music, or is it her heart pounding? The 'Whiskey-a-Go-Go' is a blur of bodies, dancing wildly and crashing into each other laughing and screaming for no reason at all. The local kids are passing joints from hand to hand and clinging to each other like a ball-up of salamanders. Everyone is dancing for sheer pleasure; no choreography, just moving to the music that blasts full volume from heavy speakers. There is no lack of partners who fill glasses with an endless supply of cheap red wine. Maggie and the others are drenched in sweat, spinning around the wooden dance floor, doing the shimmy, the frug, the jerk, the mashed potato, the twist, and the tango. Between the maze of arms and legs, Maggie can see Sophia signing autographs and Nicoletta trying to seduce the sexy orchestra leader, Jose Costa-Pinto, who everyone knows is married. *What the heck, another glass of wine and I might flirt with him, too.* Or maybe, she might just go to sleep somewhere. As they dance the night away at the Go-Go' party, a short distance away at the casino, the fancy people are sipping *Dom Pérignon Brut* champagne, eating sturgeon's caviar, and being entertained by a stoned jazz-pianist, Roy Karls, who also won't remember a thing in the morning.

Just before dawn, an explosion rocks the villa. Maggie is jolted awake, completely confused and feeling sick. From somewhere in the house there is a crash and the slamming of a door. She can hear footsteps coming to her room. Before she can cover her naked breasts with a sheet, Daniel pokes his head around the door. "Can't you knock?" she grumbles.

"That was a gunshot, Maggie, and why is your door unlocked?"

"No point locking the barn door after the horse has bolted." Maggie pauses. "Daniel, my camera has been stolen so there is not much good in a locked door."

"It is about your safety, you bonehead. If it wasn't for me you would have passed out on the beach," he replies.

Suddenly wide awake and alert, Maggie whispers, "Daniel, let's get out of here." She starts to climb out of bed pulling the sheet over her nakedness. "Go down the kitchen stairs to the garden and I'll meet you at the gate. We have to disappear."

Downstairs, behind the double doors that lead from the main hall to Herr Görlott's private salon, the body of Massimo Badalamenti is sprawled on the floor, his blood seeping through the cracks in the herringbone planks. On his face is a look of disbelief. Beside him is an Italian semi-automatic Beretta M1934 and a well-placed piece of statuary of a marble foot, most likely Egyptian. His pockets are empty except for a roll of undeveloped film. The sound of police sirens can be heard, disturbing the tranquility in the gardens of Villa Marlene and the dawn chorus of songbirds.

Twenty-four hours later, an excited group of dancers are gathered around Ronáld who is sitting at one of the trestle tables at the 'Clay Pigeon' reading out loud from *Le Parisien Libéré*. He is translating as he reads. "MAN FROM 'LE MILIEU' SHOT IN CANNES: Massimo Badalamenti, believed to be part of the Corsican underworld *Gang de la Brises de la Mer*, was shot in the back on Sunday morning; his body discovered by the caretaker of the *Villa Marlene, #4 Chemin des Rosiers, Cannes*. The Corsican gang control most nightclubs and cabarets in major centers on the Mediterranean Sea and have been linked with smuggling between Turkey and the port of Marseille." Slowly, Ronáld puts the newspaper down, "You and Daniel are billeted at the villa"? Maggie stammers, "M…mur…murdered?" Despite the rising heat of the late morning, she shivers. *Where the Hell is her camera with the film of the dead man—plus pictures taken in Antibes, Beirut and backstage in the Auberge des Pyramids, which conveniently burned to the ground the day they left Egypt?*

Everyone is laughing and joking as though it doesn't concern them at all. Gulping down her lukewarm *café au lait*, she jumps up and announces, "Enough is enough. My dream was to dance, not get mixed up in sordid backroom deals that end up with people getting killed. *Damnit!* This is *not* the life I longed for." No one is listening. Turning, she kicks her way through the soft sand to the stage door toward the girls' dressing room, to change for class. Inside the gloom of the underground corridor, she almost collides with Simone, who is hustling back and forth with racks of costumes. The rooms used by Roy and the Roylettes have been emptied and now belong to Les Ballets Jazz Europa once again. Next week there is to be another gala, this time for the French Polio Foundation, featuring American superstar, Dionne Warwick, and the whole changeover will begin again. Gritting her teeth, Simone splutters, "*Les Américains, Bah!*"

The music of Mozart fills the small salon where fourteen hungover dancers grip onto a makeshift *barre* and begin the time-honoured warm up exercises. "*Demi plie, grand plié,* one, two, three, four, inhale, exhale." Like machines, they bend and stretch, lift their legs, like hands on a clock, up, up, slowly to twelve o'clock, hold, hold, and then momentarily soar into space; somewhere between the sea and the sky. Everything else is forgotten.

The loveliest time of the day in Cannes is just before nightfall, when the baked beauties have gathered up their lotions and creams, towels and sandals, and vacated the beach to prepare themselves for the hedonistic pleasures of the night. Then, there is nothing but a silvery stretch of empty sand standing between the rows of regimental palm trees and the Mediterranean Sea, trailing off to the invisible coastline of North Africa. For the dancers, it is a nostalgic time—a brief moment, before yet another show begins.

Clipping along the *Croisette* in black, sling-back heels and her only cocktail dress; a backless, raw silk sheath, Maggie is heading for the casino piano bar. She is determined to find the Maestro alone, confess to the loss of the incriminating film, and tell him she is leaving the ballet. "He's got to be there." With confidence, she climbs the imposing front staircase and is met by the doorman in his midnight blue and gold uniform.

He immediately recognizes her and recites, "Artists may not use the main entrance," stops and winks at her, whispering, "*T'es canon, toi.*" *He thinks I'm hot,* she grins, tossing her hair back and sailing through the door before he can make a pass at her.

Inside the hallowed walls, her heels echo down the marble corridor, *click, click, click,* as she hurries toward the sound of music. There is no one in sight. She pauses at a door and listens. *Where have I heard that music before?* Stepping into the dimly-lit piano bar she hears a voice singing in English, and accompanying himself on a magnificent, nine-foot long, *Bösendorfer Imperial*; the Rolls Royce of pianos.

"It's not the pale moon that excites me, that thrills me and delights me, oh no, it's just the nearness of you."

In a flash, she remembers that night crossing the Atlantic on the Cunard liner, *Ivernia*, heading for her future as a ballerina with the Royal Ballet of London. *So much has happened. How has it been two years?* She wonders. On that night so long ago, she fell for the Chief Medical Officer with the heap of silver hair and the unusual name of Pip. But, he was heading to western Canada and she was starting her career, one going east, one going west. She felt a lump in her throat and her eyes misted. "Oh crap, I mustn't cry."

Across the room she spots the Maestro, Nikolaus Pávlos, standing by a long, curved onyx bar, immaculately dressed in a beautifully cut Italian suit, sipping whiskey from a crystal glass. His arm is around the bejeweled waist of the beautiful, but aging, Peggy Goldenstein. They are congratulating each other. As Maggie approaches she overhears him say, "I have signed the contract. We open the new season at the *Opéra de Paris*." Retreating to a long, lost memory, he murmurs, "I have been waiting years for this moment, Les Ballets Jazz Europa will present a full-length ballet unlike anything seen before, and there will be no intermission."

CHAPTER XII

Is Paris Burning?

*Nearing the end of WWII on August 21, 1944, a direct order came
from the leader, das Führer of Nazi Germany, Adolph Hitler, to the
newly appointed Commander of Paris. "Leave the city of Paris
a field of utter ruin, a Trümmerfeld, rather than hand it over to
Allied forces." The response was that "Paris must not fall into
the hands of the enemy." The city of love, founded in 259 B.C. by
a Gallic tribe called 'Parisii,' was to be sacrificed by a political
party gone mad. Only thirteen days before this edict, General
Dietrich von Choltitz, had taken up the post, and was working
from the Louis XVI style, Hotel Meurice built in 1815 at 228 Rue
de Rivoli, across from the Louvre Museum of Art. Following the
orders, bombs were placed on all bridges across the river Seine,
under the Louvre, the famous theatre, Opèra de Paris, the National
Assembly, Palais Royal, and even planted on the Eiffel Tower.
Three days later, on August 25, 1944, with the Allied forces at the
gates, General von Choltitz defied the orders to blow up the city.
What man would want to become infamous as a destroyer, when
he could be a hero? He surrendered the city to the Free French
army and the Resistance. Rumour has it that a deal was struck in
order to save his neck and his family from being shot as traitors.
The Commander, who became known as 'The Saviour of Paris'*

spent the rest of the war in an English country mansion, Trent Park, writing his memoirs. In 1965, a book by Larry Collins and Dominique Lapierre was published and adapted as an Oscar-nominated film of the same name, 'IS PARIS BURNING?'

Paris, France 1965:

Almost imperceptibly, the train begins to slow down on the outskirts south of Paris. From the picturesque fields of alfalfa and grass, dotted with cows and ancient stone farmhouses covered in climbing roses, there is a stark contrast to the dark, sooty, rabbit warren of apartment blocks in the crowded *banlieue*, of poverty on the fringes of the capital. This is the area inhabited by French-born Algerians and low-paid workers, never seen by the flood of tourists who swamp the historic center.

Maggie and Anna are gazing out of the carriage window, both absorbed in their own thoughts. "I've come full circle, Anna. From the *Gare du Nord* in December '63 to the *Gare de Lyon* in September '65. Who would have thought that my six-week contract would last for two years?" Anna smiles, but says nothing. *It's been a grand tour like no tourist would ever take,* Maggie muses. *Thank God, nothing ever came of the missing film. It just vanished with my camera. The Maestro said he would take care of it, and I guess he did.*

"Here we are," Anna announces, quite unnecessarily, as the train grinds to a squealing halt. The glass door to the compartment slides open and Rudi sticks his head in, grinning wickedly.

"Ladies! *Bienvenu à Paris.* Welcome to the city of sin and debauchery," he says.

Anna playfully throws a crumpled, brown paper bag at him, "Sod off you twit." He blows her a kiss and dances down the corridor whistling the melody of the *Marseillaise*, the national anthem of France.

Just a little to the north of the Opéra de Paris, where Les Ballets Jazz are opening the season with Nikolaus Pávlos' new ballet, lies an area called *Pigalle*, a rather seedy spot stretching from Boulevard Clichy to Avenue Jean-Baptiste Pigalle, named after a long forgotten 18th century French sculptor. Standing on the pavement, Anna, Maggie, and Talitha are staring at a sign outside a grey and black cabaret that reads, 'Le Rat Mort,' or 'The Dead Rat.' "I don't believe this is our rehearsal studio." Talitha checks the address on a slip of paper, reading "7, Place Pigalle, 75009," and pushing the door open mutters, "Appalling, where does he find these places?" Maggie is peering at the posters advertising the all-night entertainment and throws back her head and laughs out loud. *Wow! A rehearsal studio by day and a strip joint by night. I won't be writing home about this rat hole.*

September 1965:

Dear Mom and Dad:

It's hard to believe that I have finally achieved my goal after two years away from home. I have a leading role in the new ballet, "Les Arlequins," which translates to "The Clowns." The essence of the ballet is that we are all hiding behind masks so that no one sees the reality of pain. The ballet exposes the insecurities and loss that lie beneath the costumes, the make-up, and the laughter. That probably sounds gloomy but it is not. The choreography is absolutely brilliant, the most difficult of my entire life. The music has been especially orchestrated, the costumes are unlike anything I have ever seen and I am dancing in the most historic theatre in Paris. It doesn't get better than that! The Maestro has brought out the best of my abilities without me realizing it. I thought he didn't like me but he has been guiding me not just in dance but in seeing the world as it really is. He is a complicated person that has suffered a lot, but he has survived by helping others find themselves. This ballet company is his life. But now, it's time to come home. I don't really belong here and never have, but I have changed so much that I am afraid I will not fit into life on the island. Did I ever? I only wish you could be here to see me fly; to be proud of me for one moment in my life before my understudy, Zhu Li, takes my place. There is always someone in the wings who is younger, more talented and eager to jump into your pointe shoes. If you look on a map, you will see that we are rehearsing in an area of Paris called Montmartre. It is and was the haunt of famous painters: Pissarro, Picasso, Degas, and Toulouse Lautrec. Paris inspired them and that is why the Maestro chose this part of town to create his greatest ballet yet. We rehearse all day and by nightfall I am too tired to do anything but grab something to eat and fall asleep. I'll be home soon and have decided to enroll in art school. I'm not going to become a school teacher and that's that! C'est tout!

Love from your almost bilingual, Mags xxx

P.S. I do know how to swear like a French truck driver, that should be useful in North Oyster.

She folds the pre-stamped aerogram, and addresses the other side before putting it into the bottom of her giant holdall.

Finally, Les Ballets have an afternoon off, and they disappear like rats from a sinking ship. Liliane is off to meet her mother who is an usherette in a movie theatre on the Champs-Elysées, Daniel and Rosie climb on a bus heading for Montparnasse, of course, the Bobbsey twins never tell anyone where they are going and what they are doing. Rudi is taking Zhu Li to see the sights. The rest are going to have their hair dyed and go shopping. "Are you coming?" calls Talitha. Maggie, who has spent almost all her savings on her ticket home, waves a folded map of the city and jokes, "See you later, alligator." *Or not,* she thinks as she sets off down rue Blanche, hoping it leads to the river.

Longlands, North Oyster Cove, V.I. 1940's:

Maggie and her sister Geraldine are sitting on a tartan blanket spread out in the shade of an apple tree. Down the long, sloping field in front of them, bright orange California poppies dance in the slight breeze coming from the southeast. Above, perched like a Bald-Headed eagle, is her middle sister, Allister. Only yesterday she cut off her hair with her mother's pinking shears and is pretending to be invisible. All three are wearing hand-smocked dresses with prim white collars edged in lace, and have been warned not to get dirty before Sunday lunch. Geraldine is carefully braiding the fringe on the edge of the blanket and Maggie is sucking her thumb. In a beautifully articulated Scottish accent, Grandmother is reading from their new book by Ludwig Bemelmans, called Madeline.

> *"In an old house in Paris*
> *That was covered with vines*
> *Lived twelve little girls*
> *In two straight lines."*

She puts the book down on her lap. "Margaret Alice, take your finger out of your nose. That is not the behaviour of young ladies anywhere in the world." Engrossed in the story, Maggie stares at the bright green cover. Eleven proper little girls are walking stiffly like soldiers, wearing matching black shoes and ankle socks, but what catches her eye is the twelfth girl, the smallest of them all, dancing with legs and arms flying in all directions. She is the only one with carrot-red hair and having the most fun of all.

Paris, 1965:

According to the guide book, the river Seine has thirty-seven bridges in Paris alone and runs from the city of Dijon to the coastal towns on the English Channel. Maggie is leaning over the stone balustrade of the *Pont Saint-Michel**. Off in the distance, the Eiffel tower can be seen towering over the charcoal grey, mansard roofs of the seventh *arrondissement*. Below her, the river looks muddy and strewn with garbage. The bridge, still grey with wartime neglect, stinks of urine, and every few yards are brown splats of dog shit, some flattened by an unwary foot and others glistening in the sun, fresh and *odoriférante*. Not far away, a swarthy giant of a man is smoking furiously, his eyes fixed on the flowing river below. He tosses the stub of his *Gauloises* into the turbulent water and hears a voice.

"Fahad, Frank? Is that you?" Maggie rushes up to him breathless with excitement. "Isn't this fabu—?"

"Are you following me?" Frank interrupts, his dark eyes flashing. Maggie steps back feeling foolish and unwanted. "My *baba* died here," his voice is hoarse with emotion. "Murdered by the *poutain de flics*."

"The police, why… how come?"

"Four years ago, 1961—a peaceful demonstration—Algerians against an imposed curfew and *bam*. The *flics* open fire and panic… screams…guys jumped over the walls and either drowned or were shot trying to swim. Maggie is dizzy with horror. "After a few days, the press, lying bastards, *sal menteur*…said only two people died. Two, out of hundreds… Bullshit! The number…more like five hundred, and my *baba* was one of them." Maggie doesn't know what to say or how to comfort him. "I am alone…I have nothing but anger, but Nikko, he, he find me. He teach me to dance—to be part of his family." Frank turns to face Maggie and grips her tightly by her arms. "He's a good man. Never forget that. He's my father now and I would kill for him."

Most of the ballet is billeted in one room studios on rue Frochot, close to Place Pigalle. Maggie is hanging out the window watching the nightlife below in the street. Flashing lights from bars and sex shops change from red to green to yellow as the neon attempts to lure revellers inside. Sounds of drunken laughter, singing, and swearing almost drown out the music blasting from doorways. The smell of hot grease and garlic, urine, and cheap perfume drift up to the first floor window. *Is this going to go on all night?* She wonders, as she glances at her watch. Turning, she climbs back into bed and thinks back upon this extraordinary day.

In a small café, of no name, but advertising the Arabian food of the Maghreb, four dancers: Talitha, Sophia, Maggie, and Fahad are jabbering at once, interrupting each other in broken English, Dutch, German, and French-Arabic. Everyone seems to understand each other, especially after several glasses of lethal *arak* and distilled fig liquor. On a brightly coloured tablecloth, steaming platters of noodles and meat called *rechta* and bowls of *couscous* arrive from the kitchen, which is just a hole in the wall separated from the main room by a beaded door. Frank pounds on the table making the cutlery jump and bellows his point of view. *He is a completely different man than he was this afternoon. After two years with the ballet, I am seeing him for the first time. Why am I so blind? All of the dancers have a past and are struggling to move on. The one thing we all have in common is that we want to dance, to be part of Nikko's creation.* The four dive in, using unleavened bread to pick up pieces of meat, just like in Egypt but, the flavours are much spicier and hotter. "What is the hot spice?" she asks Fahad.

He replies with a smirk, "*Ras El Hanout*, made from ground cannabis, Spanish fly, belladonna, hot peppers, and cockroaches."

She laughs. "How do you say bullshit in Algerian?"

The next morning is the last run-through before they move to the *Garnier Opéra de Paris* for the full dress rehearsals, with costumes, props, and orchestra. Maggie bustles through the door of 'The Dead Rat,' carrying two cups of coffee. No one is there. "Allo, Allo, Bonjour?" Silence! *Damn! I was told to arrive early.*

I could have gone for fresh croissants. She finds a light switch and starts toward the dressing rooms at the far end of the room. Les Ballets have been using two small alcoves to change into practice clothes. She puts the cups down on a round table with her holdall, and opens the ornate door to the backstage area. Musty smells of sweat and hair oil compete with the ever-present odor of ancient plumbing. *Christ, what a stench!* The first door on the right is ajar and she snaps on the light. In front of her is a collage of men, mostly semi-naked in heavy make-up, and racks and racks of glitzy women's costumes—sequins, feathers, and rhinestones. On the shelves above, rows of female wigs. She looks in amazement. And then she sees it on the dressing table. *Holy catfish!* There is an autographed photograph of Ronáld.

The sound of a piano playing a Mozart's sonata fills the nightclub as Les Ballets Jazz take their places. No one seems to find classical music in a run-down cathouse incongruous. As usual, some are grumbling, some hung over and some just dead tired. "*Plié*, straighten, keep your arms relaxed, forward and up, *battement tendu*, close and stretch into *arabesque*. Grand *battements*, one, two, three, and hold. More stretch, lengthen the fingers." The Maestro claps his hands. "Now on zee other side. Strength comes from here," and he pats himself under his rib cage. "Maggie, *finalmente*, you stop flinging your legs, *brava*." He doesn't miss a thing, like a cat at the mouse hole waiting to pounce. "The ballet is only as good as the weakest one." He pauses for a moment, deep in thought. "Listen only to the music. That is your guide. *Die musik ist dein führer!*"

"Take five, *cinq minutes. Dahhlinks*, we start the final rehearsal in five minutes. Where's my coffee?" He is looking around the room as though it will magically appear from space. Anna retrieves a cigarette from her bag, lights it and hands it to Nikko. He never has his own. The coffee is cold but he gulps it down. "Lower the trapeze, Xavier. I want to speak to Simone about costumes." At that moment,

José Costa-Pinto comes in from the street carrying a suitcase. He has just arrived from Lisbon. The Maestro rushes over, claps him on the back and begins speaking in Portuguese. "Turn on the music for clowns," he calls to no one in particular. It blasts out of the speakers and they put their heads together, reading the score and listening.

Maggie limps to the side of the room and snatches her towel from the back of a gaudy red velvet chair. Slowly she sinks to the floor, her legs flopped out like an old rag doll, and mops the sweat from her neck, breathing deeply.

Rudi saunters by, sweat running down his face, "You want a massage?"

Maggie shakes her head. "*Merci, non.*" The rehearsal room is in a state of utter confusion. In a flash, it all becomes quite clear. *I am a part of all this; like an oboe or violin to an orchestra or a brush full of pigment smeared on a masterpiece, all of us are part of a whole. Nikko is the conductor, the artist, and he is the one who will be remembered. I am the last piece in his jigsaw puzzle.* Her eyes close in thought. *I can't let him down, let the whole ballet down. I must dance like I've never done before, not for myself, but for the Maestro who gave me the chance to fulfil my dream.*

With a burst of energy, she jumps to her feet, strides to the center of the room and starts practising pirouettes. They have to be flawless for the opening. One tiny stumble will be noticed. She takes her preparation, inhales, pauses to get her balance, marks a spot on the opposite wall, and with a pounding heart, spins and spins from one tiny dot on the floor, until she flies to that special place where only a dancer can go.

EPILOGUE

It is September 7th, 1965. A light shower falls upon the coiffed heads of Parisians, balding theatre critics, and French ballet students called '*les rats*' as they race across the *Place de l'Opéra* toward the famous, nineteenth century theatre, *L'Opéra de Paris*. Tonight is the opening of an international modern ballet's first performance in the capital.

Rainwater runs down a poster, reminiscent of a colourful cubist painting. Lying across the advertisement, a sodden paper streamer reads, '*billets épuisées*,' meaning 'sold out.'

L'Opéra de Paris présente
Un ballet extraordinaire
LES ARLEQUINS
Chorégraphie de Maestro Nikolaus Pávlos
Les Ballets Jazz Europa
Musique : José Costa-Pinto
Costumes: Inspirés de Pablo Picasso
Rudolfo Canessius Soemolang – Margaret Alice Dinsdale

Backstage, *L'Opéra de Paris*:

The tension on that fateful night in September is electrifying. Maggie and Rudi are being strapped into harnesses, waiting to be hoisted aloft into the fly gallery where they will be posed in a suspended picture frame representing Pablo Picasso's *The Circus Family*. Rudi is portraying the clown, and Maggie, the young mother. Her costume is gossamer. In the blue light of the first act she appears almost naked, ephemeral, like a wisp of smoke from an extinguished match. With a hammering heart, she is trying to remember the first few steps after she descends onto the stage. She arches her feet, over and over to soften her *pointe* shoes, and steps into the resin box twisting the powdery glue onto the leather soles. Eagerly waiting in the wings is her understudy, the lovely Zhu Li, who is a formidable dancer.

Arms grab her and Rudi whispers in her ear, "We make love when we dance, *ja!* Break a leg."

Maggie laughs, I'll break more than a leg if I fall out of the fly gallery."

The Maestro silently stands behind them. A whiff of scotch perfumes the air. He mutters something in a foreign language. She turns and sees his eyes full of emotion.

"I have all confidence *daahlink*. You are perfect in this role," and for the first time ever, he kisses her on the forehead, and backs up into the gloom beside the control panel to signal the start. "*Merde*, here we go."

A sudden hush falls over the auditorium, the gallery, and the boxes at the arrival of José Costa-Pinto into the orchestra pit. House lights dim, work lights flicker. Maggie feels a tug on her safety strap, grabs a piece of silk, and shoots into the air like Peter Pan, high above the stage. She peeks down and sees tiny clowns in their strangely erotic costumes buzzing about like brightly coloured garden gnomes taking their places for the opening. Not a voice can be heard, everyone waits for that tiny *tap, tap, tap* of the baton on the lectern and the first dramatic notes of the overture.

An explosion of sound rocks the theatre, blue spotlights search the great ceiling, an air raid siren screams while the violin section plays a lullaby. Curtains open with a whoosh. Maggie, reaches back, unhooks the safety strap, and the magic begins.

Place de l'Opéra. Paris, 1965:

The Maestro slips quietly out of the stage door and walks slowly, with a barely perceptible limp, around to the main entrance. The rain has stopped but his face is moist. At the foot of the grand staircase, he pauses, lights a cigarette, and gazes up at the famous façade, the classical friezes, statuary, multi-coloured marble, and porphyry, with a slow smile of satisfaction. From behind, the clicking of boots on pavement begin as three uniformed men approach through the fog, their breath coming in gasps as if they had been running.

"Are you Maestro Nikolaus Pávlos?" He nods, calmly removes the *Gauloises* from his lips, and drops it onto the pavement. "You are wanted for questioning for smuggling artworks stolen by the *Kunstschutz* during WWII." Shiny, stainless steel *menottes*; handcuffs, click around his wrists like cheap bracelets. At that moment, the tall ornate theatre doors burst open and the excited audience pours into the place de l'Opéra shouting *"Bravo, incroyable, magnifique."*

Vancouver Island, British Columbia:

North Oyster is enjoying what the locals call "Indian Summer." That means warm, beautiful days that continue until leaves turn russet and gold and come tumbling from the tree tops. It is also harvest time when the final apples: Gravenstein, Bramley's, and Cox's Orange Pippins are gathered safely in.

In the small cove in front of her family farm, Maggie is splashing in the cold, clear waters of the Pacific Ocean, alone yet not alone. Beneath her toes baby crabs scurry under rocks, schools of minnows dart about her bare ankles and high overhead seagulls caw while searching for food. Their cries almost drown out the sound of

206 | No Intermission

Chopin's Ballade coming from the open windows of her mother's music room. *Nothing has changed,* she muses. *Life goes on as if I had never left home. I deeply regret that my Grandmother never saw the ballet triumph in Paris. Everyone, even Simone danced like never before. No one in my family will ever know the effort it took to fulfill my dream.* She missed the chance to thank the Maestro for believing in her. After the curtain call, he had simply disappeared. Two days later, Maggie had boarded the train alone, waiting until the last second to see if he might come to the platform to see her off. *"D'abord,"* the porter had called, in the same, bored, singsong voice as always. She picked up her battered suitcase now covered with labels and flags, her square beauty box containing an Egyptian ponytail flyswatter from Daniel, her tattered purse containing Anna's gift of an Italian leather cigarette box with a lily embossed on it, a completely illegal switchblade dagger from Ronáld, and the ridiculous hubbly-bubbly from Egypt, and boarded the train to the coast.

A small, white, clinker-built fish boat trolling for September salmon catches her eye. A young man is rowing toward her, the oars dipping rhythmically in and out of the water. She squints into the late afternoon sun. *Where have I seen him before? The silver-grey hair with unusual streaks of black that can only belong to one man.*

A small smile plays across her lips and she calls out, "Caught anything, Pip?"

"Not yet."

Appendix

Chapter One: Getting There is Half the Fun

*Cunard: Sir Winston Churchill Prime Minister of Great Britain during WWII declared that the ability of Cunard to transport troops across the Atlantic shortened the war by a year. Enemy submarines could not keep pace with the fast-moving liners. Samuel Cunard (1787-1865) was a Canadian businessman from Halifax, Nova Scotia. He won the contract from the British Government to deliver mail between Britain and North America on July 4th 1840. It took fourteen days to sail by steamship from Liverpool to Halifax or Boston. RMS in front of the ship's name stands for 'Royal Mail Ship.'

*Ladysmith: On land originally settled by 'Stz'uminus' First Nations, a coal town on the east coast of Vancouver Island called 'Oyster Harbor' was built in 1898, by Robert Dunsmuir, known as 'the coal baron.' It is now a sleepy lumber port, some fifty miles north of Victoria, the capital city of British Columbia. Ladysmith lies on the 49th parallel which separates the U.S.A. and Canada. Oyster Harbour was renamed as Ladysmith, after a town of that name in South Africa, to commemorate the lifting of the siege in the Second Boer War of 1900. All coal was depleted by the early 1900's and Ladysmith has become a tidy little retirement town with well-preserved heritage buildings.

*Davis Strait: Named after British navigator John Davis in the 1580's, it is the largest strait in the world lying in Canada, between Greenland and Baffin Island, Nunavut. It is noted for its fierce gales in the North Atlantic Ocean, especially in the fall.

*Johnathan Logan: In 1944, the Johnathan Logan dress company was a high-end, high-quality dress design company that stressed very shapely, gathered full skirts and narrow waists. By 1960 Johnathan Logan sales hit one hundred million dollars and they became the first ladies clothing company to be listed on the New York Stock Exchange.

*The Nearness of You: A popular love ballad composed by Hoagy Carmichael in 1938 with lyrics by Ned Washington. The song debuted with the Glenn Miller Orchestra in 1939 and has been revised over the years by the late Ella Fitzgerald and Louis Armstrong in 1956. It was rerecorded again by the late Frank Sinatra and recently by Nora Jones.

Chapter Two: Not All That It Seems

*The Leather Boys: A nickname of the British rebels called 'Rockers' as opposed to the gangs who called themselves 'Mods' (Moderns) in the 1960's. The Mods and Rockers represent post WWII youth movements escaping the greyness and tedium of no jobs and no money. Entertainment consisted of coffee bars, music, and legal amphetamines. Rockers were wild-haired, leather-jacketed motorcycle drivers, who were fans of rock and roll. The Mods emphasised stylish clothes, Italian-influenced tailoring, and enjoyed the blues, soul music, and driving vespas. Both groups were rebelling against society, fighting for the freedom to act as they pleased. Their brawls tended to get more newspaper coverage than necessary.

*Fried Brains or Cervelli Fritti: This dish is an acquired taste. The entire brains of calves or lambs that are dipped in egg and flour, rolled in Italian seasoned breadcrumbs, and deep fried to a golden crisp. The inside remains soft and flavourless and oozes white liquid.

*Portrait of Mlle. Gabrielle Diot by Edgar Degas 1890: This portrait of Mlle. Diot is one of thousands of paintings stolen from Paris during the Nazi occupation in a 1940. It belonged to the legendary Jewish Parisian art collector and dealer, the late Paul Rosenberg (1881-1957). Mr. Rosenberg's first gallery at 21 Rue la Bóete was next door to an apartment that Pablo Picasso lived in, resulting in their long-time friendship. He was an early admirer of not only Picasso, but Brague, Matisse, and Degas. Four hundred of his personal masterworks were stolen, and sixty-five paintings have not been recovered by the heirs. The Portrait of Mlle. Gabrielle Diot by Degas is still missing. It surfaced in 1974 in Switzerland, disappeared again, and in 1987 was resold to an unknown collector by the Hass Gallery in Hamburg.

Chapter Three: A Rolling Stone Gathers No Moss

*British Air Raid, Bremen, Germany: The main target for the bombing of Bremen in 1945 was the *Valentin* submarine factory on the Weser River, the largest fortified builder of U-boats and the *Flugzeugbau* assembly aircraft factory. The 'fight for the skies' saw 13,000 long tons (2,240 lbs.) of explosives decimate the area to prevent manufacturing of war machines. Throughout Germany it is estimated that ten thousand and four hundred civilians were killed. For children born in Europe in the 1940's, survival was their primary goal. Millions of dollars' worth of the finest art treasures from the Bremen Kunsthalle Art Museum disappeared. In an ill-conceived plan in 1942, the best paintings and drawings were shipped to the *Schloss Karnzow*, the castle of Count Konigsmark and his mistress. Three years later when the Russian army attacked from the east, they found the castle uninhabited and seventeen hundred Master drawings and watercolours, and over fifty oil paintings by Raphael, Rembrandt, Rubens, Delacroix, Manet, and Durer. Most of these were stolen and sent to the State Hermitage Museum in St Petersburg, Russia, and not likely to ever be returned. The rest disappeared into private homes to be sold or smuggled to foreign countries. The bodies of Count Konigsmark and his mistress, who died in a double suicide, were found in the bottom of a nearby lake.

*****Irish Sweepstakes:** A lottery was established in 1930 to support the Irish Free State Hospital. At this time Ireland was one of the poorest countries in Europe. Although it was supposed to be a charity, it was in fact a private company run for profit, and illegal in Britain and Canada. Tickets were bought on a black market. The final *Irish Sweep* as it was known, was held in 1986.

*****Mary Quant:** A fashion icon who invented the "mini-skirt" during the swinging 60's in London was born in 1930. She is quoted as saying the mini "Indicates youthfulness and to have fun." She named the tiny skirts after her car, a Mini Cooper. Just four inches from the buttocks, a later version called the "micro mini" was hemmed at the panty line. The youngsters who wore these were called "ya ya girls" and felt very modern. Many countries, especially in Africa, banned them.

*****Vase of Flowers:** This painting by Jan van Huysum (1682-1749) was stolen during WWII by a Nazi soldier whose family later claimed he bought it. After seventy-five years and international cooperation, the Jan van Huysum painting of the Vase of Flowers was returned by the Foreign Minister of Germany and presented to the German-born director of the Uffizi Gallery, Eike Dieter Schmidt, in Florence on July 20, 2019. "It was a moral duty to return the painting." He quotes, "Today we render justice to history."

*Winklepicker boots: Winklepickers are very long, narrow-toed leather boots adopted by British rock stars, teddy boys, and mods in the 1950's. The name came from a periwinkle, a winkle or sea snail, which is a small intertidal shellfish with a sharp pimple on one side of the shell. They were made fashionable by rock groups such as the Beatles and the Rolling Stones.

Chapter Four: Pasta, Paintings and Pirouettes

*Armistice of Cassibile: Realizing that Italy by September 1944 faced destruction by uncontrollable combatants, the Grand Council of Fascism returned command of the ineffectual armed forces to Victor Emanuelle III who arrested Mussolini the next day. Earlier in July, Italy started negotiations with the Allies for an armistice in neutral Portugal. The formal agreement was signed in Cassibile, Sicily on September 3, 1944. Meanwhile, Hitler sent two divisions from France to control Northern Italy and secure the release of Mussolini. This meant that Milan, the hub of Italy's industrial and financial strength, was bombed again, this time by the American air force. Although they were targeting the Alfa Romeo plant and the railway system, they damaged many irreplaceable historic buildings in the process.

*The Spaghetti Westerns: The term "Spaghetti Western" was coined by a Spanish journalist Alfonso Sanchez to mean a low-budget movie of the American cowboy genre, but with Italian or Spanish producers. The hero was always Clint Eastwood or a rough look-alike and the other actors, Italian. The bareback riders were likely North American natives playing both the 'rojos' and the cowboys. Over six hundred spaghetti westerns were produced, providing a distraction for war-ravaged Europeans.

Chapter Five: The Agony and the Ecstasy

*Stinche Prison: Despite being such a fitting a title in English pronunciation, the ancient word 'stinche' is defined as 'a dishevelled pile of building stones.' When the Ghibellines were expelled from Florence in the late 1300's, they left debris. About one hundred years later these construction materials were used to build a tall prison, with no windows and a single entrance. The surrounding moat gave it the title '*isola*,' meaning island. Stinche was a private operation and inmates were charged for room and board. The fortress lasted as a prison, dungeon, and graveyard for four hundred and fifty years until it was converted, more happily, to the largest, most ornate theatre in Tuscany. It was built for opera, with a five-degree raked stage from the footlights to the highest point at the back of the stage, so all singers and actors could be seen from the audience. The stage door is on *Via Isola delle Stinche* so its history as a moated prison will not be forgotten.

*Pigri maici fornici: The literal translation for this phrase is "lazy fornicating pig," an insult which was aimed at Pope Paul VI, who unwisely reaffirmed the Catholic church's position on artificial birth control, namely the pill. Catholics around the world were stunned as almost half were already using some form of birth control. This mistake weakened the church's authority in the 1960's. "Pay, pray, and obey" was a hard pill to swallow, especially as the celibate Paul VI was rumoured to be homosexual with a well-known movie actor, rendering him a hypocrite in his private life. He was accused of promoting only gay men to positions of power in the Vatican which contributed to the breakdown of morality within the church. Paul was the brunt of many jokes.

*Uffizi Gallery: One of the most spectacular art museums in the world is the Uffizi which means simply, 'offices.' The large office building was commissioned in 1560 by Cosimo I de Medici for the administration and judiciary of Florence, with a U-shaped design by Giorgio Vasari. By 1581, some of the Medici art treasurers were installed in this superb building, and gradually, the art collection took it over. It was opened to visitors by request in 1769 but did not become a public museum of art until 1865.

*Sandro Botticelli (1445-1510): Possibly the greatest painter of the Renaissance, Florentine-born Sandro Botticelli's original name was Alessandro di Mariano di Vanni Filipepi. Sandro changed his alias to Botticelli, meaning "little barrel" in dedication to his elder brother, a pawnbroker, whose anatomic shape reflected the description. The family lived on Via Nuova, neighbouring Amerigo Vespucci, after whom America was named. Sandro Botticelli was trained by Filippo Lippi and surpassed him in his personal style. Although the ceiling of the Sistine Chapel in the Basilica in Rome made Michelangelo famous, both the northern and southern walls of the Sistine Chapel were painted by Sandro Botticelli. One of his most famous paintings, *The Birth of Venus*, is the subject of much speculation. Who was the beautiful model? Countless books have been written and just as many films made about the lovely Simonetta Catanea Vespucci (1453-1476), who died of tuberculosis at the age of twenty-three. She was married by the age of sixteen to Marco Vespucci, a cousin of Amerigo, and led a most enviable life admired by all Florentines. Rumours persist that Botticelli was in love with her, an idea that continues to supply novelists with endless material.

Nanaimo bars: In 1985 and 2019, Nanaimo bars were declared the number one confection in polls by the *National Post*. The Nanaimo bar's climb to international fame began in a simple cookery book in 1952 published by the *Women's Auxiliary to the Nanaimo Hospital*. The namesake is a small town on Vancouver Island, twenty miles north of Ladysmith. The dessert is made in three layers, consisting of a no-bake combination of chocolate, coconut, almonds, custard powder, and cream. It made its television debut as an ingredient in *Masterchef Canada*, was featured in Expo 86 as "the classic Canadian dessert," and much to everyone's surprise, in April 2019, its image was on a postage stamp dedicated to world-class desserts.

*Grappa: Grappa is a brandy distilled in northern Italy, made from the residue left over from wine making, called the "marc" or "pomice" consisting of the skins, seeds, stems and pulp. Grappa contains 35-60% alcohol by volume and is traditionally consumed in shot glasses. It is also popular in South America where many Italians immigrated before and after WWII.

*Caterina de Medici: As an orphaned child, Caterina was tossed about like a hot potato between feuding Italian families until her marriage. She married Henry, Duke of Orleans, which allowed her to become the Queen of France when he outlived his elder brother. A staunchly Roman Catholic heiress from the Florentine Medici family, she became the most powerful woman in Europe, as The Governor of France after her unfaithful Henry got a jousting lance through his head. She survived all but two of her ten children and is accredited with bringing dancers of the ballet to the court of France. In 1581, the first ballet to be presented in the French court was *'Ballet Comique de la Reine.'*

*Ponte Vecchio: There is a plaque on this most famous bridge in Italy recognising that Gehard Wolf, the German Consul to Florence 1940-1944 was decisive in sparing the Ponte Vecchio from destruction during WWII. Others give some support even to Hitler who had visited the Uffizi and walked the bridge with Mussolini. All other bridges across the Arno River were destroyed and the rubble of a mile of blasted stones of the houses were placed on either side to cover roads and access to the river. Perhaps the Ponto Vecchio built in 1345, would not bear the weight of tanks and heavy trucks. Gerhard Wolf was interned by the British at the end of the war. Florence begged his release. The Germans, including Hitler, tried to make Florence an open city to exclude warfare in November 1943. Field-Marshal Harold Alexander, British commander of all Allied troops in Italy, did not respond.

*Vin Santo: This is a sacred wine made mainly in Tuscany, consisting of white grapes which are dried on straw mats to concentrate the flavour. It was used as a communion wine or the wine at Mass, and the beverage given to the village priest or someone very special as an unexpected treat. It is usually sweet, but a dry variety is popular as an aperitif in the late afternoon served with a biscuit. It is sometimes spelled *vino santo* or 'wine of saints'.

*Malaspina: Alessandro Malaspina lived from 1754-1840 and was from a large and noble Italian family whose name is remembered in Florence through its famous Torrigiani Malaspina Gardens. He was an explorer who spent sixty months sailing the world, and has a college named after him in Nanaimo, on Vancouver Island, British Columbia. The largest piedmont glacier in the world on the Alaskan panhandle was also named after him.

Chapter Seven: The Grand Tour

*Goose Step: Originally, the goose step was a Prussian military or Honorary march called '*Stechschritt*' performed to show strength and stamina, and the tradition spread to Russia. It is a formal military march in which both legs are kept rigidly straight until the advancing toe is level with the hip. In military parades, Olympic games, and official ceremonies, the goose step is impressive. Although it is still used in China and many countries in South America, the *Stechschritt* is for many associated with Nazi Germany, and not often performed in Europe or North America besides as a parody.

*Aglianico grapes: Aglianico is a corruption of the word '*Ellenico*,' Italian for Hellenic or Greek origin of the grape vines. Aglianico grapes are black and considered one of the three greatest varieties of Italy. The finest bottles come from the volcanic soil on Monte Vulture, an area east of Naples.

*The Port of Naples WWII: Once the Allied forces had control of Sicily, the Sicilian airfields were within easy reach of the port of Naples. Many two-tonne bombs, the largest yet developed, enabled the Royal Air Force to destroy much of the Italian fleet that was used to ship German and Italian war materials to the North African front. After the public announcement from the Italian government September 8, 1943 of the Armistice of Cassibile, armed resistance harassed the German plan to ship thousands of Neapolitan men into forced labour camps in the north. This was despite the German threat to kill one hundred Italians for any one German casualty. This resistance was so effective that the German forces retreated, enabling the British forces to start the counterattack by land. In August of 1944, the German bombers returned to destroy the city of Naples, causing unimaginable suffering of civilians.

*Spirit gum: Spirit gum is adhesive glue manufactured in 1870 used to hold moustaches, wigs, beards, and eyelashes in theatrical costuming. It is a mixture of denatured alcohol and resin, is highly flammable and can cause eye irritation. It can be removed by alcohol and Vaseline.

*The Bombing of the Palermo: In a matter of months, the city, port, and shipyards of Palermo in Sicily were bombed by five different air forces, both allied and axis: French, British, Italian, German and American. The port suffered the heaviest, bloodiest raids of the entire war. The raids managed to destroy one hundred nineteen heritage buildings, killed two thousand, one hundred and twenty-three, and wounded thousands more. Post-war aid never reached this small island and to this day, many areas still lie in ruins.

*Lady Caroline Lamb: An Anglo-Irish aristocrat who has been described as incompatible with her age. Although married to the Honourable Viscount William Lamb, she pursued Lord Byron with a volcanic, flamboyant passion, writing novels of their brief affair and descending into madness when it was over. Her eccentric behaviour caused her relatives to have her certified insane. After her death, her husband became Prime Minister to Queen Victoria.

Chapter Eight: Alexandrian Rhapsody

*Coptic Christians: The word 'Copt' is old Greek for indigenous Egyptian. The apostle Mark, the evangelist, is said to have reached Alexandria in 33AD. His charisma spread the word of Christianity so effectively that approximately 10% of the total one hundred million Egyptians profess the religion. Another million live in the US, Canada and Australia with heavy concentrations in the Middle East. Egyptian believers of Coptic Christianity tend to be disciplined, more educated and in white collar work than the average Egyptian. Since the advent of Islam in the 7th century, there has been variable inclusion and exclusion of copts in government positions. In 1952 when Abdul Nasser came to power and the abdication of King Farouk, the Copts suffered. Nasser's dream was for a pan-Arab Muslim identity for Egypt.

Chapter Nine: Dancing on the Nile

*Leonard Bernstein: On September 27, 1957, the musical *West Side Story* composed by Leonard Bernstein and choreographed by Jerome Robbins shot to fame. The New York Herald Tribune states "Jerome Robbins has put together and then blasted apart, the most savage, restless, electrifying dance patterns we've been exposed to… in killer rivalry between Puerto Rican and white gangs in the city." The Tribune continues, "The energy, violence, and sweetness of the music by Leonard Bernstein, a first-generation Ukrainian Jew, was also groundbreaking." *West Side Story* inspired many choreographers to explore the concept of rival gangs, religious conflict, unrest, and violence to the world of ballet.

*The Pyramids: History is someone else's story so we have to treat it with respect, even though we may never get it quite right. Starting slowly about 5,500 BCE, Egyptian culture dominated the Mediterranean for 3000 years and is probably the most powerful national culture the world has known. To build the largest man-made structure ever contemplated, sensibly aware of the obstacles, sand, elevation, finely shaping the twenty-tonne blocks of limestone with only tools of stone and copper plus the labour force of four hundred thousand Egyptians. The scope of the project required an extraordinary group imagination that had to hold together for about one hundred years. The earliest pyramid was built in 4300 BCE for a queen, and the largest; the Khufu, around 2500 BCE. Blocks of limestone were floated down the Nile River, which when in flood allowed camels to bring them closer to the site at Giza. Sledges dragged over carefully wetted sand completed the journey. Around 500 BCE the iconic, inclusive intelligence of the Greeks blessed the Western world.

Chapter Ten: Phoenix on Fire

*Vickers Viscount: In 1942, Britain, concerned about commercial air flight to Europe and its colonies after WWII formed the Brabazon committee incorporating plane manufacturing and airlines. The most promising plane was the Vickers Viscount which went through innumerable developments. The prototypes were loud and rough. First flown in 1948 the Viscount entered service in 1953. After piston engines were replaced by turboprops, the ride was silky smooth. To prove the peaceful flight, the cabin staff would place a coin on edge on the seat tray and it would not fall over.

*Sand: Rachel Carson, (1907-1964), environmentalist is quoted to have said, "In every grain of sand there is a story of the Earth." Desert sand is polished by the wind, too smooth to be used in cement. A five-hundred-foot sand dune can be removed by the wind in two winters. The official size of sand grains is 0.02mm-2.0mm. Archimedes, a Sicilian Greek mathematician from Syracuse, 240 B.C estimated the size at 2.0mm. The tawny colour of sand is from iron oxide with many alternatives. Fifty billion tons of beach sand are used in construction annually, mostly from Australia. This resource is non-renewable in our lifetime.

*Château Grimaldi: The stone castle, known until 1966 as the Château Grimaldi, was built over the foundations of much earlier settlements of *Antipolis*, later known as *Antibes*. It commanded a view over the Mediterranean Sea, the vital maritime trade route and a lookout for defense. The stone fortress was built in 1309 and converted to a residence in 1620 for the powerful feudal family Grimaldi. Over the years, it has been used as a fortress, home, town hall, barracks, art studio for Pablo Picasso and finally, an art museum dedicated to him containing one of the world's greatest collections of his works.

Chapter Eleven: The Man Behind the Mask

*Camille Pissarro (1830-1903) 'Rue Saint-Honore, Apres Midi (1897): In 1939 at the beginning of WWII, Pissarro's painting of An Afternoon in the Rain on the rue Saint-Honoré, was sold by a Jewish Collector, Lilly Cassirer for '*Fluchgut*' flight money, meaning a pittance in order to escape Nazi Germany and seek asylum in a neutral country. The flight money was never received according to family members. Pissarro's painting disappeared for twelve years, popping up briefly in New York in 1951 before disappearing again until 1976.

*Edgar Degas (1834-1917) 'Five Ballerinas': Baron Mor Lipot Herzog had one of the largest and most valuable art collections in Europe before WWII. In 1939 when Nazi forces invaded Hungary, the collection was seized and only some paintings were ever returned to the family. The whereabouts of Edgar Degas' painting of 'Five Ballerinas' remains a mystery to this day.

Chapter Twelve: Is Paris Burning?

*Pont Saint-Michel (1857): One of thirty-seven bridges crossing the River Seine in Paris. Its 62 metres link the Place Saint-Michel on the left bank to the island in the middle, Île de la Cité. Although a beautiful bridge, it will forever be remembered as the scene of a massacre of innocents. On October 17, 1961 in the middle of the Algerian War, the Parisian police provoked a group of demonstrators marching for the National Liberation Front. The police attacked using clubs and guns and pushed them into the river, shooting those who tried to swim to safety. After years of denial that the massacre of innocents was intentional and motivated by racial hatred, the chief of police, Maurice Papon, was put on trial and found guilty of crimes against humanity. It wasn't until 2001 that a commemorative plaque was put on the bridge honouring the memory of those victims.

Made in the USA
Coppell, TX
30 October 2021

64917297R00129